Kathy Warwick is an English writer, t
mother. Kathy has spent the last 20
and now with her children grown up,
writing. Kathy has an extensive range of interests, including
film, outdoor pursuits, travel, wine and obviously books!
Having spent many years writing purely on a recreational
level, Emily Unchained is Kathy's hilarious debut novel.

Emily Unchained

This is a laugh out loud, exaggerated take on family life. On
what it's like to be a woman thrown back into the complicated
world of relationships - competing against women who don't
have bodies mutilated by pregnancy and childbirth, or a secret
stash of Tena Lady in the airing cupboard waiting for that
inevitable pelvic floor malfunction! Emily is an everyday
woman that many of us can relate to. Whether it's as she tries
to juggle her disjointed family with friendships and work, or as
she blindly navigates her way through the minefield that is
dating again with two nearly grown children and a regrown
virginity! Close friends Elaine and Karen add to the chaos and
humour, usually bringing wine and secrets with them.

Emily Unchained is a work of fiction. Any resemblance to
people living or dead is entirely coincidental. Opinions offered
in this book are my own and do not reflect the opinions of any
person or organisation that is mentioned in the book.

Copyright (©) Kathy Warwick 2018

EMILY UNCHAINED

PROLOGUE
1996

I had just turned eighteen when we discovered I was expecting Nicole. We sat, perched on the edge of the sickly peach coloured bathtub at Michaels house that hadn't been in fashion for two decades, at least. We were both in absolute shock, staring at the urine covered plastic stick with its scary blue line. The line that would ultimately change our lives forever. One way or another. Although what we thought would happen when we'd had unprotected sex was anyone's guess. If this were a lame daytime television drama, tear jerking music would be playing in the background to emphasise that fact that we'd fucked up massively.

"I can't believe it. I just can't believe it." Michael kept repeating annoyingly. Head in his hands one minute, eyes on the cabinet where the razor blades were kept the next. I wanted to flick the pissy stick in his face just to shock him into shutting the fuck up. Or worse, actually open the cabinet and hand him a blade. Formally assisting him out of his obvious misery. Assisted suicide was legal in these circumstances, right? "Should I do another one?" I pondered out loud. I was still feeling like I was having an out of body experience. The peach hue of the dated bathroom suite wasn't helping matters either. It was nauseating even without the pregnancy hormones racing around my body.

"Why?" His head snapped up, sudden hope in his eyes that only seconds before were deadpools. "Could the first one be wrong?" He was desperately clutching at straws here and I really didn't want to dash his hopes so I shrugged nonchalantly and cruelly said, "sure maybe".

The second test was also positive as I knew it would be. He became a broken man, well, a little boy really right in front of me. I watched him having a tearful tantrum on the linoleum floor. I guess I should get used to this. It's what parenthood must be like, on a daily basis. "Is being tied to me for life such a terrifying prospect then?" I mustered up a joke from the depths of somewhere, even though I was just as scared as him. Michael just cried harder. Snot everywhere. He should probably get used to being covered in slime and other gross stuff if he was to become a father, sorry, not if, but when. My mind was already made up.

There then followed weeks of vomiting, night sweats and the occasional nightmare - all Michael of course - I came round pretty quickly to the idea of being a mummy. He manned up eventually, resigned to the fact he was going to become a dad, not brave enough to broach the subject of, said in a whisper, abortion, with me.

"We're in this together," he said solemnly. We certainly were. What a brave soldier he'd suddenly become. But I wish he hadn't made it sound like we'd committed some heinous crime and were about to serve hard time for it. Although some might argue that's parenthood in a nutshell! My parents for example. I hadn't been the easiest child to bring up and I feared that our news might possibly send them over the edge now.

So we decided to get my mum and dad onside as soon as possible, give them as much time to process what was about to happen. We stood in my front room and I gripped Michaels hand tightly, not so much for support, but mainly to stop him running away and leaving me to do the dirty work on my own. Mum was engaged in her favourite Sunday morning activity of being a nosy neighbour under the guise of cleaning the windows. Dad was watching the golf.

It was a brave person to disturb either one of them at this time but needs must. Adrenaline was pumping. I announced loudly and more confidently than I actually felt that I wanted to talk to them both. Mum looked away from her curtain twitching for a second, and I swear looked straight at my tummy. I instinctively sucked it in a little. Not that there was anything to see just yet. Dad just sighed and held onto his remote control tighter, just incase someone tried to take it away from him. I wished someone would take it away from him actually, as I was extremely concerned that he might missile launch it at Michaels head once we'd shared our 'happy' news with them. Not that I was completely adverse to Michael having something thrown hard at his head, but it might make things rather awkward for us all in the future.

"Mummy why does daddy have a huge dent in his forehead?"
"Well darling, that was your beloved grandads fault, the day

we announced your existence he attacked him with a remote control!" It would make for an awkward conversation around the dinner table. Making a rod for own own backs, especially when celebrating special occasions in the future.

"I'm pregnant!" I announced to the room, not looking at anyone in particular. Michael gasped and looked at me in absolute horror. Leaving me to wonder if maybe I should have done some stand up comedy. Warmed them up a bit first, to soften the blow of my, sorry 'our' baby bombshell. Dad stood up. Michael cowered pathetically beside me. Mum drew the curtains. The remote control appeared more menacing in dads tight grip now he was vertical, all six foot four of him. Mum wrestled the remote out of dad's hand and then for a second appeared to be considering throwing it at Michaels head herself before hiding it in her pocket.

"How did this happen?" Dad asked pretty calmly actually for my dad. "In this day and age, how did this bloody well happen?" He was shaking his head. His disappointment was worse than his anger. I felt suitably ashamed. "We had unprotected sex," mumbled Michael beside me, finding his Reeboks extremely interesting. It was then my turn to look at him in absolute horror. "It was a rhetorical question you idiot!" I said. My dad just gave me a look as if to say 'this guy? seriously?'

Mum at this point looked like she was on the verge of a epileptic seizure, she gripped the duster as though it were my neck and started sobbing uncontrollably. "Shut up Sheila," barked dad harshly. But mum carried on crying, I thought I could make out the odd word between sobs...'shame'...'neighbours say'... "Will you be standing by her?" Dad asked. I willed Michael to realise this was a trick question with only one acceptable answer. He rather mechanically put his arm around my shoulder at this point, it felt unnatural as Michael was a whole head shorter than my five foot ten inches so it just looked as if he was trying to get me in a headlock.

"Of course. I love her don't I." He said sounding slightly backward. I inwardly cringed. Dad gave me another look as it to say 'Really? You want to breed with this guy?' "They'll be no galavanting off anywhere and leaving us with the baby you know! You've made your bed now you have to lie in it!" Said dad, very seriously. It's the longest sentence he'd ever addressed to me. I wasn't sure what galavanting meant but I highly doubted I'd suddenly take it up as a hobby once my baby was born. So I nodded just as seriously in agreement.

"You will marry of course!" Mum announced loudly, Victorian style. She'd pulled herself together enough to devise a plan in her head, a ridiculous plan, but at least she wasn't crying any more.
We all turned to look at her, even dad looked surprised. I wondered when we had stepped out of the late nineties and into a Charles Dickens novel.,,,,,

Pregnancy did not agree with me at all. I aspired to be like the pregnant model on the cover of Mother and Baby magazine, a petite blond with a small basketball sized bump under a floaty white dress. Strolling through the park laughing over her shoulder at something her no doubt equally good looking husband had just said. I, on the other hand took to wearing baggy t-shirts and jumpers and, in the later stages of pregnancy, an old tracksuit of Michaels. From a distance it looked as if I was wearing it over a fat suit. My long dark hair hung greasily, as though I had just dipped my head into a chip fryer, not completely out of the realms of possibility to be honest, snuffling for that last rouge chip. My hunger was that insatiable.

The same could not be said for my sexual appetite which was less than non existent unfortunately. For Michael that is. If I never had sex again it would be too soon. And If Michael was stupid enough to come anywhere near me with his penis I was more likely to cut it off, deep fry it and eat it for a snack and not in a perverted, deviant way either. I was just always hungry.

I had been told pregnancy was not an excuse to eat for two, so instead I ate for a family of four, a larger than the national average, possibly obese, family of four. I wasn't glowing. I was hideous.
There was no strolling in the park for me, it was all I could do to drag my hemorrhoids from room to room looking for cake. Not my finest hour it has to be said.

The labour was pretty horrific too not the beautiful spiritual experience everyone bragged about. I'm sure this was my punishment for not making a birthing plan, the holy grail of pregnancy and child birth according to the 'experts'. Three days of contractions, dilating, sweating and pushing. I'm pretty sure I pooed myself at some point, but nobody would confirm nor deny this. Swearing loudly, mainly at the complete bastard that put me in this position. Which would be legs akimbo with strangers poking around my private bits. Not fun. Not fun at all. Total bloody carnage it was. And what then felt like three weeks later, they placed a heavy, blood and mucus covered lump on me and expected me to be ecstatic.

"You forget all that pain the minute you hold your own little baby in your arms don't you," said the Irish moronic midwife who looked about twelve and clearly wasn't talking from experience but from a text-book. I shot her a look of pure loathing. "You tell that to my vagina, you'll find it down there by my ankles!" I hissed savagely at her. It was extremely out of character for me to be so vicious. I blame the drugs. Moronic midwife backed nervously away shooting Michael a sympathetic look as she left the room, obviously thinking I was a right sour bitch who deserved all my twenty four stitches.

Anyway, after a cup of tea, a measly biscuit and a huge dose of painkillers, I'd fallen in love with the now cleaned up Nicole and was ready to receive my visitors. However I was mostly ignored while Michael was greeted first like a war hero. "Well done young man, well done." Shaking his hand and clapping him on the back like he'd just discovered a cure for cancer or something equally momentous.
Yes, well done Michael, I seethed inwardly, you had unprotected and pretty unremarkable sex nine months ago and here you are getting all the credit. When I have just spent seventy two hours pushing a human being out of my fanny, but yep you're a fucking hero alright. Resentment bubbled under the surface of my now forever stretch marked, flabby tummy. I could have cried. Not that anybody would have noticed.

When my mum and dad arrived there was a slight scuffle about who would hold Nicole first. Dad won the battle while mum sulked and then finally acknowledged me, her only daughter and my rather dishevelled appearance. That was putting it politely. I was a mess. Boobs the size of genetically modified melons, over ripe and leaking all over the place. I

looked absolutely ridiculous sitting there on a rubber ring still looking, it had to be said, nine months pregnant.
"Emily, you look...well," she said giving me a look that I couldn't decipher. I'm not sure what she expected to find an hour after giving birth. Me in my pre pregnancy bikini, sipping a cocktail and looking fabulous darling?

"Mum, you'd look...ah..well, if you'd just been through what I just had," I retorted giving her a look of my own but it was lost on her as it was her turn to hold precious Nicole. I sat there like a gigantic, lactating lump being ignored.

So three years later despite knowing the horror and pain that was in store for me we decided to repeat the whole miserable process, and that was just the conception part of the plan! That pregnancy wasn't half as grim as the first. Running around after Nicole meant, although I might not have ever rivalled the cover model I had always coveted, I certainly didn't resemble an overweight wrestler second time around. And I went prepared with a birth plan! I sashayed into the labour room, well it was more like a slow waddle in reality, but the sashay was definitely intended.

Armed with my foolproof birthing plan, I placed it smugly on the table in front of my midwife, who I immediately recognised as the slightly older, but still moronic looking midwife from before. I'm sure I only imagined the evil glint in her eye as she snapped on her rubber gloves. The birthing plan was subsequently ignored and the labour was equally as horrific as I remembered it to have been, but this time a bloody and mucus covered baby boy that we called James was placed on my chest and the midwife sensibly kept her mouth shut.

My body may have been ruined beyond repair. I may have no pelvic floor muscles to speak off, thighs like a wrestler and a spongy stretch marked tummy, but my family was now complete.

But instead of that being my happy ever after it was only just the sad miserable beginning...

CHAPTER ONE

"My name is Emily Smyth and yes I was a teenage mother!"

Each week I vowed to myself that I would stand up and announce this loudly, confirming what all the other mothers thought they knew of me anyway.

And each week I didn't.

The awkward atmosphere and the forced joviality in the cold hall reminded me of AA meetings I'd seen on the television. Hard chairs, arranged in a circle, people trying not to make eye contact with anybody and nibbling biscuits they didn't really want. A group of random people coming together for a sole shared purpose. In this case a mother and toddler group. Otherwise known as sheer hell on earth. The other mums sat in their cliquey groups ignoring me after their initial smile of greeting and a generic 'hello, how are you?' Not even bothering to wait for the answer before turning back to their coven of witches.

You think I'm being harsh? You've clearly never rocked up to a toddler group alone then, hoping to make friends and then being exiled to 'the other side of the room!' The wrong side. Why did I put myself through it? I hear you ask. Well, I needed a two year old Nicole to understand there were other people in the world, apart from me, daddy, grandma and grandad! My circle was very small and very sad, made perhaps even sadder by the inclusion of the 'torture hour' as I'd renamed it.

I dutifully sat at the puzzle table, or the play dough table and interacted with my child whilst counting down the minutes in my head before I could leave the germ ridden hall of doom. The other mums however drank their coffee and ignored their own children, and more often than not I had their snotty nose kids wanting me to play with them too. And by snotty nosed, I don't mean aloof, I mean actual snot streaming from their noses, I swear some of these kids hadn't seen a flannel in days.

There was a man once, a widower apparently, who used to show up occasionally. He was very friendly and I felt less like a social pariah when he was in attendance. I thought I'd finally found a parenting buddy, but unfortunately it was too good to be true. It soon become apparent that he was coming on to me, and not subtly but in a sex pest sort of way. I soon gave him the short shrift and started talking about my huge, scary, jealous husband every time he even looked in my direction. Luckily he never asked to see a photo, or I'd have been busted when he saw puny little Michael staring goofily back at him. So he moved on to the next saddest loneliest looking woman In the room, before disappearing completely. It was eventually noted that he seemed to bring a different child each time he came, as though he were borrowing children for the sole purpose of picking up women. The lengths some people would go to get their leg over.

This wasn't the first occasion of being treated differently because of my teenage mother status. The first time being when I went to find out the results of my pregnancy test. This was before the days when you could buy pregnancy testing kits in Poundworld! I mean, who would trust the reliability of something so cheap?

The old lady receptionist grimaced at me when delivering the news that it was positive. She actually said I'm afraid it's positive. I smiled, thanked her and left, seething with indignation. So what if it was a huge shock and not exactly how I'd planned to spend my nineteenth year on this planet, I really didn't need someone else rubbing my nose in my stupidity. Would she have said that to a woman in her thirties? I think not. It was unbelievably ageist of her.
The second occasion that sticks vividly in my mind is the day I was dressing a five day old Nicole ready to take her home from the hospital. A momentous occasion in my mind. My grandma had knitted a very pretty white cardigan trimmed with red lace and matching booties. Nicole looked adorable. Pretty as a picture.

A sour faced old nurse stopped by my bed looking down at me, quite literally, and with her lips pursed like a cats bum hole she said ' you do realise that's a baby and not a dolly?'
'Thanks Janice, I'm aware she's not a doll but an actual baby, my savaged vagina bears witness to that fact you

condescending old bitch', is what I should have said but instead, I nodded not looking up because I didn't want her to see the tears that had pooled in the corner of my eyes, she'd made me feel stupid and had tainted Nicole's homecoming for me.

Although going back to the mother and toddler group, not that I ever would, not even if my life or the life's of my family depended on it. Maybe I had been unfair to those women, maybe the reason they weren't very welcoming or warm towards me wasn't anything to do with the fact I was a teenage mother. Maybe they genuinely didn't like the look of me or my clean nosed child.

My first real 'mummy' friend was a girl called Candice who moved into the flat opposite us. Maybe friend was too strong a word, acquaintance would be more appropriate. She was around my age and her daughter Crystal was twelve months older than two and a half year old Nicole. Candice was a rather odd woman with a wonky eye but she seemed pleasant and friendly enough. However, her family were the perfect Jeremy Kyle fodder. Alcoholic mother, no idea who her father was and a brother in prison. The father of her daughter was absent most of the time, until he needed money or sex, she was very open about all this considering I was practically a stranger.

My family was so vanilla it was an eye opener to see how some other families behaved, especially real life families that even Eastenders writers would deem too 'out there' for the British public.
So we began tentatively knocking on each other's door and asking if the other needed anything at the shops while we

were there. We then moved on to taking the girls to the park if the weather was nice.
Popping round each other's for cups of tea became a daily occurrence. The kids played together while we chatted. Crystal was a bit of a brat who didn't like to share her toys but it would do Nicole good to realise not everybody was as nice and kind as her.

Their flat was rather grubby too, I always felt like I needed a bath when getting back to the relative luxury of my own modest flat. Antibacterial gel became my constant companion when making visits across the hallway. I much preferred her to come to mine. Michael didn't like her, not one bit.
"I can't ever tell if she's looking at me or out the window," he complained. "Don't be so mean!" I admonished. "It breaks up my boring day talking to her and it's nice to get out the flat sometimes". The possibility of catching something contagious was the price I had to pay for not being lonely.
"I just don't want her in here that's all," he'd whined. "Why? Because her brother is in prison for burglary?" I said. Michael looked at me incredulously. "Yes, that's exactly why! And five pounds went missing the other day from my jar!"

I tutted in frustration at him, at his narrow mindedness, but vowed to become more vigilant in future. I didn't tell Michael that it was me that had actually taken the money from the jar, I'd fancied some chocolate and had no money. I felt mean letting Candice take the blame for it but it wouldn't make a blind bit of difference to what he thought about her in the end.

After a while though, Candice stopped being a nice distraction and started to become a pain in the arse. She'd had her hair cut in the same style as mine. She started wearing the same sort of clothes that I wore. It was all starting to become very

Single, White, Female. This especially freaked Michael out. "What if I accidentally mistook her for you one night?" He complained after bumping into her on the stairs one evening and mistook her for me. To be fair the lightbulb had blown on the shared landing and he'd been drunk but still, I was bloody offended. "She's a lot bloody shorter than me and a million times fatter!" I declared mutinously. He muttered something about us looking the same from behind, while drunk. Bloody cheek! "Maybe you should be more careful in future, and not go up behind woman until you know you're actually married to them!" I said, angrily.

Candice constantly wanted us to do things together, acting like we were best friends. She even started talking about going on holiday together. I could only imagine what Michael would think of that particular delight.

It soon become apparent that she was also rather envious of me and what she deemed my perfect life. How misguided was that? Making snide comments about my clever daughter, my husband that treated me right and our families that would do anything for us. The norm for most people I would have thought.

Then I'd found a bruise, albeit a small one, on Nicole's arm that had been caused by Crystal pinching her, when Nicole had tried to play with one of her toys. I wasn't having that! So, I started to ignore the door when she knocked and telling her I was busy when she invited me round.

I felt rather cruel but space was definitely needed. I couldn't tell if she believed my excuses or knew I was phasing her out. I can't imagine she was an expert on friendship etiquette. I'd not seen much evidence of any other friends visiting her in the entire time I'd known her, says me, the rather hypercritical outcast of the toddler group. I did sometimes wonder if I'd been a bit harsh. But it was Nicole, declaring in front of my mother that their flat smelt of poo, that was the final straw. Mum looked like she was going to have a coronary upon hearing her precious granddaughter was fraternising with dirty people.

Then one night an ambulance turned up, there was one hell of a racket, screaming and shouting coming from her flat. I assumed her boyfriend had turned up and started causing trouble again. Something he had taken to doing once a month, usually the day after she'd picked up her child benefit. It had become the norm now, but I hated having to listen to all the swearing of which there was lots. To our shame we pretended not to hear it and turned the telly up. Hoping that the nosy parker who lived above Candice would do the right thing and call the police. Low and behold blue flashing lights appeared not long after. We could sleep easy now. Within ten minutes of the police arriving the disturbance stopped. The blue lights disappeared. I thought nothing more of it.

The next day I received my regular knock on the door. Sighing and formulating an excuse before I even knew what she wanted, I opened the door to find Candice as expected but a Candice holding a baby in her arms. A big grin on her face. It turned out she'd been pregnant and hadn't known. The screaming had been her in labour. The absolute horror of it.

"I gave birth on the bloody kitchen floor," she announced proudly. I felt queasy, her kitchen floor was disgusting. "How have you not had a whole show dedicated to you on Jeremy Kyle?" I said, realising too late that might be considered an offensive thing to say. Candice though looked rather chuffed about it, that I'd even regarded her life that worthy of being ostracised on a day time television show by that shouty man. "Mum was on it the other week, she took my auntie on there, accusing her of stealing her microwave! She did a lie detector test and everything." She said proudly. I guess you hadn't made it, unless you'd done a lie detector test on telly in Candice's world. "And did she?" I said not caring one way or the other. But wondering how you could sneak a microwave out of somebody's house without being seen. Maybe her brother had been released early!

"Nah, it was the neighbour, can't trust anyone these days can you?" I couldn't decide if she was just making conversation or issuing me with a threat. A warning not to fuck with your neighbours.

"So do you want to hold him?" She thrust her bundle of joy at me. "I've called him Travis!" I had no choice but to hold him. Other people's babies rarely did anything for me, but I rocked him a bit, cooed at what a gorgeous boy he was then handed him back, the waft of a full nappy still lingering in my doorway. "So," I said, knowing it was rather uncouth to ask but also knowing it wouldn't bother her in the slightest. "Is your ex the father then?" I nodded towards the baby. She shrugged her shoulders. "Maybe, not sure." That was not the answer I was expecting at all! Who else could possibly be in the running?

"It could be Michaels." She retorted deadpan.

I just stared at her. She stared back at me. "I'm joking Em," she laughed punching me on the arm. I nodded, obviously you were joking Candice. But it was a step too far for me. I wanted to rub my arm where she'd punched me, but not wanting to give her the satisfaction. She tried to lighten the mood, maybe realising she'd overstepped the mark. "Trav, could be Nicole's toy boy in years to come," Candice laughed.

Over my dead body, I thought privately. If I ever mentioned that snippet to Michael he'd have us change our names and leave the country immediately. I noted unkindly that Trav rhymed with Chav. I knew that was what we'd end up calling him in private. I only hoped that never slipped out in her presence. That would be unkind. It wasn't the babies fault his mother was beginning to scare me a bit.
Thankfully, for me that wouldn't be a problem. Candice was moved into a house and out of the area not long after the birth of Travis. Although we promised to stay in touch, it was just words. I had no intention of ever going to stay at her new house, despite being invited to their house warming party. Or going to Yarmouth for bank holiday weekend either.

Three months after she'd moved, and I'd ignored numerous phone calls and the odd letter, Michael and I had moved too, into our own new house so there was no longer anyway of her finding me. The trail would be cold if she ever tried to. Not that she ever would I'm sure. So that was that.

By the time Nicole started nursery school aged three and I was pregnant with James I'd made some real 'mummy friends' of my choosing. Healthy friendships. Ones that weren't just born out of convenience or close proximity to each other. There were five of us altogether, I guess we'd be considered a clique by the other mums in the playground. Because of my poor treatment at the toddler group, I always made sure I was pleasant to everyone. Especially to the mothers standing alone, always a 'hello' and a 'how are you?' And I would actually wait for the answer and make conversation before automatically drifting towards my friends. It cost nothing to be nice and the school playground could be a tricky obstacle course to navigate at times.

I'm not sure how the five us came about to be honest, it just happened. We naturally just seemed to gravitate toward each other, our children, who were already friends, pulling us into a readymade friendship group. Not to sound like a sentimental fool but for a while we were like a little family bundling along together. Sharing the highs and the lows of parenthood. This was an extremely happy period of my life where I finally felt happy in my own skin. I wasn't that teenage mother anymore, I was Emily, just mum to Nicole and James and good friends with Sharon, Miranda, Tina and Linda. Until our children reached the end of primary school we did everything together. Play dates at our homes, picnics in the park, bike rides, trips to the zoo etc. But it was all about the children. Occasionally on our birthdays we'd go out without the kids and have a meal and a drink, but our main common interest were our children. All good things come to an end, and our children went their own separate ways at secondary school, although Nicole and Miranda's daughter Grace were still pretty friendly. One by one we all started not being readily available to each other as before. We all had other commitments, jobs, relationship issues, new friends. And it just petered out naturally, no nasty fall outs, we just stopped hanging out. We were all friends on Facebook now and we kept up to date with each other's business, what they had for dinner and how many times they'd been to the gym, that sort of thing. And we always tried to meet up at least twice a year. Well except Linda who was no longer with us. Nope she wasn't dead. Five years ago she'd left the country with her toyboy lover, dumping her poor husband and leaving him with the kids and nobody had heard from her since. Her Facebook account now deactivated. There was always one nutty slightly odd friend in every friendship group and she was ours. I guessed in my current friendship group that position was probably held by me.

CHAPTER TWO

Michael and I ended up separating eight years ago after thirteen mediocre years of togetherness. It had been a long time coming, a welcome relief for me, a bit like removing a painful splinter from deep under your skin after it's been festering there for a while going gangrenous. For him? I guess it was like having the rug pulled out from under him with no warning, although the constant arguing, permanently chilly atmosphere and absence of sex for two years should have given him a heads up to what might eventually happen and it wasn't a happy ending. I used those metaphors when explaining the breakup to my friend Elaine.

"It's just so sad," she'd said squeezing my hand. "But it wasn't all bad was it? You were happy once?" It seemed really important to her that there were some good times in my sad little marriage so I quickly racked my brain and came up with an occasion just to appease Elaine, a hopeless romantic. "Of course, there was the time Michael went on a rugby weekend with the lads, we were both pretty happy then." She'd just looked at me. "That's just so sad," she'd repeated but in a slightly different tone than before. Elaine was my oldest friend in the world, oldest in time not years by the way, she wasn't ancient. I don't as a rule socialise with the elderly, apart from my grandma on special occasions, such as the upcoming Easter circus at mums house.

My friendship with Elaine went right back to our early school days, becoming firm friends over our shared love of Sylvanian Families after I spied a Mrs Badger tightly gripped in her sweaty little hand on day one of infant school. A kindred spirit, clearly. After our initial bonding moment in the playground, we'd both bring in our creepy little animal figurines dressed as humans and play with them every chance we'd get. Obviously alienating ourselves from all the other girls who didn't have weird obsessions with hedgerow creatures, but not caring that we'd become social outcasts of our own making. Until that fateful day when my mother rabbit went missing from my desk. A man-hunt was launched, everyone giddy with excitement at getting out of glockenspiel practise (as small kids we loved a bit of drama and I remember it being a thrilling time despite my eventual and sad loss). Mother rabbit was discovered floating without her pink tunic, upside down in one of the boys toilets. Devastated wasn't the word, especially as little Johnny had peed all over her first before running to tell the teacher of his discovery. I never did find out who cruelly robbed a rabbit family of their mother but rumours were rife at the time that it was Mrs Middlebrook the piano teacher. I forget the reasoning behind the absurdity of that particular rumour, but it was something to do with her pet rabbit dying of myxomatosis and it sending her a little doolally. Luckily our friendship survived the Sylvanian Families ban that was imposed soon afterwards and we bonded over our joint hatred of little Johnny instead. Whose only crime, it would appear looking back, was having a weak bladder.

So I agreed with Elaine that yes it was sad that we'd been unable to make it work. However, it was definitely sadder for Michaels mum, when he moved back into her spare room for the foreseeable future. On the plus side it was an amicable split, so amicable in fact that I'm pretty sure the kids, Nicole then aged eleven and James aged eight, hadn't even realised he'd left home, as he seemed to spend more time with us than he ever did before.

"Just passing," he'd say as he turned up on the doorstep again, with some other lame excuse for being there. Funny thing was we lived at the bottom of a huge housing estate and down a cul-de-sac of just four houses, so the chances of him 'just passing' were pretty slim. I humoured him anyway, perhaps this was rather unkind of me in the long run but I was actually changing the habit of a lifetime and trying to be nice to him.

After a few weeks Michaels permanent presence at the house was becoming uncomfortable to say the least. Turning up to return random things of the children's that kept turning up in his car. I was pretty sure he was stealing some of them from the house just so he could have an excuse to come and give them back. "Ah yes I've been looking for that slightly greying old sock with a hole in the toe for ages." I'd say deadpan when he'd turned up one day proudly waving it around as though he'd just returned my lost purse full of money. "Oh sorry am I interrupting your dinner?" He'd asked looking past me into the house where he could clearly see the kids eating. "Well, it is five o'clock, and that's the time we have dinner," I smiled tightly, adding silently 'as well you bloody know'. "There's some spare spaghetti if you'd like to join us," said grudgingly hoping he'd say 'no thanks that would be hugely inappropriate'. So this was how I ended up eating dinner with my estranged husband more nights after we separated than when we were actually together. It was the morning when I was happily soaking in my bath and the distinct smell of bacon came wafting enticingly up the stairs that finally propelled me into action.

At first, stupidly, I thought it was the kids making me breakfast and I felt touched at their thoughtfulness. Then I remembered that my kids were lazy little sods who were still snoring in their pits and that they wouldn't know how to use the grill without specific written instructions anyway. Also, we had no bacon.

"Would you like tomato sauce in your sandwich?" Called a voice that sounded suspiciously like Michaels. I sighed, hurriedly got dressed and explained kindly to him as if he were a simpleton - obviously between bites of bacon sandwich - that he couldn't keep doing this and could I please have my bloody key back. He was clearly embarrassed, and had kept nodding, I tried to ignore the tears glistening in his eyes and the quivering bottom lip. "So you understand?" I asked, wiping sauce from my mouth. "Of course Emily, I'm so sorry." He smiled bravely at me. Phew..."I'll phone in future and knock before coming in." Clearly not then.

"You do realise that at some point it's all going to kick off!" Karen my close friend and next door neighbour said at the time. "When he realises that there's not going to be a happy reconciliation between you both, because that's what he's hoping will happen. He probably thinks this is just a silly stage you're going through and when you're bored of being on your own you'll let him come home." She was talking from experience having split with her long term partner Paul a year ago. Paul unfortunately did not go quietly, he pitched a tent in their back garden instead and camped out for three long weeks causing untold trouble, until Karen called in the big guns i.e. his mother to take him home to her spare room. There appeared to be a reoccurring theme happening here and I vowed that as soon as James had left home I'd take preventative measures and turn his room into a gym or office just so he couldn't come back every time he broke up with a girlfriend.

"Karen, that won't happen. We are both mature adults with only our children's best interests at heart, we won't have them in the middle of rowing and nastiness." I said naïvely and perhaps a little patronisingly. Karen kept quiet. I'll give her her due when the shit hit the fan two weeks later and she caught me running down the road throwing flower pots after Michaels hastily retreating car as the kids watched traumatised from the doorstep she didn't say 'I told you so!' She just handed me a glass of wine.

Old John from across the road had also witnessed my crazy lady display. I was too angry to feel the mortification I should rightly feel. "Hello young Emily," he called in greeting, I heard the disappointment in his voice. I'd become one of those unstable women. I assumed he'd been married to one of them at some point. His own flower pots were removed from the front of his house that night as if he thought I might suddenly go bat shit crazy again and launch his lovely blooms at Michael instead of my own dead, sticky offerings. I also got the impression he avoided me after that.
I said as much to Karen, who scoffed and said I was being paranoid. "Why do you think that?"
"Because I never saw him again despite him not moving away for another four years, which he did while I was on holiday."
"Paranoid!" She repeated, less convincingly.

Anyway back to the day I found out Michael had moved on.

"He's met someone. Already!! Tara!! At a friends wedding apparently!! Well that's a lie to start with, he has no friends it must have been online!! She could be anyone!! I won't have her around my children." I'd ranted, it was a little over the top it had to be said. "Are you jealous?" Asked Karen mildly.

"Jealous!?" I spat, "God no, but...he makes me so angry." I wasn't jealous but I was slightly put out how quickly he had moved on.

Michael had taken on the arrogant swagger of a man suddenly getting female attention and probably more sex than he'd had in recent years, which wouldn't be hard as he'd had none. I'd likened his foreplay technique back in the day to the 'stretch and sweep' the torture a midwife administered to your cervix to try and induce labour. I only hoped he'd improved somewhat since then or Tara was in for a real treat.

He'd started to wear chinos, a crease ironed down the middle instead of his usual jeans, and polo-shirts instead of his tatty football tops. His hair now had a centre parting. He looked like a prize twat. He'd been due to have the children as it was his weekend but had cancelled the day before citing a "personal emergency". Maybe he'd finally looked in a mirror and discovered what a wanker he looked. I was seething as I'd made plans to go out myself. "What's the problem? You thought I'd hang around forever waiting for you to take me back, I'm not your puppet!" He'd hurled at me. "IT'S NOT ABOUT ME IT'S ABOUT THE CHILDREN! And I've never treated you like a puppet, a MUPPET perhaps but not a puppet." I yelled.

Cue months of furious arguments on the doorstep when he could be bothered to pick the children up that is and nasty phone calls about maintenance and pretty much anything else we could find to argue about.

There was one particular instance that sticks in my mind, a ridiculous argument about a plant from the garden that Michael wanted me to dig up and give him. "I bought and

planted it." He said matter of factly. Pompous arse. "Planted in my garden." I shot back. "Then, it was our garden." "But I've watered it and nurtured it." This was a lie, I didn't even know what stupid plant he was talking about.
"Nurtured it? How?" He asked incredulously. "By talking to it obviously." "Like fuck you do!" "Prove it!"
"You are such a child," he shook his head in a mock sadness gesture. "No you are." I said, all but sticking my tongue out, proving him right.

The following week I dug up the bloody plant and left it on the driveway for him to find when he came to pick up the kids. "That's not even the plant I wanted, anyway I've changed my mind. Plus I live in a first floor flat I have nowhere to put it." He said as if I was the stupid one. I had to count to ten, very slowly otherwise Michael would have ended up at A&E having a plant removed from his anus. The plant then died. There were no winners that day.

My children would now be the product from a broken home, who knew what lasting damage this would cause them. I felt incredibly sad, horrendously guilty and furiously angry all at the same time.
Had I made a mistake?

Unlike Michael I decided not to put all my proverbial eggs in one basket when it came to dating again. Well, after my first initial dating disaster that is. Instead I played the field for a time. Though after a while it felt more like I was working that field. In fact it really wasn't that much fun at all sifting the wheat from the chav!

Once again I asked myself if I'd made a huge mistake ending my marriage to a reliable, hardworking, decent, boring, hypercritical, argumentative...nope I'd definitely made the right decision there and even if I never dated another man again and had my virginity grow back I'd still be better off without him.

My first dalliance was with Irish Benjamin from Ireland who now lived in England! I'd met him online and yes his profile really was as vague as it sounded. Yes I know that I kicked up a stink when I thought Michael had met Tara online, but this was different, this was me and I trusted my instincts. I was sure I could spot a rogue a mile away (pah ha!). Plus his profile picture was really nice, a bit blurry in places, especially around the facial area perhaps, but I could see he had nice green, possibly brown eyes and a pleasant smile, which is what all women want don't they? Blurred, pleasant features!

Benjamin will be forever known as 'The Mistake'. So much for trusting my instincts, I felt very cross with myself afterwards, which is a huge understatement! We 'talked' online for a month before arranging to meet up.

"So he's like your pen-pal?" Joked Karen one evening after a glass or two of wine. For some reason this observation made by her really bothered me because in my head Benjamin and I were in a relationship! God, how I cringe when I think back. I think I must have been suffering from a form of mental illness, it was the only explanation for my ridiculous behaviour. We swapped phone numbers at my insistence and I phoned him straight away, wanting to move our 'relationship' forward with immediate effect (cringe again). But whenever I phoned him he never answered, eventually texting back an hour, maybe two hours later citing being busy at work or not hearing his phone and then giving me a specific time to phone back which was pretty helpful in a way because it meant I could prepare myself.

The first time, I locked myself excitedly in the bathroom, ran a deep bubbly bath and waited and true to his word he phoned me when he'd said he would. In the privacy of my bathroom we chatted for the first time and the conversation flowed really nicely, well as nicely as it could when talking to an Irish man for the first time, I think I only said 'pardon what did you say?' about seven hundred times. It was all going swimmingly well until someone started pounding on the bathroom door! "Mum let me in I need a poo!" Shouted James! Shit, was there anyway Benjamin might not have heard that? But just in case he hadn't! "MUM I NEED A POO LET ME IN!" Screamed James louder, "ITS COMING OUT, HURRY."

Suffice to say the mood had been broken and Benjamin rang off before I could say "Did I not mention I had children?" So awkward and yes so cringeworthy! So, to cut a very long, mostly embarrassing, on my behalf anyway, story short. I was mortifyingly stood up by Benjamin once at a hotel that I then had to pay for. I was then blown out by him six times in a row with the most far fetched excuses ever used by a man before. Before meeting up with him twice rather unsuccessfully in the eight months that he occupied the obviously vacant space in my head. After a little bit of investigating via social media it turned out that Benjamin actually had a girlfriend, which explained why he was never able to answer his phone, despite the fact when I did meet up with him that bloody phone appeared to be welded to his sodding hand.
He also had several fake profiles that I'm guessing his girlfriend was blissfully unaware of. Obviously I made sure she became aware of what a cheating arsehole bastard her beloved boyfriend actually was. I then blocked him and her

very quickly, as we all know it's the messenger that tends to get shot rather than the accused.

I was mortified to have been taken in like that but even more so that I'd actually allowed him to do so, over and over again. "One day you will laugh about this!" Karen used to say to me, usually when I was sobbing my heart out at her kitchen table drunk or when she was holding my hair back as I was throwing up in her toilet. Also drunk. "Never!" I meant it then, but now seven years later she was right, it was absolutely hilarious what I put up with. The excuses, the lies and the blatant bullshit that was so glaringly obvious that I just couldn't see back then. Some might say I was extremely naive all those years ago or maybe just agree with Karen's opinion that I was 'just fucking stupid'.

If truth be known I think I was simply in mourning over my failed marriage. Karen supported me immensely during this dire part of my life. Not just by being there to clean up my drunken vomit. She was also there to wipe my tears, of which there were many. Mainly tears of guilt though. Personally, I was perfectly happy about my single status, even if the single mother stigma was a bit embarrassing. Not so much for me, but for my mother who seemed to take it so personally. As if I divorced Michael on purpose just to cause her maximum mortification with her snooty peers. Michael in the beginning when he'd been acting like a lost puppy who'd been kicked, elevated the guilty feelings I had. But looking back perhaps that was all just an act because as soon as he got a whiff of a new bitch to play with, boring her to death instead of me he soon turned into the cocky shitbag I now had to endure.
I say it was a dire time because although I was practically giddy at the thought of not ever having to have sex with Michael again, I had effectively caused my children pain.

Although they hid it very well. They were now thriving in the less chilly atmosphere, but maybe that was just a passing warm front before a real storm hit.

Nicole and James both ended up going through a rebellious stage at school, though thankfully not at the same time and it hadn't lasted too long either. Every other day or so it would seem like, I'd receive a voicemail from a harassed teacher inviting me to come in and discuss their destructive behaviour. They always made it seem like I had a choice in the matter. I wondered if it would be considered bad form to decline their rather unappealing invitation. Obviously I never did, I dutifully turned up to hear how rude, sullen and argumentative my child had become time and time again. While my rude, sullen child sat there and argued that the teacher was lying. It was painful. They were both intelligent children, who were throwing away their education, according to the teachers in question. Personally they just seemed like normal teenagers to me, fighting against the system. Not wanting to conform. But what did I know, I was just a former teenage mother. The rather scary head of the science department showed me Nicole's exercise book one time, it was perfect as far as I could see. Lovely handwriting, the worksheets stuck in straight. Lots of ticks and A's on show. There had to be a catch! Obviously, it turned out that it wasn't Nicole's science book after all. She pulled Nicole's out from under the table. I had to cover my mouth. The front cover was hanging off and water stained, the worksheets crumpled and not stuck in neatly and not a lot of ticks or much else could be seen in between the sticky pages. Despite the seriousness of the situation I wanted to smile, it was why I'd covered my mouth. I knew I couldn't meet Nicole's eye because I would start laughing. It was slightly funny I had to admit. Although I would of course punish her when I got home.

"Is everything alright at home?" A sympathetic teacher would always end up asking, knowing full well that dad wasn't around anymore, because I'd been up front and told them, it wasn't a secret. I'd smile and lie that everything was fine, well until we got home tonight that is and I confiscate his bloody PlayStation until he can behave himself and save me the embarrassment of being patronised every other day.
At first when the school contacted me, I'd call and ask Michael for support too. "They're teenagers," he'd retort. "Of course they're moody, rude and argumentative!" "Will you have a word with them?" I'd ask knowing full well he wouldn't. "God, do you not remember what absolute shits we were at school?" He'd laughed. Yes Michael I do and look where it got us you twat! I did not want my children ending up like him or indeed me, so I stopped asking him for help and dealt with it myself. Story of my bloody life. Eventually they stopped behaving like fools and knuckled down and the phone calls became less and less. It appeared Michael had been right, not something you'd hear me say again or ever admit to him.

I just hoped they wouldn't turn out to be psycho weirdos when they were adults. I selfishly hated the thought that they might one day be asked the question 'so tell me about the relationship with your mother!' By a therapist trying to get to the bottom of their destructive behaviour. However if they wanted to blame the father, I'd be ok with that. I'd hate them citing the main reason for being so fucked up is the excuse of coming from a broken home, ' it was mum who broke up with dad, just so she could go out and get drunk with her friend Karen!' Not the main reason of leaving Michael clearly, but going out and having fun was a definitely a plus point to my newly divorced status. Please remember that while all my friends were coming of age and legally going clubbing and

getting off with random guys, I was at home breastfeeding and wearing easy access bras. Not sexy, not sexy at all!
I'd felt like a middle aged woman before I'd even left my teens. So, I'm afraid the also newly single Karen and I reverted back to behaving like teenagers, dragging Elaine along too for the ride when she wasn't too busy being Miss sensible and a tad judgmental it had to be said.

"Should you be going out, again?" She'd said when I invited her one night to a foam party at the local club. A flier had been shoved through my letterbox, probably aimed at the horny teens in the area but intercepted by a 'desperate to have fun' me. "It's called having fun!" I replied rolling my eyes at Karen who was jumping up and down in excitement a shower cap on her head in preparation behind me.
"I can't I'm busy!" Said Elaine pompously. Probably balancing her cheque book I'd said to Karen. We both laughed unkindly at her and her sensible ways. I wasn't a very nice person back then, especially after a drink or two when I felt I wasn't being supported, and support from my closest friends was what I needed, misguided support or not. Unfortunately, for Elaine, she got the brunt of my meanness. She was always so sensible, like the good cop to Karen's bad cop sitting on my shoulder, wittering in my ear telling me to do the right thing when all I wanted to do was get drunk, forget my responsibilities and have a bit of fun for once. I wondered occasionally if my mum had paid her a consultancy fee to keep me on the straight and narrow.

If the truth be known I think she was just concerned about me, that I'd get myself into some sort of trouble. Maybe a night in once in a while wouldn't hurt. Not every night out had to result in getting wasted and suffering for it the next day. Yet I'd spent years doing the right thing and being sensible, so I wanted to do the opposite for a change. When I say reverting back to teenage antics, I don't mean we were getting drunk on cheap ciders and lying in fields. Although Elaine and I had done that a lot when we were younger (before all her sense of fun had been extinguished by real life and sense of responsibility). We'd pretend that we were staying at each other's house instead. I'm still surprised that we got away with that time after time considering my mother was like a cross between Hyacinth Bucket and Columbo on speed.

Karen and I were classy ladies in our thirties when we'd become single, we obviously had a little more dignity and behaved with more decorum than that. So instead we went to our local wetherspoons, drank the buy one get one free shots and jugs of cocktails through straws. Then made huge prats of ourselves on the dance floor, throwing some shapes around (does anyone under the age of seventy even use that saying anymore?) whilst taking photos of the whole car crash to upload to Facebook when we got home at silly o'clock in the morning.
Please note my children weren't home alone during this time. I was recapturing my lost youth not attempting to get my children put on the at risk register. They were safely ensconced with their father on 'his weekend' when he could be bothered. I'd become one of those people now, someone who could use the excuse 'sorry no can do, it's my weekend with my kids!' Whilst pulling a sad face."Do you know what the hardest part of being a single parent is?" I slurred at Karen one time after a mad night out. Karen shook her head drunkenly, eyes closed. I think if there had been a speech bubble above her head it would have read 'I don't care, fuck off home Emily I'm tired!' "All of it!" I said, banging my hand hard down on the table, making Karen jump, waking her up in the process. "Surely it's just the same, except there's no man

there to leave the toilet seat up and create nasty smells," she reasoned sleepily, picking up her empty coffee cup, sipping its empty contents then putting it down again. Her eyes sliding to the kitchen clock that was reading the ungodly hour of half past four, in the morning. "No,no!!" I cried dramatically. "I can't even say 'just wait until your father gets home anymore!' When they are being shits!" "Did you ever say that to them?" She said, snorting with great mirth. Which then made me snort, snot shooting out of my left nostril which I unceremoniously wiped on my sleeve. We both sat at Karen's kitchen table laughing uncontrollably. As if either of my strong willed children would ever be that bothered if I threatened them with their flaky father. After a minute we'd forgotten what we'd been laughing about and Karen managed to manoeuvre me to the door. I probably only imagined the sound of Karen double locking and bolting her back door as I let myself into mine.

Clearly Karen didn't care what the hardest part was, she wasn't a parent so it was all rather irrelevant to her. So just in case you cared, the hardest part about being a single parent is the loneliness. The absolute tediousness of it all. Oh and the lack of any worthwhile support from their absent father.
I remember there was a period where Nicole had turned into an insolent little madam, back chatting me at every turn and I'd rather foolishly asked Micheal for some backup. I'll never forget that look on his face, an air of triumph blowing around him. "You wanted to become a single mother Emily, maybe you should have thought about the consequences of your actions." "I ended my relationship with you, not your relationship with your children!" adding a silent 'prick' to the end of that sentence. Needless to say I never asked him again. I did what any good mother would do and turned off the wifi. "That'll bother you more than it will bother me," she said

bravely, but I saw real fear in her eyes. "Maybe, but that's a sacrifice I'll have to make." It wasn't, I automatically connected to Karen's wifi next door but Nicole wasn't to know that. After two nights of no internet and no amount of stamping her feet and crying at me to change my mind, she knew I was deadly serious and apologised, albeit grudgingly, but stopped with the undulant attitude. A huge victory for the single mother going it alone! Go me. Nicole was about to start secondary school when we'd first separated. I think Michael believed it was a trial separation, I let him think this whilst knowing I'd never go back. Because as lonely and tedious as being a lone parent was, it was nothing compared to being trapped in a loveless marriage. It really was bad timing to grow a backbone and break up the family whilst Nicole was on the cusp of adolescence though. Not only did I have to deal with her raging hormones and changing body alone, I also had to deal with the ridiculously long uniform and equipment list that accompanied secondary school admission on my own. I considered, very briefly, asking Michael for extra help regarding the never ending list of stuff needed, but couldn't find the nerve, knowing he'd give that smug smile and say 'surely that's what my maintenance is for Emily?' Nice one Michael, thanks for reiterating the reasons why I despise you. Your maintenance hardly even pays or their food! That list gave me nightmares the entire six weeks holidays. The pressure was on. That rugby top, the one that should have been bloody designer considering how much it cost, that MUST HAVE for outdoor PE rugby top, well it was worn about five times then lived at the bottom of the washing basket for 4 years, that's how important it was to have it! I should have started charging it rent it stayed in there so long. I would have brought it out of retirement to pass down to James when it was his turn but typically they'd changed the design and made the new one ten times more expensive, rendering it obsolete.

The 'absolutely must have' football boots and shin pads also hardly ever worn. The track suit ditto. Can you spot a pattern emerging here? As for the compulsory gum shield? Well that never came out of its packaging, so at least I was able to slip that into James PE bag, saving myself all of £3.99 when the time came. So when James didn't actually use it either, I decided it might be nice to pass down to his kids, kind of like a poor version of a family heirloom, one that isn't actually worth anything. Shame that can't be said of all the one hundred and two other "essential" items on the list. My other major bug bear was that everything had to have the school logo on it, so it wasn't even possible to buy cheaper alternatives elsewhere. It all had to be bought from the official online outlet! Money grabbing bastards! Thank goodness for tax credits, the one good thing about being a single, working mother.

CHAPTER THREE

The Easter weekend was fast approaching bringing with it the annual Easter gathering at my parents house. I'm not sure when this stopped being a no strings attached casual family get together to a compulsory, you must be there or else kind of thing. My family, just in case you wondered were not in any way, shape or form religious. We didn't ever go to church, we didn't care much if we missed an episode of Songs of Praise and there were no creepy Jesus pictures adorning the walls of my parents house. But for some peculiar reason, Easter meant something to our parents. Well more to my mum actually, I'm pretty sure my dad could have done without the whole rigmarole of the Easter celebrations. He much preferred to be on the golf course with his beer buddies as he was every other Sunday of the year. I remember one year, forever known as "CrazyMumGate" when my brother Simon threw a crucifix in the works by citing a work emergency and tried to pull out of dinner. Well, the fall out was massive, tears and tantrums, accusations of not caring about family traditions. There was even talk of Simon being written out of the will at one point. Although to be fair it was me who started that particular rumour, trying to inject some humour into the situation that was threatening to spiral out of control. It was only a roast dinner after all. Mum gave him the silent treatment, she even phoned him up especially to give him the silent treatment. So, needless to say he managed to get out of his work responsibilities and be there. It meant that he was passed over for a promotion a few months later because of his lack of commitment to the job but at least mum was happy. It had been a tense five days and a pretty strained Easter celebration that year, but it had served as a warning to others, do not even think about trying to break tradition or incur the wrath of crazy mum. Later on it was revealed that our mother was 'going through the change' which explained her crazy lady behaviour somewhat, well some of it. She still had the tendency to go way over the top at any given moment, for any given reason. "Do I have to go?" moaned James this year. "Seriously what's going to happen if I don't go!" He said whiningly, an air of defiance swirling about him in amongst the hormones. "Nothing! Nothing will happen. If you are prepared to phone Grandma yourself and explain that playing grand theft auto with your friends on PlayStation is more important than her family Easter tradition I'm sure she'll understand, darling, here phone her now." I passed him the phone. He pulled a face and mumbled "doesn't matter", the defiance dispersing as quickly as it came, unfortunately the boy smell still lingered after he'd stomped off. "There's a good lad." I said feeling smug.

Mum phoned a week before the feeding of the five thousand to confirm details, I suspected an ulterior motive behind the phone call. I was right. "Oh Emily how very rude I've been!"

Mum exclaimed as if reading from a script, I now had a feeling what was coming next! "Obviously your friend Graham is invited on Sunday too, I should have said before." I sighed and rolled my eyes, here we go again.
"Oh don't worry mum," I said breezily "Graham is working Sunday but maybe next time." It had been my standard answer for the last four months, and every time mum had suggested a meeting. Why I'd even told her I was seeing someone was beyond me, oh that's right I hadn't. Nicole had ratted me out.
Mums displeasure was obvious, lots of tutting and huffy sighing. "Are you ashamed of your family Emily?" She asked ridiculously, crazy mum putting in an appearance once again.
"Of course not, maybe next time." I said a little more forcibly.

The truth was Graham wasn't working and would have jumped at the chance of meeting my family but I was dragging my feet about that particular milestone, I'm not sure why. Graham was my boyfriend, excuse me while I swallow the little bit of sick that just came up, 'boyfriend' is such a hideous word to describe a grown man, but that's what he was I suppose. I had met him in the the local co-op, we both reached for the last reduced pork pie in the chiller cabinet and our eyes met. I fluttered my eye lashes a bit hoping he'd be a gentleman and let me have it but his grip definitely tightened around it protectively. But while I considered wrestling him for it, my handbag was wrenched off my shoulder by a spotty youth who went to run out the shop with it. "Stop him!" I yelled. It was very Carry On material.
Graham acted instinctively and threw the reduced porkpie at my muggers head. I'd love to be able to tell you that it hit him hard and knocked him off his stride. Giving Graham time to catch up with him and save the day, but that would have been a lie. What actually happened was the pork pie sailed through

the air, missed mugger boy completely and hit the young cashier behind the till, who yelled 'oi', catching the attention of my actual saviour. Who was in actual fact an eighty eight year old lady who tripped him up as he went to run past her with her walking stick, he fell flat on his face! Graham then grabbed him and rescued my bag and held onto the delinquent youth who looked rather shamefaced, and who I recognised as one of the boys in James's year at school, until the police arrived. We got ourselves a half page spread in the local paper, well, myself and Doris did anyway. A photo of me the poor victim together with the hero of the hour Doris and her cane. Graham got a small mention at the end of the article as Gary aged 58. Obviously it was a typo but a devastating blow to Graham as he'd told everyone he knew an exaggerated more heroic version of the actual story, he was ribbed about it for months. By me mostly. "I'm forty bloody four, where did they get fifty eight from?" He kept repeating over and over again. "And your name is not Gary!" I added dryly. Fifteen year old Davey Jones got a suspended twelve month sentence and a lifetime ban from all co-ops. His rather scary mum also made him write me a sorry letter. Which is still on my fridge as a constant reminder to James to not be a criminal arsehole. But anyway, 'Gary' and I swapped numbers and when he ended up asking me out for a drink I just thought why not? He wasn't my usual type, if I even had one, which I didn't. He was a few years older than me but not the thirty years the paper unfairly stated. He had curly dark hair and the less than glamorous job title of a postman but he was nice, honest and most importantly kind.

Introducing Graham to my children, even though they were almost adults themselves, was a huge deal for me. A nerve wracking ordeal in fact. Not once in the eight years of singledom had I ever bought a man into our home and into their lives. Don't get me wrong I'd not be mistaken for a celibate nun in a police line up but I'd hardly be counted as promiscuous whore either. I'd dated a bit, but all behind the scenes of family life, when they were safely cocooned with their father on 'his weekend' or in the loving four walls of my parents abode being fed homemade cake. As far as my kids were concerned, I'd sacrificed my love life to be the perfect mum to them, albeit a drunk one at times who occasionally lost her shit over stupid things, phone calls from the school, missing biscuits, lights left on all night, the usual bollocks that all mums complained about, whether single or not. My main reason of resistance was because Michael had introduced his new girlfriend Tara within weeks of meeting her and months of us splitting up. It made me more wary, more aware of the damage we could possibly impart upon our impressionable children. I didn't want to be that stereotypical teenage mother whose kids had numerous 'uncles' trailing in and out of the family home over the years.

Karen and indeed Elaine found this hilariously funny when I'd spoken about my fears. "Nicole and James are almost adults, and not once in your eight single years have you ever introduced an 'uncle' to them," laughed sensible Elaine uncharacteristically. Tears of mirth running down her face. "Just do it, what's the worst that could happen?" Karen was of the same opinion but for different reasons.
"Bloody hell Emily, are you joking? Or is your resistance more down to you worrying about what your children may think of Graham?" Damn you Karen! I thought, she always cut straight to the chase and was spot on. Yes, Graham was a nice man but I could imagine that my children might find him less than worthy of their mother. A bit wishy washy, or to quote Nicole 'a bit lame'. I didn't want my children to judge me. I didn't want to be seen as just settling. Anyway, regardless of any misgivings I might have had, I approached the subject with Graham, who

as I thought was more than up for meeting my children. In his eyes, I guess, he saw it as part commitment on my behalf. Maybe I was more of a catch than I thought? That was preferable than thinking of him being more desperate. I then approached the subject with Nicole and James who were both less that enthused. "So do we have to go out for dinner and make polite conversation with this man you're seeing?" Asked Nicole contemptuously. "Can't he just come here and say hi, do we really have to spend a whole evening with a guy who can't even throw a pork pie at a target!" Eyes rolling so far back into her head i was seriously concerned she was having convulsions. James was even more contemptuous. "Do we have to meet him? I mean what's the point! It's not as though you'll get married again, I've heard you say to Karen that you'd rather kill yourself than chain yourself to another arsehole again!" Oh god, my kids would so end up in therapy because of my ability to use my indoor voice. It was only when I said, out of absolute desperation, that Graham had suggested taking us to a theme park for the day, an idea that I'd vetoed immediately because it was one of the stupidest ideas I'd ever heard, that they both changed their tune and backtracked and said 'sure why not!' FUCK IT! When he first suggested it I'd laughed and said 'over my dead body'. Only a man who didn't have kids or had never actually been to a theme park would suggest going to one with two stroppy teenagers. I'd had my fill of theme parks over the years. God awful places of hell, almost on par with mother and toddler groups. Not only did you have to sell your soul to the devil to be able to afford to be even admitted to the place and that was with the buy one get one free vouchers I'd procured from cereal packets. But you then needed a second mortgage to be able to afford a can of coke in one of those places. The huge packets of sugar puffs, minus the vouchers I'd ripped off, took up valuable space in the cupboard under the stairs. It was such as shame that none of us actually liked those bloody puffs of nothing. I still rather hoped one of my children might suddenly wake up one morning and declare 'they rather fancied a big bowl of sugar puffs!'

So off we went to Chessington World of adventures. Graham and his band of miserable men. He wanted to leave early, to beat the traffic. That was such an old man thing to say, reminding me so much of my dad. Many an annual holiday to Cornwall when Simon and I were kids saw us leaving at silly o'clock in the morning, only to arrive early and have to wait in a lay-by for six hours until we could get into our caravan at four. Nicole and James, behaving like zombies, because they'd been deprived of a few more hours sleep grunted a greeting before sticking their headphones in and ignoring us for the entire journey. They weren't creating a great impression it had to be said. Graham and I shared a bag of lemon sherbets and talked amongst ourselves. We arrived before it had even opened but we still had to queue. It turned out to be good practise for the day ahead. I had offered to bring my BOGOF vouchers, which was such a mum thing to say, but Graham had said no, this was his treat. Fair enough, he'd couldn't say I hadn't tried. I think Graham was going to be in for a shock when he realised he could probably buy a new car with what he was spending on his "treat" today. Low and behold when it came for him to hand over the cash I saw him visibly blanch at the cost. My vouchers not looking such a mumsy thing to suggest, not so ridiculous now. Something told me he'd regret turning down my offer of bringing a picnic lunch too. The unappetising anaemic hotdogs we ended up eating, did not satisfy the hunger pangs and cost more than a three course meal in a restaurant would have done. So to sum up our rather unsuccessful day. We went on only three rides while there, despite queuing up for a total of six hours, yes six bloody hours to experience those forty five adrenaline fuelled minutes. For five and a half of those tedious hours queuing with the masses, Nicole and James didn't look up from their phones. Graham and I chatted amongst ourselves, like they weren't even there. We'd run out of intelligent conversation within an hour of the first queue and began repeating ourselves like an old couple suffering from dementia. Why hadn't I stuck to my guns and insisted on a meal out instead of this long day of nothingness and possible bankruptcy? His bankruptcy, I had actually come away with more than I started out with in my purse when I found a twenty pound note on the floor of the women's toilets. He tried not to look bitter, but failed miserably, putting on a brave face. "Finders keepers," he sang jovially. "Losers weepers," I sang in response. "Not that I think you're a loser!" I backtracked. Great now he did look like he wanted to weep.

It was the first hint of a smile on James's face all day. Nicole just shook her head at us both rolling her eyes, she did this so often now I was started to think she'd developed a tic. I'm sure I heard her mutter 'lame' under her breath. I hoped she meant him not me, but reckoned it was the both of us she was referring too.

The last half hour, Nicole and James entered the conversation but only because their phones had run out of charge and they were trying to establish if Graham had the means to rectify this in his car. The answer to that was a no. So they sulked and then slept the entire trip home. I bought us all fish and chips on the way home, it seemed the least I could do. James shot me a look I couldn't decipher, although at a guess it was probably something along the lines of why would I want to prolong this already torturous day. I thought it myself but I couldn't send Graham away hungry after all the money he had spent. But that said, the hour sat at the kitchen table, in my house with our fish and chips was the best part of the day.

Conversation passed back and forth and Nicole and James acted less aloof and sullen than they had all day. Then when they left the table, Graham and I shared a bottle of wine and smiled tentatively at each other. All's well that ends well. Even though Graham would probably have to sell a kidney to get himself solvent again after today.

So the kids liked him. Well, tolerated him more like, as they didn't actually like anyone, but they weren't adverse to him either which helped. He didn't have any children of his own which meant he didn't have a clue how to act around two stroppy teenagers. So when things got awkward he'd just shove some money at them, which was probably why they weren't adverse to him! They soon cottoned on to the fact that the more awkward and teenagery they behaved around him the richer they then became. He'd never been married before but had had several long term relationships that hadn't worked out. I made it quite clear early on that I'd done my time as a mother and that I would rather eat my own excrement than ever have another baby. Maybe a bit presumptuous so early on but I needed to get it out there before he got his feet under my table, if you know what I mean? Yes, I meant sex was ok, but no children, just in case you were wondering. The only person who hadn't warmed to Graham, at all, was Karen, which was odd as Karen liked everyone. I put it down to I'm ashamed to say, jealousy that I now had someone and she didn't. "I just don't trust him. How can a man get to his age and not have been married or had kids?" She'd exclaimed. I'm not sure if my facial expression gave me away or if a speech bubble appeared over my head displaying the words POT. KETTLE. BLACK. "So, okay I may not have been married or had children but I was in a serious and long, too long relationship with Paul!" Karen defended her opinion about Graham with a pout. "And not having children was a decision made by us both! We wanted to enjoy our money, holidays, cars without being tied down!" I believed her, of course I did! But I wonder now, now that her relationship with Paul was over if she ever regretted that decision? It was a question I never dared ask in case it opened a can of worms. I mean what if she met someone else right now who wanted children? More mature mums were quite fashionable right now. "Plus Graham has dishonest eyes!" That was her opinion and she was sticking to it. Maybe he couldn't have kids, I'd said. She didn't appear to believe that at all, preferring her theory of him being a weirdo. I often looked at Graham's eyes wondering what dishonest eyes were supposed to look like, but they just looked like normal eyes to me, a boring shade of grey. Graham did admit to me on our second date though that he thought I'd been having some type of epileptic seizure when I'd fluttered my eyelashes at him that day. How very embarrassing, no wonder he didn't want to relinquish the pork pie from my grasp, but I made a note to work on my flirting and seduction techniques for future reference.

Anyway, Graham and I had been seeing each other (I refuse to say that we were going out as that would make us sound like twelve year olds. Or courting, as that would make me sound like my mother) for about six weeks when the decision was made that he'd stay overnight for the first time. The decision was made by me, after a few wines one evening. A decision I wished I could take back the next morning when hungover but sober. Nicole and James were sleeping at their dads. It was Michaels birthday weekend so I assumed he'd arranged his annual sleepover to coincide with this occasion, in the hope of receiving a present. Maybe I was just being suspicious and nasty. It seemed like the perfect opportunity to move our relationship on to the next level. Even though, if truth be told, I was quite happy just hanging out with him without the complications of conjugal relations. However I realised that Graham probably wanted more than companionship. After all we weren't elderly.

I'm not one to kiss and tell but the actual deed was pleasant enough and that's all you need to know. It's not as though I'd ever had much to compare it with. I had been slightly bored during the actual event. Is this normal? With a new partner? Boredom is what I encountered with Michael after years together. Should I have been laying there wondering what to have for dinner the next day? No, I thought not. I was deliberating between pan fried salmon and a roast, just in case you were wondering. Don't get me wrong, he wasn't selfish, he was very giving actually...just not good at the execution...anyway, moving on…..Turns out I am one to kiss and tell.

However, it wasn't until the next morning that I realised just how inexperienced Graham might be in all things female I woke the next morning, with familiar stomach cramps and realised my period must have come early. Although I knew I had enough lady supplies to last the day, when Graham announced he was popping to the shop I asked him to buy me some sanitary pads. A simple request one would think. Micheal for all his faults was perfectly comfortable when buying anything of a delicate female nature. Even thrush treatment. This was his only redeeming quality now I think about it. Well, anyone would have thought I'd asked Graham to pop into a sex shop and buy me the largest vibrator available. He turned white and started nodding and mumbling, I was concerned he'd had a stroke at one point but he shuffled off to do my bidding, so no harm done. He returned an hour later and said he'd put them in the bathroom. I thought no more about this.

The kids returned home at lunchtime. Nicole put her head around the door. "Can dad use the bathroom? He's desperate." I rolled my eyes but agreed. Five minutes later he stuck his head around the door to thank me. A slight smirk on his face."Thanks for that Emily." "Sure, although next time go before you leave your house." It was such a mum thing to say. He snorted with mirth. "That's rich coming from you," he chuckled as he disappeared. I thought no more about this. Nicole's friends turned up not long afterwards, getting ready at our house for some occasion or other. In and out of the bathroom. When it was time for them to leave, Nicole put her head around the door again. "You knew my friends were coming round, you're so embarrassing." She hissed at me before flouncing off. One, I had no idea her friends were coming round and two, I could only presume that me laying on the sofa in my dressing gown a hot water bottle on my tummy was what had offended her and her friends. Despite the fact none of them had actually set foot in the front room and actually seen me. I thought no more about this. That was until Karen turned up wanting the gory details of the night before. She even brought wine. Well, obviously I skirted over the major issues I had. After all imagine her reaction if I told her I was thinking about dinner when Graham was showing me his best moves, she'd have said stuff to make me doubt my relationship with him. I already doubted it, I didn't need her doubts thrown in as well. She popped to the toilet an hour into our dissection and when she came back down she looked amused. "So we are good friends aren't we?" She asked. "Obviously," I replied, I wouldn't have shared my boring sex stories with her otherwise. "I had no idea you were having problems," she said cryptically. Oh goodness me, had she guessed that sex with Graham was a bit vanilla, bland even. Should I fess up? "Look why don't you come to yoga with me next time, we work on pelvic floor muscles." "I have no idea

what you are talking about." I reply blankly. She produced a huge box of incontinence pads, she was doubled up. I looked at the box in confusion. What the? Then it dawned on me. Bloody Graham! I explained to Karen what had actually happened in between her hysterics.
"Why doesn't this surprise me?" She gasped trying to catch her breath. I'm glad my mortification amused her so. If she kept this up she might need a Tena Lady or two herself. Oh Graham, surely this was a joke you can't have possibly thought thought these were every day sanitary protection. No wonder Michael was amused! I bet he was still chuckling with Tara about it now. And I can understand Nicole's embarrassment. No teenage girl wants their friends to think that her mother wets herself. "Don't be too hard on him," Karen mused. What was this? Karen sticking up for Graham?"He can't help being a complete fuckwit!" Cue more laughter at his expense. Indeed. I felt indignant on his behalf. If only pity were an aphrodisiac.

After I put the phone down to mum it rang again, this time it was my friend Elaine. "I need a favour," was her opening greeting. She sounded very far away and the telephone line was cracking a bit. It was difficult to make out what she was saying, she sounded very hyper but was probably just drunk. Like me, Elaine loved a drink or two. "Where are you?" I asked feeling slightly concerned. "I need you to cover for me, please!" fired back Miss Straight-laced never done anything wrong in her life! Lots of crazy thoughts ran through my mind at this point, money laundering, drug deals, bank job, an alibi for why she couldn't make church on Sunday. Elaine, was as perfect a person as you could get. She worked for a boring insurance company. She'd worked her way up to the important position she was now in (I don't know what position that actually was because everyone knows Insurance is mind numbingly boring!) I had a tendency to switch off when she talked shop. Plus I got worried she'd try to sell me something I didn't want if I looked too interested. She'd paid into a personal pension plan since she was about ten years old and never even had a library fine, detention or cross word from a teacher or manager, ever! I wasn't sure what to make of this odd phone call, maybe she was stoned or having an early mid-life crisis. "Cover for you!!" I exclaimed wondering if I heard right, "Why? What have you done? Are you in some sort of-trouble?" Well duh, obviously. You don't ask someone to cover for you if everything is hunky-dory in your life. She sighed, she actually sighed at me, Elaine was never impatient. "Look, if my mum phones you asking where I am just say that you've spoken to me, I'm fine but you don't know where I am, ok?" "But that's not covering for you, that's telling the truth! What's going on?" I practically shouted down the phone. "Can't say at the moment, but I'm fine and I just need you to trust me! Mum might not even call, this is just a precaution. I just didn't want you to worry about me if she did make contact. Speak soon Hun." The phone went dead! Hun? She'd never called me Hun in her life. I wondered if that was our safe word for something? "If I ever call you Hun, phone the police immediately I'm being held hostage!" Nope didn't ring any bells! I wondered if I'd blacked out for a moment and was daydreaming, the phone call was so out of character for stoic Elaine and surreal.

Oh well all I could do was wait for the next instalment and in the meantime I could drink wine. I reached for the bottle and poured myself a generous glassful and watched absentmindedly out of the window thinking about Elaine as Mike the sexy builder roared past in his van, his god awful rock music blaring and assaulting my ears as he pulled onto his driveway. Mike lived in Johns old house, he was the latest in a long line of people who'd lived there. Mike a was a rather good looking, macho builder. He was friendly and always put his hand up in greeting. I bet he wouldn't hide his flowerpots from me.It was only after he stood there waving cheekily at me that I realised I'd been staring at him without seeing him. I waved back feeling embarrassed, although I waved back with my wine glass. I hoped he didn't think I was inviting him round! I wasn't that kind of neighbour, it wasn't that kind of neighbourhood. I also hoped he didn't think I was stalking him, watching at my window for him to come home. I watched him as he disappeared into his house, turning back when at his door to see if I was still there presumably. I ducked, but not quick enough. Damn, I'd made it worse, now it looked like I was stalking him and trying to be sneaky about it. More wine might help, so I reached for the bottle.

It was times like these that I wished I still smoked. That I could pop outside, taking five minutes to process what had just happened. Can you see what you're doing to me Elaine? Your cryptic phone call is making me yearn for nicotine again. I felt like I needed to keep my hands busy and out of the biscuit tin and away from the wine! But I'd given up that enjoyable, filthy habit six and a half years ago.
I'd been smoking on and off since I was a teenager. Coincidentally the off bits were when I was pregnant and a nursing mother and the on bits were all the parts in between. I'd stupidly started again just after I'd made myself single. On a night out a cigarette had just appeared in my mouth, so I decided to become one of those mythical creatures you sometimes hear about a 'social smoker'.
Didn't happen, they don't actually exist. I found that when I was home alone, with no children around to witness my apparent lack of willpower, I'd quickly pop outside and have a crafty one. It seemed so naughty. So unlike me.

Karen was livid with me, when she caught me one day over the fence. I tried to turn it around on her.
"Are you spying on me Karen?" I'd said, self-conscious of the fact there was a cigarette in my hand. It was like being caught by a parent. She didn't bother to acknowledge my pathetic attempt to make her out to be in the wrong. Having never smoked herself, she thought it was absolutely ridiculous that I'd take it up again, after the hard time I'd had giving it up before. Sometimes she actually refused to let me into her house if I smelt of it. It soon started to become a daily occurrence again. I'd become very stealth like getting in and out of the garden without the kids noticing. It always felt like a small victory if I managed it. Most of the time they were oblivious to everything I did. Paying me no attention at all. I could be pole dancing in the front room and unless I was in the way of the telly they wouldn't notice. Until that is I actually wanted them to not notice what I was up to, then they went all Inspector bloody Clouseau on me. "Where have you been?" "What were you doing out there?" "Is that a polo in your mouth? Can I have one?" The morning that Irish Benjamin cancelled our meeting with a made up story about having his wallet stolen, I was in a right state, my head told me a cigarette would make it better. Calm me down, and other such crap us smokers tell ourselves, when justifying why we smoked those cancerous little sticks of heaven. However there was an obstacle in my way. James, who was sitting at the table eating his breakfast, slowly. One rice crispy at a time by the looks of it. I'd stood in the kitchen tapping my foot impatiently. Normally he bloody inhaled his food. Actually he probably wouldn't even notice if I opened the door and went out..."Where are you going?" He piped up. Damn him. "Checking the weather. Yep, it's still cold." He eyed me suspiciously before turning back to his bowl of now soggy cereal. "You need to hurry up, it's bath time." He just looked at

me. I'm pretty sure he'd had a bath the night before but I was hoping he'd forgotten that. "I'm not dirty!" "Germs are invisible James!" "I don't want a bath!" "You don't want to smell do you?" "I don't!" He said outraged. "Well, I didn't like to say but actually..." Don't worry I judge myself! Would I be considered a terrible mother to 'accidentally' tip a glass of juice over him? It's ok, I already knew the answer to that one.

Eventually he left the kitchen. I retrieved my secret stash of cigarettes and lighter from where they were hidden in the cleaning cupboard, let's be honest they would never find them there. I opened the door ready to make my escape when..... "I'm starving, can you make me some scrambled eggs?" said Nicole, who normally slept until lunchtime, who didn't grace me with her presence unless I shouted and screamed for her to get up and dressed. Well, Nicole had appeared in the kitchen, on her own accord for the first time ever. It was a bloody miracle. I found I couldn't answer her, the screaming in my head was too loud. So anyway, after eighteen months of illicit smoking and getting away with it, I was busted one afternoon. Unbeknown to me they'd arrived home from their fathers early. I'd quickly gone out to have my last cigarette where I wouldn't have to hide it, when two little faces appeared at the kitchen window. Two sad little faces. Was there any chance they hadn't seen what I was doing? "You were smoking?" cried James heartbrokenly. "You're going to die and we will have to live with dad!" He sobbed. He seemed to have inherited my mother's prone for overreaction gene. Nicole on the other hand just shook her head in disappointment, and turned away. I was embarrassed. Then annoyed, I'm an adult I can do what I want. Then embarrassed again. I decided to give up then and there, nothing was said, they both appeared to be giving me the silent, guilty treatment. I'd be lying if I said I hadn't had a cigarette since, it was bloody hard to give up cold turkey, for two weeks after getting busted

I'd had a few cheat days but nothing again for six and a half years. I fought temptation now and had a kit Kat instead, okay two kit kats and another glass of wine. Damn you Elaine.

CHAPTER FOUR

The phone call I'd been dreading came on Good Friday. Early in the morning, rendering it not so good after all. Too early in the morning for a precious bank holiday, disturbing the lay in I'd been looking forward to all week. I was dozing starfish like in my king sized bed when the sound of my fake telephone voice came drifting up the stairs. Over and over again. The caller hung up, didn't leave a message as instructed and redialled. It was exactly the sort of thing my mother would do. 'Hello there's no one here to take your call please leave a message after the tone...BEEP!' I sounded less posh and more inbred every time the message was repeated. I buried my head under my pillow willing whoever it was to just fuck off. I reassured myself that if it were a genuine emergency that the person trying desperately to contact me before sunrise, would call my mobile phone instead. Cue my mobile phone start to vibrate on the bedside table next to me. Bugger it. I mumbled something unintelligible into the phone. "Hello dear, sorry to ring so early but I didn't know who else to call," said a mum, not my mum but Elaine's mum. Double bugger. How did she get my number? "Oh hello Sandra, I hope everything is ok?" I answer rolling my sleep crusted eyes at how false I sounded. My mind started racing, it had gone completely blank, what was it Elaine had said about her mum? "I hope you don't mind dear but your mother gave me your phone numbers." I noticed she said numbers, plural. Of course she did and probably my email and bra size too. "Well, everything isn't ok really dear, you see Elaine appears to have disappeared. I haven't heard from her in days. I phoned her manager at work and they told me..." I think she choked back a sob here "...that she'd taken all her holiday in one go, all twenty one days of it. She's never done that before. Do you know where she is? Or should I call the police? It's very out of character for her." So when Elaine asked me to cover for her she didn't really give me any specifics and it was too early to make up a believable lie on the spot. Sandra sounded pretty distressed so I told her the truth. "All I know is that she's alright, she sounded happy enough and wanted me to tell you not to worry, ok?" I said kindly, willing that to be the end of the conversation, willing Sandra to say cheerfully 'oh ok dear, bye for now!' "But why didn't she just tell me that instead of involving you?" she said sounding very confused. "She's not answering her mobile phone either." Well, precisely, I was wondering the exact same thing myself, maybe I should be cruel to be kind. "Well, Elaine is thirty seven years old and doesn't really have to tell you what she's doing all the time, does she?" It started out as strong statement but ended up as nervous question. This was met with silence and not of the comfortable variety. "She probably just needs a break, she works so hard..." I trailed off in trepidation of Sandra's response. "Maybe she's met a sexual deviant online, posing as a nice man. Maybe she thought she was going to have a pleasant time. Maybe she is now being held hostage somewhere and about to be sold for sex slavery or worse!" Sandra said very calmly for a mother who was imagining the very worst that could possibly happen to their only child. Right, well yes we could focus on the 'what if's' I suppose, but I'm not sure what could be worse than human sex trafficking aside from death that is. "Or," I suggested alternatively, "she just needed a break away from it all!" Meaning you, I added silently. Seriously Sandra was worse than my mum, something I thought near impossible. I thought my mum was a crazy one off. "If you hear from her in the next couple of days, I trust you will let me know immediately, if not I'll be phoning the police and reporting her missing officially." Gone was the sweet mum I knew of old. The one who used to make me fish finger sandwiches after school. She was replaced with mean hard don't mess with me mum. "Ok of cour..." But she'd already hung up. Great thanks Elaine, now I'm a disappointment to your mum as well as my own. I texted Elaine.

PHONE ME NOW!

She did not.

Easter Sunday eventually arrived, I gathered my young and herded them to the car. They were moaning and groaning at being woken up so early at the weekend. Bloody lunchtime was not early. I knew that they secretly enjoyed the celebration at their grandparents house, especially the Easter egg hunt despite them being nearly adults now. If I'm being honest I did too, it was family tradition. Of course the never-ending supply of alcohol that accompanied any gathering at my parents house helped tremendously. I was just about to get into my car when Graham's silver BMW pulled up outside the house. Mike the sexy builder just happened to be at his garage in the shortest of shorts, he had nice muscly legs. He gave me a wave and I waved back but willed him to disappear before Graham got out of his car. I'm not sure why. Maybe I didn't want Graham to notice the frisson of attraction I felt towards Mike. I wasn't sure I could hide it. What did Graham want? Was my first thought, he knew we were going out. I felt suddenly very annoyed with him, I slammed my car door shut again and gave him what I hoped was a welcoming smile but in truth was rather an impatient grimace. Mike, now shirtless, appeared to be tinkering with his engine and no that wasn't a euphemism for anything else. His extremely cute eight year old daughter Kimberly, who was visiting for the weekend was riding her bike up and down the paths of our cul-de-sac. She was looking adorable in her little cycling helmet. I remembered when my own two were that cute, now I struggled to recognise them under all the hormones, pimples and attitude. "Hello Em," Graham said cheerfully giving me a kiss and pulling me in for a hug, clearly not noticing how distracted I was not to mention annoyed. He surely can't have noticed my resistance to the hug. But if he noticed it he ignored it. "Hi, sorry Graham, have you forgotten we're going out today." I winced at my poor choice of the word 'we're' as obviously he wasn't included in the going out part? I tried to keep the annoyance out of my voice. Nevertheless, I felt frustrated with him. "Nope I've not forgotten. I just wanted to give you your Easter gifts that's all," he said, pulling out two posh gigantic eggs from the boot. "For Nicole and James," he said with a flourish. Both kids looked up from their phones when they heard their names mentioned, both expecting to be underwhelmed by Graham's offering. But their eyes widened in delight when they saw the sheer size of the eggs. Suddenly gone were stroppy Kevin and Perry and in place were two polite angels I didn't recognise, well, that I'd not seen in a while anyway. "Wow, thanks Graham," gushed Nicole uncharacteristically as she skipped from the car and then gave him an impromptu quick hug. Graham looked a little shocked at first, then embarrassed by the physical contact. He then quickly and rather bizarrely reached into his pocket and gave her a ten pound note too. Nicole looked like she couldn't believe her good fortune. Graham then did the same for James. He shoved the money at him quickly just in case James tried to hug him too. "Cheers Graham you're a legend!" whooped James happily whipping the folding from his hand. "That was very kind of you," I said warmly and meaning it, once the kids were back in the car. "But I have to get going, if

I'm more than five minutes late she'll send out a search party," I joked. I gave him a quick hug and went to get back in the car. " I'll see you tomorrow." I said firmly. "Well hang on Em, don't forget yours." He reached back into the boot and bought out another humongous egg, a bottle of good wine (and by that I mean something that cost more than five pounds) and what looked like a large bottle of my favourite but expensive perfume. I was conscious of the fact that I might be being watched but when I discreetly checked, Mike and Kimberly had disappeared. I didn't know what to say, thank you seemed a bit lame. I wanted to ask him if he realised it was just Easter and not a special birthday but that seemed a bit ungrateful and a little churlish. We'd only been dating four months. Given that he'd spent a fortune on a charm bracelet for my birthday just last week, it all seemed rather over the top to me.

"Thanks Graham," I said. Yep that sounded completely lame. He smiled happily, a little gormlessly at me, oh God was he waiting for something in return? The problem was it hadn't even occurred to me to buy him anything. I quickly racked my brains in case there was something indoors I could give him and pretend that it was a well thought out Easter gift. I didn't think an already opened bottle of warm white wine or a double Kit Kat with a finger missing would suffice. Then, to make it worse. "Oh, and this is for your parents," he produced another bottle bag containing wine, "have a great meal, see you tomorrow darling." He kissed me goodbye and got into his car, although he seemed to take an awfully long time pulling away from my house.

What do I do? I now felt torn. Should I now invite him along to my parents? They wouldn't care, they'd be over the frigging moon, that their spinster daughter might have met a mate. Nicole and James thought Graham was alright too after his chocolate offerings, so they wouldn't be bothered in the slightest. Something was stopping me from calling out to him and inviting him along. The truth was, I didn't want him to come! What did this mean for our 'relationship?' Should it be this awkward and stunted so soon? Surely I should want to be in his company instead of making excuses. I had some thinking to do. So I pathetically waved him off feeling like a shit as he drove off at two miles an hour and eventually disappeared. I'm sure I only imagined the impatient thump on the steering wheel as he rounded the corner, he was probably just tapping a tad too enthusiastically to his rock ballads CD that he seemed to have a weird attachment to. If I ever heard Alice Cooper's poison again in my lifetime it would be too soon.

We arrived at my parents in good time and in good spirits, despite the fact I had to endure endless car selfies with the kids along the way. Easter egg selfies and other such like crap to be uploaded to their various social media accounts. I pouted on demand and asked not to be tagged otherwise I'd be uploading my embarrassing photos of my own. Of which there were plenty in existence, mainly of them running around the place naked. As toddlers, not the moody teens they were now. I didn't facilitate that kind of deviant behaviour in my house. I wasn't that kind of mother. When we arrived Nicole and James disappeared immediately into the front room half a stone heavier. Their mobile phones in hand checking out their various likes on their various social media applications. Meanwhile I struggled alone getting the Easter gifts for my parents out of the car, trying not to drop anything. Cheers kids. I poked my head around the lounge door and saw my lovely Grandma in the best armchair of the house, also known as 'dads chair'. Fred was laying by her feet, Fred was her smelly poodle, not my grandad by the way. I gave Grandma a big hug and a kiss. I handed over my Easter gift of yellow daffodils, which she announced as her favourites. I could have given her a bunch of pond weeds and she'd still have declared them as her favourites. My Grandma was lovely and maybe a little bit senile. Grandma in turn handed over an envelope filled with cash. I surmised that she was having to move some of her pension money around again before the authorities found out and cut her benefits. It felt a bit like a drugs deal going down. Instead it was daffodils for cash but I thanked her profusely and gave Fred a conciliatory ruffle. He then growled and farted at me so I ruffled him harder, smelly little fucker. I assumed the kids had also received an Easter envelope filled with tax payers hard earned money, due to the smug looks on their faces. Nicole was now taking selfies on the sofa with a bunch of tenners instead of the half eaten chocolate egg discarded at her feet. Fred shuffled over and gave it a lick. These kids didn't know they were bloody born. When I was a kid I'd got an Easter egg. A regular sized one with maybe a mug. No money ever exchanged hands, not at Easter. "Happy Easter dad!" I gave him his gift of a bag of chocolate raisins, which happened to be his favourite confectionery and a bottle of red. "Thanks Em," he said not taking his eyes off of the golf, his iron like left grip on the remote control, the other hand sporting a can of Stella. He may be sulking about losing his favourite chair to Grandma but he wasn't going to lose the right to watch his beloved golf. "Your mother is in the kitchen." I guessed I was dismissed then. "Hi mum, is there anything I can do to help?" I call out as unenthusiastically as possible as I wandered towards the kitchen. I was hoping she'd call back 'no thanks love, go and sit down and put your feet up, like every other bastard that walks through the door expecting to be fed for free!' "Yes please, the table needs laying, the gravy needs mixing and I could do with a stiff bloody drink!" Mum was like the Tasmanian devil whirling around the kitchen, sweating profusely and breathing heavily like she'd just run a marathon. Damn it, I wasn't expecting that. I give her my present of a 'nice' bouquet of flowers and Graham's wine (deciding not to mention it wasn't from me just yet, I didn't want to start her on the subject of Graham again). I then poured her a large rose wine and started laying the table, which mum then completely relayed, following behind me. Changing cutlery around and refolding the napkins I'd just folded, muttering under her breath 'never rectangles always triangles'. Like it bloody matters anyway we're all just going to wipe our gravy covered mouths with them. "Thank you Em, where are my lovely grandchildren?" She asked almost downing the glass of wine and wafting the tea towel around her like a fan. I shrugged " I have no idea, but Nicole and James are in the front room," I said. Mum smiled and flicked me with her tea towel slash fan. "Stop it, they are great kids, don't you ever doubt that, they are a credit to you!" We then shared a moment of reflection about what a useless twat Michael was as a father! "I bumped into Sandra in Sainsbury's yesterday, poor woman is beside herself, whatever possessed Elaine to disappear without telling her mother where she was going?" "The fact she's thirty seven, single and has no ties," I say. "So what if she wants to go off on holiday, she works hard why shouldn't she treat herself!" I argue absent Elaine's cause for her, feeling resentful about it at the same time. "I have tried phoning her but it's either switched off or goes unanswered. Mum gave me a steely stare. " I'll remind you of that if Nicole should ever disappear without a word to you." "Slightly different mum Nicole is just a child maybe if Sandra had more going on in her own life she wouldn't be so involved in Elaine's!" "Yes well easier said than done when you're lonely," she said." And Nicole is nineteen, an adult, single with no ties too!" mimicked mum. "Hardly the same thing at all," I exclaim. Although thinking about it, it was exactly the kind of the same thing. I decided I needed a subtle change of subject. But before I could broach a safer topic mum then announced that

Sandra was now coming for Easter dinner!,"She seemed so low, I thought it might cheer her up," said mum.

Yes I'm sure being surrounded by somebody else's loving family when her only daughter has fucked off to God knows where, with fuck knows who will really cheer her up. Sandra right now would be the top of my list of people I wouldn't want to sit with at a dinner party! "She'll be good company for Roger" added mum, oblivious to my face pulling and eye rolling. So scrap that, Roger would be at the top of my list of people to avoid sitting next to, opposite, or in the close vicinity of at a dinner party. He was the exact definition of a bore and maybe a bit of a sexual predator too, but don't take that as read that's purely my opinion. Mum and dad sometimes liked to invite their stray friends who were at a loose end to our family get togethers. I never really minded but if had to sit next to permanently unattached Roger with his porn star moustache, a clue perhaps to why he was at a loose end year after year, listening to his hilarious (totally made up) stories again I would pull 'an Elaine' and disappear too next year. No way was Roger ever mistaken for Tom Selleck in Asda. However if he'd have said Saddam Hussain, that I'd have no trouble believing, he had that look about him. Clearly Roger had a penchant for the younger lady too, which was hugely apparent when he tentatively propositioned me in the utility room not long after I'd split up with Michael. It was probably just the gin and tonics talking, but he'd said he'd love to be able to 'look after me'. I presumed he meant financially as he couldn't possibly have meant sexually! I wasn't even sure he had a penis he seemed so effeminate in his fawn coloured slacks. I let him down gently explaining, although some might say lying out of my arse that I was a lesbian. Saying that was the real reason my marriage ended. I also told him hadn't 'come out' to my parents yet, so could he be a dear and keep it under his moustache. He couldn't get out of the room fast enough, it was as if I was about to pistol whip him with my strap-on! That still didn't stop him sitting next to me every bloody year after that without fail and asking me in a loud stage whisper 'have you told them yet?'

Suddenly the messiah that was my younger and more successful brother appeared in the doorway, his halo glowing gloriously, temporarily blinding me as I stirred the gravy. My hair going frizzy in the gravy steam. He was wearing expensive sunglasses (even though it wasn't sunny), a polo-shirt and jeans that clearly weren't a supermarket own brand. It was obvious that his whole outfit probably cost more than my months rent. I fiddled with my Lidl vest top self consciously. Please don't ask me what my brother does as a job because I don't rightly know (or care), all I do know is it's something in London to do with computers or banking and our mother is so very proud of him. "Hi mum is there anything I can do to help?" he said as unenthusiastically as possible as he kissed her in greeting. Hoping she'd say 'no thanks love, go and sit down and put your feet up, like every other bastard that walks through the door expecting to be fed for free!' "No thanks love, go and sit down and put your feet up!" The rest went without saying. Well there you go! Favouritism or sexism? You decide.
Before he could disappear into the sanctity of the front room, with mums blessing, the front room came to him. First dad, offering him a cold beer, hand shakes and 'let's talk about the football son'.
Then Nicole and James wandered in, probably wondering what Easter gift he'd bought them this year. They were followed by Grandma limping in with her walking stick, she quickly slipped an envelope into his back pocket with a wink. Even fucking Fred the poodle walked in to welcome the boy

wonder, gave him a friendly sniff, aimed another fart in my direction then waddled back to the front room.
Eventually the welcoming committee left the kitchen with Simon in tow, leaving just me, mum and scary Cassia languishing almost unnoticed at first in the shadows! Cassia was my brothers girlfriend, a particularly loathsome creature that Simon had dated for six months now, she was tall and willowy and believed any woman under six foot tall was jealous of her height. Pah, not all women wanted to look like a tree and play limbo every time they walked through a door. She had huge amounts of blond hair worn in the late Amy Winehouse beehive style, her skeletal body frame made her head look huge much like a lollipop. She certainly had the whole Ethiopian chic vibe going on. I had more fat on one bum cheek than she had on her entire body. She also talked like she had a couple of plums in her mouth, like royalty. Totally fake as it happens, because every time she didn't get her own way, when she thought nobody was listening, an Essex twang would escape from her pumped up trout pout, hilarious! Not that she talked much in our company anyway. I always was under the impression she felt we were beneath her. I once asked Simon what he saw in her. He couldn't really answer so I presumed it was something to do with sex. There wasn't much else going for her. He'd met her in Waitrose one Saturday afternoon. "Do you mean she works there?" asked mum. A shop assistant clearly not good enough for her precious son. "No, she crashed her trolley into the back of me, we got talking and I asked her out." Simon had shrugged as if it were normal to pick up dates in the frozen foods aisle. I might have to try it in my local Lidl next time. "What does she do for a living?" mum had pushed. "A model, but she's in between jobs right now and works at Costa." Mum looked horrified, stacking shelves at Waitrose not so terrible now. "Has she ever been in anything I might have seen?" I pushed.

Simon shrugged. "Not sure, a few catalogs maybe," he didn't have a clue. I bet she was lying. My poor gullible little brother taken in by the pretty coffee maker. I bet she'd rammed her trolley into him on purpose because he'd looked rich. You did hear of those things happening to people, I bet she'd been watching him for ages. To me it seemed Cassias aloof attitude was simply a fake persona for our benefit. Almost like she was playing a part in a play. Cassia the model was the character, playing her mute and stuck up was her interpretation. She must be different when alone with Simon. I mean, they had a conversation in Waitrose. I'm sure she didn't just say 'ya ya' in response to Simon's questions and him suddenly think, 'God yeah let me start dating this mute model immediately!' "Hi Cassia, how are you?" I asked being deliberately controversial. She didn't DO niceties and I knew she would struggle to answer. "Ya, ya good." She said staring out the window, looking pained at having to converse with the little people. "I love your dress, where's it from?" I continued. I caught mums eye and she smirked, mum was not a fan of Cassia either. She didn't think she was sane enough for her darling son. The dress in question was actually hideous, it was as though a cat had thrown up on a scrap of hessian and somebody, probably an expensive designer decided to call it a dress and charge the earth for it. Cassia ignored the question and mumbled something about finding Simon, she walked off like she was on stilts in the direction of the loud chatter and laughing now coming from the front room. The golf clearly not as important now Simon was here. Only once had Cassia appeared normal, at a meal out to celebrate my dad's birthday, it was probably the second time we'd ever met her, and she'd actually made conversation, all be it stilted. The posh was there but she had answered questions as though she was a normal human being and hadn't come across as ignorant cow material. But she'd been watchful, taking it all in.

Very bizarre behaviour for a young girl, with the whole world at her feet. I wondered briefly if she was on drugs. Not illegal ones but prescription ones, maybe lots of them. It might be a possible reason she seemed a little unbalanced at times.
I caught the tail end of the conversation as I wandered into the front room, all hot and sweaty after stirring the bloody gravy. Why mum couldn't just buy instant gravy was beyond me.
"...so while I was in New York, eating in one of the best restaurants on expenses, who should walk in but only Jennifer Aniston and Courteney bloody Cox!" We were all Friends fans so this was huge, gasps of amazement from the kids. "Oh my God! What did they look like?" I squealed excitedly clapping my hands. "Well," said Simon leaning in, all of us all leaning in with him, as though he was about to tell us a big secret. "Courtney looks exactly the same as she does on tv but Jennifer... Jennifer is actually Chinese in real life!" Cue hysterical laughter at my expense. "What a silly question," laughed my Grandma disloyally, Fred also appearing to be sneering at me, mutley style.

Simon and I had a tricky relationship. As adults we never quite connected in the same way we did as when we were small. As children we rubbed along together quite happily. We were the generation of children that played outside. "Go and play outside," said mum approximately twenty eight thousand times a day. There could be gale force winds and torrential rain and mum would just tell us to do up our coats. Or put on a hat. So we'd hang around the garages like a couple of losers and wait for the other mums to send their children outside too. Inevitably they always did. As soon as a mum saw that another mum had sent their children outside it was a cue to send out their own. It was like a poor man's version of keeping up with the Jones. "Go and play outside with the other children." "But it's hailstoning!" "You'll be fine, quick go before the other children go in!" Panic in mums voice, lest the others disappeared back indoors before we'd manoeuvred ourselves into a full snowsuit. There was no sexism or age limit, if you were a child you could play. As long as you all pretended not to know each other at school, it was fine. Manhunt was the game of choice back then. As there was sod all else to do. Although sometimes the older kids would organise a scavenger hunt. Great times, especially if it was starting to get dark. It seemed so thrilling to be outside when the street lights started coming on. Then, almost inevitably, the mums would see us having fun and would ruin it by telling us to 'come inside' 'right now'. Mostly though, the time playing outside meant sitting on the kerb, playing with a stick, feeling really cold and wishing we could go and play inside for a change. Then I hit that awkward age where I became a walking misery of hormones and scowls. I picked on Simon terribly then, just because I could. "One day he'll be bigger than you," was mums favourite thing to say, after I'd made him cry for the hundredth time that day. What a wuss! I'd only accidentally stood on his Lego fire station, that he'd spent all day building (outside on the patio obviously) smashing it to smithereens. Mum eventually stopped telling me to play outside with Simon then and was perfectly happy for me to stay locked in my bedroom all day. Listening to Take That on my cassette player. Lusting after Robbie and writing profound stuff in my diary, you know like 'I heart Robbie' 'I wish he was my boyfriend' that kind of literacy gold. I wasn't at all jealous the summer Simon and the other kids made a go-kart out of abandoned pram wheels and bike parts. It took meticulous planning and took them weeks to make it. Ok, so I was a little bit envious when they all then took turns going down the big hill on it. How I ached to go out and have a go but my pride wouldn't let me. Then luckily for me one of the wheels fell off at thirty miles per hours and Simon ended up with a head injury, but back then it was nothing that a plaster wouldn't fix. I felt smugly justified in my decision not to join in. And went back to mooning after Robbie.

By the time Simon took his turn at being that walking misery of hormones and anger, I'd found myself pregnant and moved out. I guess if I hadn't have got myself knocked up we'd probably have reconnected again at some point. Simon then became the ambitious freak he is now and left me behind. So while I was changing nappies and becoming an expert in different types/textures of baby shit, he went to university and became mummy's successful, brag-worthy favourite child. We never really got that easy 'lets play with this stone for a couple of hours' relationship back.

In the end a great time was had by all this Easter, apart from Cassia who moaned and sulked because she didn't have Simons undivided attention. She ended up meditating at the bottom of the garden after dinner, although I swear she really went down there for a cheeky cigarette. I think she was hoping he'd go after her but he hardly noticed she'd gone. He was too busy winding up James about his lack of girlfriend, although if he kept this up he too might be girlfriendless, and wouldn't that be a damn shame. I wonder if she'd give him a hard time when they got home, he didn't seem unduly bothered if she did. I assumed that she had a duel personality. Simon didn't suffer fools gladly. Simon handed over his Easter gifts, all of which seemed to be freebies from work, not that anybody was complaining. They were great. An exclusive spa day for mum, football tickets for dad, Chelsea flower show tickets for grandma. A ridiculously expensive PlayStation game for James and a makeup set for Nicole that I'd seen online and knew it retailed for a lot of money. I was obviously in the

wrong industry. All I got from my customers were complaints and grief. And for me a bottle of champagne.
"It's a good one sis, Curious cove, a client gave it to me but I couldn't accept it, it's considered a bribe you see as it costs over fifty quid. It was raffled off and I won it anyway!" He seemed to be of the same idea as Graham when it came to extravagant Easter presents, totally over the top despite them being free. Mum clapped her hands in glee at her incredibly generous son. I thanked him but gazed longingly at Nicole's makeup set. Would it make me a terrible parent if I asked her to swap? "I don't think I've seen you since your birthday night out?" Simon laughed as we hunted for our Easter eggs.
"Did I even see you that night?" I asked puzzled. My birthday bash in town last week was a rather sore subject actually. First I'd been refused entry to the club because my name wasn't 'down'. Obviously a technicality that was soon rectified, but not before I'd made a complete fool of myself by saying 'of course my name isn't Dan, I'm a girl!' I genuinely believed all these years they were saying if your names not Dan, you're not coming in! I then got ridiculously drunk, started dancing on the tables and then I was thrown out by the same, smug doorman that originally stopped me from entering. A mere half hour after arriving. "I knew you'd be trouble!" He said gruffly as he dragged me across the dance floor. I then started singing that Taylor Swift song of the same title. Excruciating.
I vaguely remembered Karen and a suited stranger putting me in a taxi. "Oh that was you was it?" My brother hadn't been invited out on my girls night obviously, but coincidentally been in the same place at the same time. Karen rather strangely hadn't mentioned mentioned my birthday night since, unusual for her as we normally dissected everything that had happened on a night out. Of course, she had had to put me to bed in the recovery position that night in case I was sick in my sleep. It had taken me days to recover. "You were a mess," he

laughed. "Great." How a woman loves being told that. Not. Especially by her younger more successful brother. The Easter egg hunt in the garden was as standard, all chaos and arguing about who found more, but entertaining and funny nevertheless.

Cassia who rather predictably didn't eat chocolate, refused to join in. She sipped her iced water on the outskirts of the fun, glaring daggers at Simon the whole time. How dare he have fun if she was not. I was getting the impression that things weren't going well between them. Simon seemed oblivious to her looks of death. This was making her madder. It was entertaining to observe. I reckoned Simon needed to be careful if finishing with Cassia anytime soon, she had the definite aura of bunny boiler about her. It also made me realise I was very glad not to have invited Graham. I couldn't imagine him fitting in here at all. This didn't bode well for us and the future.

Sandra, although a bit chilly towards me at first, warmed up after a few glasses of wine and apologised for putting me in a 'difficult position'. I'd also had a few bottles of wine myself and I said that I understood and that the person who actually put us in that 'difficult position' in the first place was Elaine. We both had a moment of silence thinking about how we were going to punish her sorry arse when she eventually put in a reappearance, if she put in a reappearance again. The possibility of sexual slavery was still on the table. However, the biggest surprise of the day was Roger. A moustache-less Roger no less, who looked so much better for not having that hairy monstrosity assaulting his top lip. Not enough for me to let him ever support me financially but enough that he lost the whole sexual predator vibe he'd once had. It was an Easter Miracle.

This year he didn't even try to sit next to me at dinner or even enquire about whether I'd left the closet. His penchant for the younger woman replaced by a yearning for the older more plumper one. He sat with Sandra the whole time giving her all his undivided attention while she giggled away like a tipsy school girl enjoying his conversation. Well someone had to I guess. It was nauseating to watch, especially as he recycled his Tom Selleck story again. Elaine's sudden unexplained absence seemed long forgotten. I wondered if mum had paid him to be so attentive, then I felt horrible for being so mean. They got on like the proverbial house on fire. I wondered why they hadn't got it on before.I asked this of mum whilst helping her clear the table afterwards. Everyone else had disappeared into the lounge to play a board game. I'd rather handcuff myself to Cassia for the evening than play Trivial Pursuit with competitive Simon and James. It would end in carnage I'd wager Grandmas Easter money on it. "They've only ever met a handful of times, briefly. If I'd known this was going to happen I'd have invited Sandra years ago, then we'd have been spared having to have Roger permanently sat at our table year after year. It was only in the taxi on the way home that I realised that I completely forgot to mention to mum and dad that the wine I'd brought them had actually been from Graham. Whoops. It also occurred to me that mum was a bit slow on the uptake lately for not cottoning on to the fact that, as Graham was a postman, he wouldn't be working on a Sunday! I'd had a lucky escape there, phew!

CHAPTER FIVE

"Mum can I have a sleepover?" yelled James from upstairs. I was in the kitchen at the time so I prayed I'd misheard him and that he'd actually said 'mum I'm going to do my homework now'. I hated sleepovers with an almighty passion. Just those words make me want to reach for the vodka and start drinking it from the bottle. No good ever comes from having other people's children staying in your house overnight. They never bloody sleep anyway. Little Billy ends up falling out with Little Joe. Sides are then taken and before you know it world war three has broken out and sweets are unceremoniously crushed into the carpet. With me then contemplating bashing them all over the head with my empty vodka bottle. A night in a concrete cell being preferable to being a sleepover mum. Hell on earth, even rivalling mother and toddler groups. So, no, James you can't have a bloody sleepover. I heard his footsteps come pounding down the stairs in search of me, so I did what any good mother would do and quickly snuck out the back door, over the fence and into Karen's kitchen. "I'm escaping for an hour," I call out "shall I put the kettle on?"

"Yeah sure, or I have wine in the fridge if you'd prefer?" She called back from the depths of the house. Silly question, I grabbed the wine bottle and two glasses. I could hear James's dulcet tones through the walls as he went from room to room calling out for me, before thankfully giving up and going back upstairs probably with the four pack of chocolate muffins I'd left on the kitchen table. He was very easily distracted, typical male. I thanked my lucky stars it was just food for now and not boobs, well not that I knew of. I should really check his internet history once in a while.

Karen was slightly older than my thirty eight years not that you'd ever know it to look at her, she was petite, perky and blonde. She just radiated youth and vitality. She worked in retail, at a higher end department store, so she always looked the part, nails manicured to perfection, eyebrows threaded (I didn't even know what that meant as I'm a plucker) makeup that looked like there was no makeup, so you just knew it took hours to apply. She did Pilates three times a week and a spinning class twice, which I naïvely thought was people just spinning around for half hour getting dizzy much to Karen's amusement. I really was not worthy to be her friend. My idea of exercise was to buy a celebrity fitness dvd, do it once then let it gather dust on the side. Then stuff myself every evening with Jaffa cakes watching pointless crap on telly promising to do better tomorrow. Knowing full well that tomorrow never came. Don't get me wrong, I was hardly ugly sister material. I was tallish, slimish, attractive..ish with lovely chocolate coloured hair. I just always felt a bit clumsy when I was alongside Karen. "So what's new then?" She asks, sipping her wine. I tell her all about Elaine's strange phone call and about how her mum was freaking out about it. The three of us were great friends. We'd had some epic nights out over the years. Some of the best, being while Karen and I had still been in long term relationships with our exes. Our nights out then were like being released from prison. We always met at Elaine's flat during those times, loving the freedom our prearranged plans gave us. I used to count down the weeks, days and hours until I was free from the confines of my boring four walls. Even though Elaine and I had been practically inseparable while at school, we drifted apart after we'd left. Elaine was very academic and had aced all her GCSE's, securing a place at the sixth form college out of town to do her A-levels. Whereupon I, who did pretty well considering I'd not revised much, attended the local college enrolling on a leisure and tourism course. Until I'd given it up when I found out I was pregnant. I didn't see much of Elaine while the children were babies, because she was away at university, being clever. We'd been going in separate directions for a while, but she'd stop by occasionally when she was back, though it became obvious we had nothing in common any more. I was jealous of her life, if I was being honest. I adored my children but it was mind numbing at times. My jealousy was probably pretty obvious to her, I didn't hide it. I started to make up things so she didn't think I was boring, exaggerating my new 'friendship' with Candice. I just hope she never bumped into her on the stairs. She stopped coming around for a while. My life was boring, my conversation was boring. Who cared other than me and my mum whether Nicole had pooed in the potty or not that day. It was only after she moved back to town again, after graduating that we tentatively reconnected and she became part of my life again. Karen and I however had clicked immediately after I moved in next door to her. Obviously I was extremely wary about becoming close to a neighbour again, after the Candice debacle, but once I'd established Karen wasn't likely to start trying to be me, our friendship just happened naturally. Chats over the fence and cups of tea at each other's houses then lead to nights out drinking wine or whatever else we could get our hands on.

Michael hadn't liked Karen much either but this time it was jealousy, of how much time I spent with her rather than with him. Paul hadn't warmed to me much either. Men always felt threatened by their partners good friends, it was rather pathetic to be honest. I judged them because of it, it was no wonder the relationships hadn't lasted the distance. Be thankful you stupid idiots that your wife had someone, that wasn't you to complain about stomach cramps, boredom, bad sex...on second thoughts, maybe it was obvious why they'd prefer their other half to be isolated instead.

I introduced Elaine and Karen to each other one night over wine at my house and we'd soon become a nice little threesome. We'd meet for lunch, that more often than not turned into drunken afternoons. We were there for each other in the shitty times, I always had wine to help ease whatever issue had arisen. There were lots of good times too. The only thing we hadn't done together was a girls holiday, but considering I couldn't afford to take my children away some years, I couldn't justify going on a drunken holiday with my friends. It was on my bucket list. A drunken girls holiday at some point. Being a teenage mum had put paid to that particular milestone, but I was determined it would happen one day. The thing we now had in common was that we were all unlucky in love, although some might say losers. Elaine would take first prize in that category having never had a long term relationship, that I knew about anyway. I could never understand this because she was gorgeous, tall, slim luscious long red hair. It made no sense. Elaine had the reputation of being a hopeless romantic, falling in love quickly, becoming besotted and then having her heart broken when it all started to go wrong usually within the month. My conclusion was she was too clingy or maybe she just hadn't met the right man yet. Karen, although having been with Paul for many years, had not really been with anyone since, unless you counted Dylan which none of us did. He had been fifteen years younger than her and a cocky, good looking doorman. Don't get me wrong it was great fun that he always let us in our favourite venue for free when he was on duty. Plus he'd drive us home saving us money on a taxi, but he'd messed with Karen's head something chronic. And Karen wasn't one to lose her head easily.

"It's not serious," she'd say. "Just sex!" On his part yes, but after eighteen months of this I was assuming Karen wanted more than a shag at the end of the night but just didn't want to admit it to us. It all went wrong anyway when he was sacked from the pub by the landlord and ran away with the landlords wife. He hadn't even bothered to tell her, she had to hear it from Barry the other, slightly wimpy doorman that also had a crush on Karen. Karen was heartbroken, even though she pretended she wasn't bothered. She wasn't like me, she didn't like to talk about it. She dealt with her pain in private. I was a more wear my heart on my sleeve type of girl. "I'm assuming that she's met someone, there's no other explanation for it. I just can't understand all the cloak and dagger behaviour. The funny thing is if she'd have just told her mum 'hey mum I'm going away for a few days', Sandra wouldn't be worrying and I probably wouldn't know anything about it until she came back!" "I take it you've tried phoning her again? Sorry stupid question, alcohol dulls the brain cells." She said draining her glass and topping it up again. "Obviously, but it's either turned off or it rings out to the answer phone. I've been keeping an eye on her Facebook too, no activity for at least a week, maybe Sandra's right and we should be concerned." I suddenly felt guilty for ridiculing Sandra's concerns. Karen

pulls a face and I know she's debating whether to say something or not. "I thought I saw her the other day actually, Saturday morning in-fact, the other side of town, just coming out of the newsagents along Churchill Road. I tooted her, but I'd driven past before she could register who I was. I'd put money on it being her though." We both look at each other and I know that if Karen says she saw her then she probably did see her.
Curiouser and curiouser, the mystery deepens. "I know let's send her a message, telling her to get in touch otherwise you'll go to the police, because let's be honest this is totally out of character for Elaine and actually she's being pretty damn selfish! I understand not telling her mum what she's up to, but we are her best friends what's the big fucking secret here?" Fuelled by copious amounts of wine we came up with a message that sounds like we mean business but was extremely supportive at the same time. "How were the Easter celebrations at your parents!" Karen asked pouring us another drink. "The usual. Simon monopolising proceedings by being flash, Cassia sulking because Simon ignored her the entire time and world war three broke out between Nicole and James over a history question during Trivial Pursuit! I answered her. I suddenly remembered my birthday. "You never mentioned my brother being at the club on my birthday!" I raised my eyebrow. "He mentioned it." "God, I'd forgotten about that! We were ridiculously drunk though!" This was very true. Karen had been rather elusive this week but I let it go. Although I did wonder what was going on in her life right now. She was being rather vague. I wondered if she'd met someone at last?

Graham was coming round for dinner tonight. I had intended on making him my signature dish of chilli con carne, the only meal I could cook well from scratch. Well from a packet really but it was still very delicious. I did have to chop my own onions you know, so to me that constitutes as homemade. I felt a bit nervous about tonight. I felt bad about his Easter generosity and how lacking I'd been in that department. I'd seen a flash of disappointment cross his face even though he tried hard to hide it, yet at the same time I wasn't feeling 'us' anymore. This had nothing to do with my secret crush on Mike across the road and more to do with me realising I just didn't fancy Graham. There I said it. Maybe we could still be friends.... I wondered if I would even be brave enough to broach the subject of calling it a day. Unfortunately I was pretty sloshed when I got back from Karen's and couldn't actually be bothered to open packets and start chopping onions. So I texted him and asked him bring a takeaway instead and more wine. Yes, I'm aware I was making him pay and bring his own last meal to the table. I never said I was a particularly nice person. Just ask Michael. He could write a book about nasty Emily. Graham agreed to bring an Indian takeaway as I knew he would but he sounded disappointed about the chilli! I debated whether to ask Karen to join us. Perhaps it would force the outcome I wanted but I decided that might actually be rather cruel. Graham was expecting a nice cosy family meal, not an evening where he was going to get dumped with an audience. I'm guessing it wouldn't make for a nice atmosphere if Karen came anyway, because of how much she actively disliked him. Which of course he was very aware of and a drunk Karen could be very mean Karen. I was still hoping that Graham and I might stay friends. Best not involve Karen then. Nicole came wandering into the kitchen with my entire mug collection in her arms and dumped them all in the sink before attempting to wander back out again. "Excuse me," I called "what do you think you're doing?" "Walking out of the room, well trying to anyway!" "You're just going to leave those cups there for me are you?" "I've just tidied my room!"

"Are you expecting a medal?" I ask incredulously. "Wash them up please." "I can't I'm going out and I'm late, I'll do it later." She complained. Knowing full well I'd end up doing it because I can't stand the clutter. "Do I take it you're not eating with us tonight either then?" I sighed, so much for a family meal, plus if Nicole was there I could put off the inevitable. "Hadn't planned on doing so, why?" "Graham's coming round." "Oh quick let me change my mind if Graham's coming round...no I'm going out mum." Sarcastic little madam, obviously due on. "Fine, I really don't care. But wash up the sodding cups first please, you're nineteen years old not nine!" Well anyone would have thought I'd just asked her to lick them clean, my mugs got washed up but they probably had a few more chips and cracks in them than they did before, she stormed out of the house. "When are you back?" I shouted out, no answer forthcoming.

James jumped on me as soon as I got back from Karen's, hoping to take advantage of the fact I'd had a wine or two, demanding a sleepover which I obviously said 'hell no' to, so he stomped upstairs, went on hunger strike and was playing his dreadful music at full blast. It was going to be a long night. I sighed dramatically, and reached for the wine.

Nobody tells you the hardest thing about having children is when they grow up.

Sleepless nights, dirty nappies and cracked nipples are nothing compared to the sleepless nights inflicted upon you where you simply have no idea where your child is. Especially when the mobile phone that you pay through the nose for, that's permanently clamped in their sweaty little hand, is not being answered! Dirty dishes that simply seem to breed like bacteria whenever a teenager is near the kitchen are equally frustrating. Why use one saucepan when you can use them all, and the bloody wok! Still, it's that feeling of absolute dread that accompanies the moment you discover a lighter and a packet of cigarettes hidden at the bottom of their school bag. That is just the worst feeling. Well, unless it's a bag of weed or a positive pregnancy test. That would be worse of course. Why in this day and age do these young idiots start smoking? Knowing all the risks that comes with it. Obviously to look cool in front of their mates is one reason, that goes without saying. I repeat, idiots. I'm not sure what sort of mother it makes me, that I pinched one of the squashed cigarettes and smoked it. On the decking, in full view of anyone that cared to see. I wondered briefly how cool I must look, I watched myself in my reflection in the kitchen window. Needless to say I didn't look cool and it was vile. I stubbed it out immediately. I hadn't smoked for nearly six years. Worse, now I had probably voided my life insurance. Teenagers are slightly evil caricatures of the sweet child they had once been. Underneath all the hormones, make up and attitude they were still there. That small, innocent little person that loved you so much that they wouldn't even let you go to the toilet alone. Needless to say I've been able to go to the bathroom on my own for a while now.

The evening was a catastrophic disaster, as predicted. I should never have drunk that second bottle of wine. That was fast becoming my catchphrase of late. I could tell Graham was slightly humpy with me anyway when he turned up with the takeaway, his greeting was lukewarm and his conversation was stilted. We watched the soaps on telly in near silence, instead of our normally running commentary throughout. I rambled on about Easter Sunday, about Elaine, Roger and Sandra. He remained stonily silent. "Wow, this is the best korma I've ever had," I exclaim in a jolly voice forking curry

into my mouth. It was as if I hadn't eaten for a month. My mouth was so dry I was finding it rather tricky to swallow though. He nodded, "yeah it's alright," pushing his biryani round the plate with his fork.
"I'm sorry about the chilli, maybe next time!" Why did I just say that? Offering him false hope. There would be no chilli con carne for Graham. He threw the fork down on the plate. "Remind me why our plans changed tonight?" He all but barked at me. "Oh," I felt caught on the hop, "well, because I popped over to Karen's and time just seemed to run away with us." I pulled a 'sorry face'. "Would it hurt just for once to put me first? He ranted at me uncharacteristically. Seriously, I'm always playing second fiddle to bloody Karen, to everyone in fact, the kids, your parents." "Excuse me?" I replied coolly, surprised at his animosity. Maybe he was going to make this much easier for me. Easier to finish with someone who's being an arse than a clueless buffoon. Which is how I've often, rather affectionately thought of him. "We've been together for over four months now. You don't want to introduce me to your family. You didn't invite me to Easter dinner but then proceed to tell me that's it's pretty much open house at Easter. I'm clearly I'm the one exception to that rule!" He had a point. "How do you think that makes me feel? You're always with Karen, talking to Karen, talking about Karen! Where is this relationship actually going?" He stood there staring at me, looking extremely hostile. I didn't feel threatened yet, but I wasn't sure I liked this darker angrier version of the normally nice, kind Graham. "I don't appreciate being spoken to like this Graham, especially in my own home. I have no idea where we are going, it's very early on and does anyone ever really know where a relationship is going until it gets there?" Clearly It's not going very far, I wanted to add. Although his animosity was unwelcome, he was, strangely, making this less hard for me. "Do you love me?" He suddenly asked looking

vulnerable. I felt very embarrassed for him and wished the floor would open up and swallow him whole. Of course I didn't love him.

I gulped. I actually gulped, cartoon style, but before I could reply my phone started to vibrate on the table, it was Elaine, I had to answer it. "I have to take this. I'll be right back." I left the room with Graham staring after me, an unreadable expression on his face. I'm also pretty sure he muttered 'fucking Karen again' under his breath. "Elaine." I answer coolly and loud enough for Graham to hear, that'll teach him to jump to conclusions. There was a slight hesitation before she answered me. "Emily, I'm so sorry I haven't been in touch, it's just been a crazy time. I wasn't thinking straight and I shouldn't have got you involved." She grovelled, too little too late, I suddenly felt very resentful. "Yeah well I've had grief off my mum and your mum, I've felt guilty for not actually worrying too much about you in the first place and then I get images put in my head by your mother of you being shackled to a bed somewhere about to be sold in a sex trafficking scam by a conman you met off the internet!" I felt out of breath after that sentence. "So yeah I wish you hadn't got me involved in whatever it is you've been up to and just manned up." I snapped. "I mean why say anything at all, just call her every couple of days and she'd never have known you weren't at work!" I ranted, suddenly feeling very angry and tired of the whole sorry mess. This was met with awkward silence. "I know I've been an absolute twat, I was just high on the recklessness of it, me just doing something out of my comfort zone!" She sounded contrite. "So it's a man?" This was met with another slight hesitation. " Yes." "What's the big secret? Is he married?" "No of course not!" Sounding indignant. "You obviously haven't gone very far either. You were seen." "So Karen did see me that day then?" sighed Elaine. "Don't sound too surprised, I'm guessing you weren't wearing a disguise so

the likelihood of being spotted was high, in our home town where everybody knows each other! What's his name then? Do I know him?" "Jack... and I think it's going to work out this time, it's...different." Whoop-e-do I felt like saying, how many times have I heard that one before. "Seriously go and see your mum, she's been beside herself."
"I've tried phoning actually but there's no answer, I hope everything is ok?" She said sounding worried. "A bit late to be worrying about her now," I retort feeling furious, "don't worry she's probably out with permanently unattached Roger. Turns out, he is a right stud muffin without his creepy moustache! Look, I've got my own shit going on here so I'll speak to you later." With that, I hung up before she could ask 'who the fuck is Roger'!

I took a deep breath and returned to the front room half expecting and half hoping that Graham might have disappeared quietly into the night never to be heard of again, but nope, there he was, unfortunately, shimmering away with frustration by the window. Damn! I was hoping against hope that he'd forgotten the question but I was sorely disappointed. "Do you love me?" he asked again, looking at me with sad eyes. I closed my eyes, so as not to see him, because the truth was I didn't, I cared for him at a push, but no it certainly wasn't love. I shook my head, tears squeezing from the corners of my eyes, not because I felt sad but because I hated any kind of awkward confrontation. Even my marriage break up wasn't as cringeworthy as this. Michael and I had been sitting on separate sofas on opposite sides of the front room, the metaphor speaking for our entire relationship actually. We'd been watching an old episode of Friends, the one where Joey and Rachel decided to be one of those couples that didn't have sex. We'd then looked at each other a little uncomfortably and I simply blurted out that I didn't love him

anymore! He looked shocked at first, then upset, but eventually, mutually we decided to call it a day. Just like that. Understanding that we were both young enough to meet someone new. Both realising that there had to be more to life than the sad, loveless one we were living. We then had a beer together. Something out of character for me as back then I didn't drink, especially at home, how times change with circumstance. He moved out the next day. Easy peasy!
"Right well, that's fucking brilliant, cheers Emily, you let your kids use me as a fucking cash machine. I do anything you ask of me and you had no intention of this ever being a serious relationship!" he practically spat at me. Whoa there tiger. "I need you to leave please," I suddenly felt very weary, fed up of expectations being put upon me. "I haven't misled you in any way, we were dating. I could have lied to you and said I loved you but that would be so very wrong, I like your company, a lot actually. But for me, no, I don't love you, maybe I would have done in time...but now we'll never know." I said sadly, willing him to leave quietly. I felt a bit mean turning it around so he looked the bad guy, but secretly I was relieved. I took off the charm bracelet and held it out to him. He snatched it from me.
He looked at me in disgust and shook his head, I finally understood what Karen meant about his dishonest eyes. Steely grey eyes staring angrily at me. "You owe me!" he said as he walked out the door. I kept my mouth shut so not to antagonise him further. Well I did for precisely two seconds but then curiosity got the better of me. "I owe you? What exactly do I owe you?" I ask incredulously. "I've spent a fucking fortune on you and your bastard children! Take, take, take the lot of you, and nothing much back! Not even a thank you from your parents for the wine I sent them!" Shit, he'd got me there, but seeing as I hadn't remembered to tell them it was from him in the first place he wasn't likely to have had a

thank you. I should have remembered to lie to him a thanks from them both, mum would be mortified if she'd thought people knew she hadn't acknowledged a gift. "Well, if you constantly feel the need to buy people..." He then completely lost the plot and starting shouting. "You condescending little bitch..." He made as if to grab at me but a loud voice behind him stopped him in his tracks.

"Em, is everything ok?" It was sexy builder Mike looking quite big and menacing in the dark as he walked up my driveway towards us. Thank God for sexy builders. "I'm fine thanks Mike, Graham was just leaving, weren't you? Goodbye, take care of yourself," I said meaning it. I wanted to add 'and maybe check into an anger management group as soon as possible'. Graham checked out the size of Mike and deciding that actually he probably wouldn't stand a chance against him backed off and got in his car. Mike watched him silently, this must be what it was like to have a burly bodyguard, I could get used to this. "You are a complete bitch Emily do you know that?" With that as his parting last words he drove off erratically. I hadn't even realised I was holding my breath until he'd driven away. I let it out and felt my knees buckle a little. Mike threw out an arm to steady me. "God what an arsehole," I'd laughed nervously, "thank you, not sure what he'd have done if you hadn't intervened." Mike then put a big hand on my shoulder and peered at me in concern, "are you sure you're ok? Do you think he'll come back?" "No, he won't come back," hoping that were true. Actually Graham had drunk a bottle of wine to himself so he really shouldn't be driving, I wondered whether I should call the police and shop him but I suddenly realised Mike was talking to me. "So, that was your boyfriend then? Not to be the nosy neighbour, you've already got one of them," he'd laughed gesturing towards Karen's twitching curtains "but I've seen him around quite a bit." "We'd only been seeing each other a few months, he was getting too serious too soon. I just didn't expect him to behave like that. I ended it tonight." I smiled up at Mike, "thank you again, great timing." I wondered if I should ask him in for coffee or a beer as a way of thanks. "Look I'm on my way out," well that put paid to that idea then. I felt stupidly disappointed. I realised that actually he did look quite smart and he was probably off out on a date, silly me. I then felt ridiculously jealous. "Let me give you my number, if you need me at all call me ok?" "Are you sure? I mean..." "Seriously, call me if he comes back or if you need anything, the guy sounded like a right twat, call me," he looked genuinely concerned. "Thanks Mike, that's really nice of you." We exchanged numbers and after squeezing my shoulder again he wandered off in the direction of town. I sighed and made my way inside. I was a single lady again. Beyoncé singing "all the single ladies" like a mad woman in my head.

CHAPTER SIX

It was the morning after the night before and I woke up feeling like I'd been hit by a truck. No scrap that, by a convoy of trucks in quick succession of each other. I had what felt like a pneumatic drill going off in my head trying to crack through my skull. My tongue felt too big for my mouth and it was covered in fur. I was pretty sure if I made any sudden movements the evening would play out right before me but in reverse, if you know what I mean. There was also a pain somewhere else on my body that I couldn't quite place just yet. For ten blissful ignorant seconds I lay there feeling like death but oblivious to the drama that had unfolded last night. Then it hit me, like a rogue truck that had got separated from the others and came thundering out of nowhere. Bang! Last night!

Elaine not smuggled in the back of a lorry bound and gagged about to be sold for sex slavery, simply shagging a new man in secret. It was a bit of an anti climax to be honest. I'd at least expected a frantic trip overseas with a dramatic helicopter rescue thrown in for good measure. I'd have been hailed a hero by the newspapers for rescuing a lorry full of women destined for sexual slavery. I think perhaps I've been watching too many Silent Witness reruns. I must start watching something less trashy and a bit more intellectual. Still, at least she was safe, if somewhat boring and predictable with it. Then, I remembered the biggest shock from last night, Graham and what an absolute knobcheese he turned out to be. My stomach heaved a little bit when I remembered the aggression towards me and the spiteful words. Thank God for Mike being in the right place at the right time. I dread to think what might have happened otherwise. I'm pretty sure Graham was all wind and bluster but just goes to show how little you know someone. I think I'd had a lucky escape with that one. It had left a bad taste in my mouth and nothing to do with the Korma and copious amounts of alcohol I had consumed. I hadn't had to call Karen round, she'd heard it all through the wall. Not that she'd been purposely listening of course, although there was a faint mark on her face where it looked like she'd had a glass pressed up hard against the wall. She'd been armed with a frying pan, waiting by the front door just in case it had got out of hand. She came straight round armed with another bottle of wine, and we then put the world to rights until the early hours. By that, I mean we slagged off Graham and dissected my 'relationship' with him, coming to the conclusion that he did indeed have dishonest eyes and maybe an unhealthy pork pie fetish.

"And he did the lottery every week with his mum, the same numbers. Probably his mums birthday, his mums house number, his mums bra size!" I had been very unkind. I'd also in my drunken wisdom decided to text Mike and say thank you for his help. What had I been thinking? He was on a date, he didn't want to hear from me, he was probably in mid shag! I might have put him off his sexual stride.

The text went something along the lines of.

THANKS SO MUCH FOR LAST NIGHT. SO GLAD YOU WERE IN THE RIGHT PLACE AT THE RIGHT TIME ;) SEE YOU AGAIN SOON XX

As of yet he still hadn't replied. I wasn't surprised in the slightest, I'd used a lame winky face after all.
The sudden urge to urinate washed over me like a crashing wave so I pushed aside my duvet and to my horror of horrors found that my left ankle was a rather unattractive shade of purple and at least four times its normal size! It pulsated angrily at me. I perused the depths of my hungover ridden mind and came up with the conclusion I'd had an accident, just call me Jessica Fletcher, blimey I was detective material alright. An accident possibly involving Karen's garden fence and another bottle of wine but not necessarily in that particular order, I'm sure it would come to me eventually. I couldn't put any weight on it and it was now throbbing so painfully that there was only one thing left to do, go on my hands and knees it was that or end up wetting the bed. That was a humiliating stage too far even for me!
Thank god there was no one to witness my degrading crawl of shame across the landing, my lardy bottom mooning out from beneath my too small bed t-shirt and my boobs swinging precariously underneath beneath me, free from the confines of a bra. I was just about to use my head to butt open the bathroom door when it swung open before me and I came face to hairy shins with a pair of legs.
"Who the hell are you?" I squawk shrilly from my prostrate position on the floor. "It's Billy," replied the legs nervously "I slept here last night". I looked up and unfortunately looked straight up the leg of his rather baggy boxer shorts! Well, I didn't know where to look, I focused on the slight damp patch instead! ON THE WALL, such filthy minds you have! Little Billy wasn't so little any more, this really was an excruciating

moment, please don't tell your mother I silently urged him. She still hasn't forgiven me for the sleepover incident when he was eight. Somebody drew a beard on his face in permanent marker but that would pale into insignificance if she found out about us both in this disturbing position. Yep, the final piece of the jigsaw slotted into place and I now had a vague recollection of James sitting on the stairs looking sad and concerned waiting for me to come in from my break up with Graham. "Are you ok?" He asked in concern giving me a hug. A rarity indeed for sixteen year old James who thought public displays of affection especially with your mother should be made punishable by law. "I'm fine, Graham isn't coming back." "Good! The man is a twat!" he said with force. "You didn't like him?" I asked in surprise. "Not really. I mean, his money came in handy but who does that? Me and Nicole just felt he was trying to buy us all the time." I was more shocked that him and Nicole had actually had a real conversation about this than by what he just said. He looked down at his feet, this was the nearest we'd probably come to having a grown up conversation. One that didn't involve me shouting at him about his PlayStation or me saying no to something he wanted. So I did something very selfless of me given the circumstances. "Phone your friends, you can have a sleepover!" The happy look on his face was priceless and so worth it, until now! Right now I was regretting my generous nature big time. "Right well off you go Billy, and let us never speak of this again...to anyone!" I took charge. He stepped over me, 'don't look up, don't look up' I repeated in my head and he scurried to the safety of James's bedroom. "Don't look back, DONT LOOK BACK!" I yelled at him, suddenly aware I wasn't wearing any knickers and my bare bum was on show, I frantically tried pulling my t-shirt over my behind. I'm never drinking again!

An few hours later I felt in a much better place. Taking double the recommended dose of painkillers and coffee you could run your car off tended to have that effect on you. I hated coffee but it was a necessary evil. Nicole had unsuccessfully done first aid on my ankle having just done a course at work, apparently. The bandage hung limply off my bad foot. "Wow, I hope to God none of your customers ever require your nursing skills, seriously," I waggled my foot in her direction and the bandage fell off onto the floor. "I didn't say I was any good did I?" As she did it again, this time succeeding in cutting off my blood supply to my toes instead. We hadn't mentioned the Graham issue, but seeing as she was being nice to me for a change I assumed James had filled her in already, which was bloody handy as I really didn't feel like talking or thinking about him right now. "Oh, did I mention that dad and Tara have split up?" Nicole said out of nowhere. "What?" I exclaimed loudly, spitting out my coffee. "No way? Why?" I loved a bit of drama that didn't involve me for a change. "Don't know," she shrugged. "Tara changed her relationship status on Facebook to single. She raised her eyebrows at me in question. "I haven't spoken to your father for at least two years, it's highly unlikely to have anything to do with me!" "Maybe he still lurves you mum," Nicole joked while I tried to keep the bile down. Wow, how strange. Both of us breaking up with someone on the same evening. I didn't give it too much thought as it reminded me I had to change my relationship status on Facebook too. Wondering, would mine and Michaels mutual friends put two and two together and come up with eleven? Did we even have any mutual friends anymore? Nope, it would be far too controversial, I shall wait. I'd never wanted to change my status to in a relationship if the first place but Graham was insistent. I did delete him.

The phone rang. It was Elaine. Big sigh. Nicole wandered off muttering under her breath about embarrassing parents. "Mum has disappeared!" Was Elaine's greeting. What fresh deja vu reverse hell was this!?"And by 'disappeared' you mean…...?" I asked. "I went round this morning and she wasn't there!" She said as if talking to a dumb child. "So by disappeared it could also mean popping out to Tesco to buy some broccoli?" I said sarcastically. "Oh, and I know who Roger is, he's that guy from your parents, the sex pervert guy!" she accused. The apple certainly doesn't fall far from the tree in Sandra and Elaine's case, such overactive imaginations. "No that was me being funny, I'm sure he's a really nice man actually." I felt the need to stick up for Roger. "You've decided to come out of hiding then?" "Yes, you made me feel bad," she said sulkily. "Anyway," I carry on "last week your mum could have been banging Fred and Rose West at the same time and you wouldn't have had a clue because you were nowhere to be found! So get down off your high horse and calm the fuck down!" Silence, then a snort of laughter."Reasonable point, sorry Em I'm being a twat again." "Yes you are," I agree "but your mum is fine. Seriously her and Roger got on like a house on fire, your mum needs something other than you in her life to worry about and you know it." "I guess I'm just feeling guilty, sorry I shouldn't have taken it out on you," she said. "Forget about it, look I..." I was interrupted by the house phone ringing. Only two types of people ever ring the landline, cold callers and mums! "I'll call you back Elaine."It was the latter of the two, my mum. Unfortunately not someone's else's this time. I wasn't sure I was in the mood for this.

"Hello darling, everything ok?" It was like on some level she knew that something untoward had occurred recently. She was like a witch with her uncanny intuition. Either that or she'd bugged the place. I wouldn't have put it past her. "Yes, all is well," I said sounding stilted as if all was clearly not well. I must start acting better. "That's good," mum clearly had other things on her mind than giving me the third degree. "Right, that spa day your brother gave me," mum said briskly, "well apparently it runs out in a weeks time, so I've booked it for Saturday and I'm taking you with me!" "Do I get a say?" I wondered. Mum carried on as though I hadn't spoken. "I'd have preferred to take Barbra, Anne and Jayne but there you go, you can't always get what you want. Too short notice apparently!" It would appear mum had the hump and possibly with Simon too, that was a cause for celebration. But a spa day with my mum, noooooo! She totally wouldn't 'get' the point of a spa day at all. "I've asked Sandra and she's asking Elaine too, it's for four people you see." Maybe it wouldn't be too bad if Elaine was being forced along too. "Have you spoken to Sandra then?" "Well obviously, when I asked her to come to the spa with us." My mum tutted impatiently. "Keep up Emily." "Is she still seeing Roger?" I queried nosily. "I presume so. Roger just updated his profile picture on Facebook to a selfie of them both!" Oh dear, I'm not sure what was worse, the fact Roger was taking selfies or the fact he was uploading them onto Facebook. "Talking of Facebook, why haven't you accepted my friend request yet?" Mum asked. Oh God I now knew what was worse than Roger being on Facebook and that was my mother being social media savvy.

So this was how Elaine and myself found ourselves sitting in the back of my mums car on Saturday morning, a 'fun' day ahead of us at the spa. "What have you told your mum?" I whispered to Elaine not wanting to put my foot in it. "That I'm under enormous pressure at work and needed some space." Yeah, that would make sense. "But she knows I'm seeing someone, I just haven't given details." Mum had already moaned and shared with us all that she was severely constipated and would have to take laxatives throughout the day to ease her condition. Gee thanks mum for that information, could have done without it to be honest though. I'd left Nicole instructions to feed her brother at some point during the day. "What do I give him?" she asked blankly as though he were a stranger she'd never met before. "There's ingredients for fajitas in the fridge," I answer. "Or a freezer full of food, you have eyes, read the instructions! I'm not asking you to cook a bloody banquet." "But I'm going out tonight!" she moaned. "Well feed him before you go out, seriously you're an adult now, help me out please!" Stomp, stomp, stomp! Something told me the ingredients for the fajitas would still be in the fridge when I got back and there'd be empty pizza boxes strewn around the kitchen.Dealing with children in the disguise of being an adult was so frustrating! I was in a foul mood anyway. Nicole had gone awol the night before and not answered her phone for hours. I was convinced she'd been abducted and was in the boot of a mad mans car. In actual fact she'd been at the cinema. She had told me, apparently. She had not.

A whole evening wiped out by worry. I couldn't even drink wine, I needed to be sober incase I had to be part of a rescue party. "So what do you do at these spas then?" asked Sandra nervously. She was behaving as though she was being driven to the morgue for the day instead of to a luxury spa centre. "Relax and enjoy the facilities." I answered rolling my eyes at Elaine in expiration. "Mum did you book our treatments?" I personally couldn't wait for my back and shoulder massage, so many knots to be worked on. "Yes of course there's a list of times somewhere." mum said vaguely wincing in pain. I hoped the laxatives weren't doing their magic right now, whilst we were all trapped inside a moving vehicle with no means of escape. "So is it salads and super foods for lunch, green tea and vegetable smoothies that sort of thing? That'll help ease

your problem Sheila," Sandra said distractedly. Her phone went off again and she quickly answered her text, presumably to desperate Roger who hadn't let up since Sandra had climbed into the passenger seat. Elaine, pulled a face. "Seriously can you put the phone down, we are supposed to be having a mother daughter day, can Roger not leave you alone for a few hours?" sulked Elaine. Sandra just gave her a look as if to say 'really? After your disappearing act you dare to judge me?' I also gave her the same look for good measure. "No! It's not healthy foods, It's prosecco followed by a three course lunch, this is a spa retreat not a health farm." I answered impatiently. "You can chill around the pool, have a sauna, have a facial, that kind of thing."
I knew they wouldn't 'get' a spa day, it was so wasted on them. "When you get there you put on your swimming costumes and a robe..." Continued Elaine but was interrupted by mum. "What do you mean? We have to eat lunch in our dressing gowns?" mum sounded aghast. "In our housecoats?" repeated Sandra looking just as shocked! Somebody shoot me now and what in bloody hells name was a housecoat?

We arrived, checked in and managed to get mum and Sandra changed into their spa gear without too much fuss. Although as we walked out of the changing rooms to the pool area anyone would think they were walking to their deaths. Pulling their robes tightly around them as if they were about to be mugged, walking gingerly as though they'd never worn flip flops indoors before. I gave them instructions to find a table whilst Elaine and I ordered a pot of tea and cake. "I've only been in their company an hour and I want to smother them both!" She said. "With their own housecoats!" I said and we both sniggered childishly. It turned out housecoats was a posh name for dressing gowns. Who knew? As we returned to the table, the mums appeared to be having a whispered conversation about one of us or maybe both. They stopped talking immediately and tried to smile innocently. "All girls together," trilled mum annoyingly sipping her tea. "Yes how lovely, I know, let's talk about how you girls are getting on with your boyfriends," Sandra spoke as though reading from a script, my mums script probably. I felt Elaine stiffen next to me and sigh. "For God's sake mum, I've told you what I want you to know, please drop it, it's early days and I don't want to tempt fate." She hissed through gritted teeth. I still personally thought Elaine was seeing a married man, or a young man, not too young that it would get her on the sex offenders register but a toy boy perhaps. Or even an old man, a sugar daddy. I made a note to get her drunk soon and find out the big secret. I couldn't understand the drama surrounding this new relationship. Both mums nodded, understanding the force of fate, they then both turned eagerly to me. "I'm sorry to disappoint you ladies but Graham dumped me the other night so I'm now single again." I sip my own tea, wishing it was a gin and watch their faces fall. "Oh dear," said Sandra sadly "was it something in particular that made him end the relationship?" she queried in a knowing way. Mum just sighed and looked disappointed in me, again. "He thought I had an unhealthy friendship with my friend Karen," Sandra nearly choked on her cake, mum back slapped her. "Truth was I was supposed to have cooked him dinner and instead I got drunk with Karen and it didn't go down well I'm afraid."

"You didn't make him dinner and he got the hump and dumped you? What is this? The 1950's? You're better off without him!" said mum uncharacteristically sticking up for me for a change. Wonders will never cease. Sandra reached over and squeezed my hand and whispered something in my ear. I didn't quite catch what she said, I'm sure it was supportive but it sounded like 'whenever you're ready love!' The mums went off to have their top lips waxed while we stayed and relaxed in

the hot tub. It was while we were sitting there that I noticed a couple sitting to the left of us, there was something very familiar about the way he clutched his mobile phone tightly in his sweaty little hand… "Oh my God it's Benjamin!" I whispered and grabbed Elaine's arm. "What?" She said squinting in the direction I was head gesturing to. "Irish Benjamin?" " No, Lithuanian Benjamin, of course bloody Irish Benjamin, how many Benjamin's have I dated!" I gave her a disparaging look. She shrugged as if to say 'how would I know?' "Was he always so fat?" She asked wrinkling her nose. "Well, he was big built back then but not fat as such I suppose. It was eight years ago, he's certainly stacked on a bit of timber since." "Did he always have a lazy eye?" She asked again, peering at him obviously, pulling a face.
"Well...can you stop it? It was a blurry photo, alright!" I snapped back crossly while she sniggered.

Just seeing him, and it definitely was him, I recognised his hairy back (gag) made all the embarrassment and resentment come bubbling up to the surface. He'd completely humiliated me on more than one occasion and I'd been in such a bad place emotionally back then I'd let him get away with it. I'd been so desperately trying to compete with Michaels new relationship and get one over on him that I let myself be used by a fat and had to be said ugly bastard like Benjamin. The only thing going for him was his Irish accent and that, to my shame, one blurry photo. I'd met up with him twice. The first time I'd spent the day before preparing myself, by which I mean, shaving, plucking, moisturising myself to within an inch of my life. Unfortunately I'd shaved my downstairs area with a bluntish razor and by the next day my fanny was covered in a hugely unattractive, red raw shaving rash and was so bloody itchy. I was like a dog on heat, wanting to rub myself up against anything I could find to relieve that horrendous itchy feeling. I constantly had my hands down my knickers when I didn't think anyone was looking, scratching away, I'm pretty sure he thought I had a sexually transmitted disease. By the end of night, it should have worried me that he still would have had sex with me. If it had been anyone else I might have come clean about the real cause of my problem and then both have a laugh about it but I didn't think he'd find it that amusing, a sense of humour not appearing to be a personality trait he possessed. I'd lied instead and told him I was on my period. Not that I'd ever have sex on a first date or anything but i just wanted him to be aware that sex was definitely off the table that night. His reaction was one of being massively put out, and the date was rather awkward. I naïvely put it down to first date nerves, maybe he was new to all this as well. I'd never really been on a date before as Michael and I had met at school and had just hung out, maybe all dates, were this difficult, stilted and plain boring. It was made especially awkward as we were staying in a hotel together for the night, we ended up both being asleep by ten, not touching at all. He then blew me off three times after that, first excuse was he'd had his wallet stolen and was at the police station going through cctv images. The second time his uncle had died! The third his appendix had burst. I believed them all, like a fool. Don't worry, I judge myself also. Fourth time lucky, or unlucky some might say.

We met up for dinner, he took me for a curry. He seemed to be competing for some kind of world record, who could eat the quickest. He was a bit stingy with the drinks and embarrassingly didn't leave a tip. However, he bought a bottle of value vodka at Tesco on the way back and we went back to the hotel, got drunk and had sex. Unremarkable, boring, missionary position sex! Benjamin went from kissing to stripping naked as though his clothes were on fire, never have

I seen a man remove clothing as quickly as he did. He stood awkwardly, naked in front of me, one hand covering his old chap! 'Your turn.' He said impatiently, jigging from one foot to the other. I decided to inject some sexiness into the proceedings. I popped the button on my jeans. 'Why don't you help me.' I had said huskily, laying back on the bed in a way that I imagined was irresistible to any red blooded male.

He sighed and rolled his eyes. 'Fine.' He yanked at the bottoms of my jeans. I not so sexily bounced down the mattress, I even had to hold on to the sides to stop myself being pulled off the end of the bed as he relieved me of my skinny jeans. That's when it all went further downhill, fast. He climbed on top me, kneaded my tits like they were two balls of dough and started pounding away on top of me as though his life depended on it. At one point I was actually concerned he was actually having an epileptic seizure on top of me as I was getting nothing out of the experience apart from friction burns in a delicate place. I then angled myself in a way that could possibly be to my advantage but Benjamin stopped and told me I was putting him off his stride so could I possibly lay flat!! The worst part is I actually listened to him and lay flat. Two minutes later he came. Two minutes after that he rolled over and started snoring, leaving me wondering if I had just taken part in a pornographic version of Beadles About. Would he turn around and say 'only joking, your turn', obviously this did not happen and I lay there feeling like a complete idiot.

I SHOULD HAVE LEFT THEN.

Hindsight is a wonderful thing I'm sure you'd agree. I woke up next morning to find my eyes stuck together with mascara gloop, I then suffered a mini attack on the bed thinking I'd gone blind, before I realised that wasn't the case. My stomach was churning with curry and alcohol, nausea radiated out from me, like a poisonous aura. So I farted, it was loud, long and smelly! I realised a second too late that I wasn't alone and my eyes whipped open, ripping off my eyelashes in the process, just in time to see a man scramble out of the bed in a big hurry. Benjamin stood, naked at the foot of the bed looking at me as though I was the most repulsive thing in the world. 'Oh my dear God, Emily!' He then started to retch, a tad over the top, it was only a trump after all, but it was humiliating nevertheless. Why couldn't he have done the gentlemanly thing and pretended he hadn't heard it, although you'd have to have been born deaf, with no sense of smell and possibly in a coma to have let that one go unnoticed.

Right now I really wished the floor would open and swallow him whole. 'Jesus bloody hell Christ!' He marched over to the window, opened it up and started gulping fresh air in. 'Sorry I forgot you were here.' I wailed in embarrassment. 'You should get that looked at love, I reckon something crawled up your arse and died!' he said still retching dramatically. I took at look at Benjamin standing there, his flaccid penis hanging limply between his legs. His stomach large and OH MY GOD a hairy back and shoulders, cue a serious dry retching moment for me too. But it was then that I noticed he didn't have a scar. How can you have your appendix removed without leaving a scar?!

It's to my immense shame that I never confronted him about it. The arrogant arse who hadn't even tried to hide the fact he'd lied so blatantly. He clearly had no respect for me or any genuine interest. I mean he could have drawn on a scar for my benefit, I'd have had a bit more respect for him then. I mentally woke up at that point and felt physically ill, vowing never to let a man play me like that again.

Anyhow, back to the here and now. I watch as Benjamin got up waving his phone at the woman he was with, indicating he was going to make a phone call. To his wife maybe, or one of his many girlfriends, while his latest bit on the side lay on her lounger oblivious. A plan for revenge began to form in my head. My window of opportunity was small, I had make it count. I'd never get the chance to get my own back on him again, and he so deserved a dose of his own medicine. Or to be more exact, my mums. "Elaine do me a favour please go and make conversation with his girlfriend or whatever she may be and get her away from the pool side for a few minutes." "What? I can't do that? Why? Do you still like him? Surely not!" She gaped incredulously. "Of course not he's a fat lump, but please and be quick, I'll explain after!" I pleaded with her. "Ok, ok...the things we do for our bloody friends, but this is far worse than me asking you to cover for me to my mother!" She muttered as she wandered off to make what I thought would be polite conversation with a stranger but what she actually did was 'accidentally' trip whilst drinking from her water bottle and tip it over the poor girl. The poor cow shrieked loudly and I heard Elaine apologising profusely, Then leading her away to grab her a clean towel and buy her drink to say sorry for her clumsiness.She was an acting genius! She was wasted in insurance. I made sure no one was looking while I grabbed a handful of mums laxatives out of her bag and walked over to where Benjamin had been sipping his pretentious cafe latte. Luckily it was almost full and still steaming hot, so I dropped the laxatives into it and gave it a quick stir, making sure I was not being observed by anyone, then I quickly jumped into the deep end of the pool feeling exhilarated at being so daring and so very naughty. I bobbed nervously in the water while I waited for Benjamin to come back, quickly followed by Elaine and the girl, a quick three way conversation ensured, some polite chatter and a sugary sweet final apology from Elaine, she was good. I was suitably impressed. I made sure he'd drunk some of his coffee before grabbing Elaine promising to explain later, got our stuff and got the hell out of there before the shit hit the fan, literally!

Lunch with the mums was a riot. Seriously, I wasn't even being sarcastic this time. The prosecco had gone straight to their heads, so they were all mellow and being a little bit silly, finally enjoying all that the spa had to offer them. I'd rather unselfishly not had a glass and offered to drive mums car home. It was, after all, mums Easter gift. I was such a good daughter. They'd thoroughly enjoyed their massages, although mum thought it was highly unnatural for another woman to be touching her like that. Elaine looked a bit uncomfortable at mums loud opinions, then Sandra then got a bit cross with her and said there was nothing wrong with it and maybe she should be more open minded about things before giving me a sympathetic smile. They both had hilarious patches - due to their waxing - under their noses giving the impression of red moustaches, that kept me and Elaine amused for half an hour. Sandra waxed lyrical about how happy Roger had made her. Mums eyes glazed over presumably having heard it before. Elaine looked like she wanted to throw up. I just wondered if she was talking about sex! Were they doing the deed? "All these years on my own and finally I've met my prince charming," she gushed. Mum reached over and patted my hand. "See, there's hope for you yet love. Let's find you a Roger." I gagged on thin air at the thought. The absolute highlight of my day had to be when mum told us the hilarious but humiliating story of the poor man who'd had an 'accident' in the swimming pool!! "He was beside himself with embarrassment, poor lad, it must have been a bug, it came on so fast, one minute he was doing widths in the deep end then the next he was running to the toilet holding his bum cheeks together, but not tight enough it would seem. Irish guy he was. His girlfriend didn't know where to look, poor girl." Elaine gasped and looked at me wide eyed a big smirk on her face, and maybe a little bit of respect there too. "People were actually filming him, probably to upload to the Internet later no doubt, who'd want to see that? Shocking. He was so humiliated!" said Sandra. Who'd want to see that? Who indeed? Me perhaps? Revenge was certainly a dish best served cold or in a latte with your mothers laxatives.

Nicole's pungent perfume still lingered in the hallway, so I knew she hadn't long gone out. Predictably there were two empty pizza boxes on the worktop and a sink full of dirty dishes. I yelled at James to come downstairs. It took him a personal best of six minutes twenty eight seconds to materialise. "Wash up please," I demanded pointing to the overflowing dishes."That's not fair," he complained. "Life isn't fair!" "Cassia was here earlier." He mumbled grumpily. "In the house?" "No, standing outside just staring." "Did you talk to her?" "No, when I opened the door to the pizza man she saw me and got back in her car." "Was it definitely her?" Why would Cassia be here of all places. We were hardly bosom buddies. I doubt she was popping in for a catch-up and relationship advice, from me of all people. "Yes, I recognised her cardboard trousers." Curious. I text Simon.

WHY WAS CASSIA AT MY HOUSE TODAY? X

WHAT? NO IDEA!

CAN YOU NOT ASK HER THEN??

YEAH OK WILL DO!

Simon as helpful as ever. I hoped I hadn't caused problems. Then I found I didn't care if I did. He didn't get back to me. I then text Karen.

I DON'T SUPPOSE YOU NOTICED MY BROTHERS GF HANGING AROUND TODAY DID YOU? XX

NO I'M OUT! WHAT WAS SHE DOING? XX

JUST STARING AT THE HOUSE. MAYBE SHE WANTS TO BE MY FRIEND LOL XX

YEAH MAYBE XX

Then nothing. Conversation over. What was going on in Karen's world I wondered? It felt odd to be on the sidelines for once.

CHAPTER SEVEN

For several days now I'd been feeling rather down in the dumps. I wasn't sure if it was the fact I was single again. Although I'd pretty much spent the last eight years with the single status hanging over my head like a guillotine, so you'd think I'd be used to that feeling. I just couldn't be bothered to do anything, anymore. Including housework. Maybe I was depressed. The hidden disease it was called. Although I looked like crap too, so not completely hidden, there were the obvious signs, bags under my eyes and deep roots showing being a couple of the giveaway signs. The house was looking rather shambolic of late too. Some might go as far to say like a shithole. Some people being my mother, of course. I as head of the household had to hold my hand up and take full responsibility for it, well most of it anyway. I'm not a bloody martyr. I did have two other able bodied people living with me, for all the use they were. Sometimes it was quicker to do things myself. Only I wasn't at the moment. I felt like I was existing in a vicious, mucky circle.

So I decided to pay an unexpected visit to my parents. There was nothing like the comforting feeling of returning to the home you grew up in to make you forget your problems for a while. It would have been nice to lay down on my bed in my old bedroom and stare at my Take That posters for a while.

But my room had been turned into a study before I'd even pulled off the driveway all those years ago.
Simon's bedroom was still intact. Just saying. A shrine some might say. Some, being me. There might be some homemade cake going begging. Mum made good cakes, even before The Bake Off made it fashionable to rise a good muffin. Mum would be so pleased to see me. She was always saying she didn't see enough of me. So I turned up after my rare half day on Friday, only to find a large white van on the driveway. I went to walk in the front door as normal but it was locked. So I had to suffer the indignation of knocking and waiting to be let in. Mum answered, looking flustered. "Darling, how lovely to see you," the words not matching the tone in which it were said, nor the look on her face. She ushered me in, not to the kitchen where the cake might be but into the front room closing the door firmly behind her. "So," she said "what's up?" What's up? When did my mum ever ask what's up? She was acting decidedly shifty. "I was feeling a bit fed up, so I thought I'd come and see you and get some TLC." I said, feeling silly now I'd said it out loud. As delivering TLC to her only daughter was obviously the last thing on her mind. Mum sighed and absently patted my knee. "Is it because you've been dumped?" The look on my face must have said it all because she then quickly said " because he sounded like a tool, you're better off without him!" Said more soothingly this time. "I know that. I'm just..." I just trailed off because I didn't know what was wrong. Was it Graham's extreme reaction to our breakup? I won't lie, it scared me a bit, being shouted at by a mad man wasn't a pleasant experience.

Karen hadn't been around much in the evenings either lately, so I was drinking alone. Elaine was tied up with her new relationship and didn't have time for me either. And Simon was now ignoring my texts so I had no idea what Cassia had been doing at my house. It was bugging me. Making me anxious, making me feel sorry for myself. A loud bang came from the kitchen. We both turned toward it. Mum looking more jumpy than ever. "Is dad out there?" I ask. Thinking of the strange work van on the drive.

"No. Look why don't we pop out for a cuppa and cake..." she sounded desperate. "Mum what's going on?" I stood up, mum stood up too, to bar my way into the kitchen. "Are you cheating on dad?" I ask incredulously, trying to go past her. Mum looked at me with a horrified look on her face, before dissolving into tears. Tears of laughter not sorrow as it turned out. "You silly girl, of course I'm not." She wiped her tears of mirth. "Well, I can't keep it secret now you're here, come on." I followed mum with trepidation. The kitchen and dining room was filled with cardboard boxes. "Oh my God, are you moving? Without planning on telling us?" "Yes, Emily that's exactly what we were planning on doing!" I assumed it was said with sarcasm, she hadn't quite pulled it off though because I was still wondering if that's exactly what they were doing.

"We are having an extension built. The boxes are from the garage, all your childhood memories as it happens." I was determined not to be swayed by the lure of childhood memories. Tempting as it were. "And the secrecy is because?" I was truly stumped. "Your father! Who else! He was worried you'd be concerned we were taking on too much at our age, and that we were spending your inheritance. Or that we might be conned by dodgy workmen!" "Thanks for that Mrs B!" said a very familiar voice. I turned toward the source of it to find Mike. "Mike!" I exclaimed. "Emily!" He exclaimed back. "You two know each other?" Asked mum. "Yes!" We said in unison. "Oh!" She said. We all looked at each other. Mike breaking the silence. "So Mrs B is your mum? Obvious now I know, it's where you get your good looks from Em," he smarmed. Mum giggled and looked coy. I pulled a sick face at Mike. He just grinned sexily at me. "Cake anyone?" offered mum. About bloody time. It turned out mum and dad were having a two story extension built, using the garage as ground floor base. Mike and his team were overseeing it. Recommended by their next door neighbours/nemesis's Janice and Roy. I decided not to ask the rather obvious question of why they needed more room in an already too big house. There were only the two of them after all. It all seemed a bit pointless to me. But knowing my mother the way I did, I guessed it was her love of keeping up with the neighbours that swayed them. If Janice and Roy had a new extension then she must have one too. Mum liked to overtake them at speed making obscene hand gestures as she passed. They were great friends though! Plus, rather selfishly I realised, if the house were bigger it would push the house into the extortionate inheritance tax bracket! The three of us sat around the kitchen table, surrounded by boxes making small talk eating battenberg cake. I tried to put the fact that Mike hadn't responded to my text message the other night out of my mind, although it clearly bothered me still. He gave no indication he was bothered in the slightest. He probably received all manner of texts from random women all the time. What was one more unanswered one. A dusty old version of Monopoly caught my eye sticking out of a box. "This was banished to the loft wasn't it?" I said laughing. In 1988 to be precise, after the game turned particularly nasty one evening. Simon had always been a bad loser.

"Yes," agreed mum. "You always were such a bad loser!"

"Her memory isn't what it was." I counteracted. Mum glared. Family game night with my own children had ceased to be a 'thing' for a long time now too. This was after a game of Monopoly (Monopoly was clearly an evil game designed to split up families) had turned particularly nasty and the board and all its contents were tipped over in anger. By whom, I can not honestly remember, it could have been me for all I knew, according to mums recollections. Even before we had begun there had been false allegations of cheating, the incessant winding up of James (me again possibly) and the confiscation of the dice "they're my dice so you're not playing with them". James had snatched the dice out of Nicole's hand. Nicole had then started to make her own dice out of paper, just to wind him up even more. Subsequently the game was then abandoned, tears were shed and accusations of favouritism were flung around. It was all sounding extremely familiar. Though unlike my parents I had no favourites. I found both my children equally annoying. We ended up in separate rooms sulking for the duration of the evening, well the kids were sulking, I was just majorly pissed off. Monopoly was subsequently added to the ever growing list of banned board games in the house. We ended up selling all banished games at a boot sale! Made a measly profit of five pounds and fifty pence for the lot. "Nice school photo Em?" He said gesturing towards the back wall where my gormless face stared down at us. "Thanks," deciding it was pointless to be embarrassed of my frizzy hair, spots and inane grin. At the end of the day that's exactly how I looked aged 15 and a half. "I'm sure you were an Adonis." I laughed. He grinned. "Sure if an Adonis had crazy curly hair and a slight easy left eye." Mike was then shivved on by mum to get on with the job. "Time is money, you can't sit here eating cake all afternoon," she declared. Mum has morphed into Alan Sugar all of a sudden. Mike laughed. "If only I could," he said. "See you soon Emily," he waved as he disappeared to the building site that used to be my parents garden. "As for you young lady, the advice I can give to you is stop drinking!" Before I could protest lamely she carried on "You drink way too much." I had to concede on that point. "Take control of your life. Take up a hobby. Don't let men control how you feel. And...you could do a lot worse," she said gesturing towards the garden, presumably meaning Mike and not the seventeen year old labourer on his phone, scratching his balls, a cigarette hanging out of his mouth who was now standing by the door.

Before I could protest I found myself also shivved on and out of the house with a couple of boxes of memories to root through. I woke up the next morning and decided enough was enough. Time to take back control. The kids bedrooms, not normally high on my agenda, if I'm being completely honest, had taken first precedent. Especially after discovering my expensive eyeliner had gone missing again, I'd made the mistake of marching into Nicole's room without protective clothing to find it an absolute shit tip, and that is an understatement. A potential health hazard would be a more accurate description. I quickly backed out of there, holding my breath before I picked up a new but nasty strain of air borne bacteria. The eyeliner was eventually located in James bedroom but it was ruined beyond repair. No, he wasn't actually using it for its real purpose (for sexy, smouldering eyes) he'd used it as a pencil for his art homework!! It was while in there that I'd first noticed an undesirable smell, not completely uncommon in James's bedroom but this definitely had a more sinister undertone about it and then I discovered a lunchbox of questionable content in the corner of his room, on closer inspection there was definitely something growing inside it. Gag, gag! "Oh my God why do you do this mother?!" exclaimed Nicole when I tried to pick them both up on their slovenly ways in a calm and measured manner. Well ok, I kind of screamed at them and totally lost my shit. "We will tidy our rooms in our own time, they're not that bad!" "That is a matter of opinion. I am only surprised that lunchbox hasn't morphed into a killing machine and killed us all in our sleep." Mealtimes had become a bit hit and miss too, ready meals being our preferred option lately and way too many takeaways. None of us sitting down at the same time anymore. This wasn't a family it was more of a dysfunctional house share of people who just happened to be related.

I knew if we carried on this way the children would develop rickets or some other such deficiency due to lack of vitamins and minerals. I couldn't allow that to happen. I was The Mum. I'm sure society, i.e. my mother again would blame me if the kids got scurvy and quite rightly so. It was time to regain some of the control. So I called a house meeting. I'd never called a house meeting before in my whole life so the kids were a bit wary. "What's going on?" said James looking worried. "You've always said before that families who have 'house meetings' are pretentious wankers!" "It's time to get our family back on track, we are like three strangers living under the same roof!" Ignoring James and his profanity because it's true I had said that in the past. "You are my children and we need to spend more quality time together as a family!" "Do we though?" Nicole groaned. "Are you drunk?" asked James. I gave him a look, Nicole sniggered. "From now on we are going to eat together as a family at least three times a week!" I announced unrealistically. "And cook a meal together at least once a week." said even more unrealistically. "We will be like the Walton's." "Who are they?" asked James confused. "Pretentious wankers?" Suggested Nicole. I sighed. "Well it can't be a Monday, Wednesday or Friday," they are the days I go to the gym after work," said Nicole matter of factly. "I just have a salad those days, or a KFC or whatever!" "I can't do Tuesdays it's football training seven till nine." Said James triumphantly, thinking he could get out of it. "And I can't do Thursday's," I sighed, "as it my late shift at the hotel. "Well, that's just great then, failed at the first hurdle before we've even begun!" I felt disheartened already. "You'll both end up with rickets then, or your teeth will rot and fall out!" I said feeling a little tearful, maybe I was due on. I clearly heard

James mumble under his breath something along the same lines. Nicole clearly took pity on me and came up with a possible solution. "How about a Sunday?" she said. "Sunday can be our day to sit down together and eat, we could even all help make a roast...if we are all in of course." Then when seeing my face fall again she amended it to "we will make sure we are in!" It was a start and I would take whatever I could at the moment. "But from now on I will be making healthy nutritious meals, that you will eat and heat up if you have to, no more ready meals or crap. Ok?" "Ok." They said in unenthusiastic unison. I then decided to take up mums suggestion of a hobby. And running was the winning activity. To keep myself fit and active. And away from the wine bottle. My ankle wasn't so badly swollen now, in fact apart from a little bruising it was absolutely fine, but I strapped it up just incase. So there I was warming up in the front room trying to look like I knew what I was doing when Nicole walked through, took one look at me and snorted in great mirth. "What do you look like?" She asked, standing there looking at me with great amusement. 'I'm dressed for running!' I replied tersely. 'What does it look like?' I stretched my calf muscle, well I think it was my calf muscle, it could quite easily have been my hamstring that I was stretching, I don't know. I'm a novice. 'It was a rhetorical question mother. I can see exactly what you look like.' she snorted again. I personally thought I looked rather swish and athletic actually. I was wearing a pair of old leggings and I had borrowed a pair of James's trainers, a bit big for me but I'd tied the laces tight. I'd also found an old T-shirt of my own at the back of the wardrobe that had a picture of the Cookie Monster on it, actually, thinking about, it I believe it could possibly be one of my old pyjama tops, but so what, it was dark and nobody would see me. I didn't have a sports bra because let's be honest sports bras are really ugly and unflattering and I haven't taken part in anything remotely sporty for like a billion years, so I was making do by wearing two of my old ones at the same time. My boobs were squished to within an inch of their lives but they weren't going to be bouncing anywhere anytime soon. I started to jog on the spot, James walked into the room and burst out laughing, then turned serious. "You're not going out like that are you? In public?" He stood mouth open wide in horror. "No darling, I was going to run around the front room a few times then up and down the stairs," I said sarcastically, "of course I'm going out like this...like what actually?" I ask indignantly. Ok so I'm not a slim Lycra clad beauty but I was going running, who cares what I looked like? It would appear James did, very much. "You are so embarrassing, what if my friends see you running about in your pyjamas, they'll think you're mental!" "So I'll leave my 'hello I'm James's mum' banner at home tonight, a little support would be nice kids!"

James mumbling something about not liking change as I stomped outside. God it was cold, brrrrr. Right off I go...nice and steady I start to pad softly down the drive, along the path towards the main road...wow this was easy peasy. I could easily be the next Sally Gunnell, she was the only runner I could think of. "Hi Emily," boomed Mike from his garage "are you going for a run?" What does it fucking look like Mike, I wanted to shout back but instead I merely put my hand up in greeting and shouted back "cant stop" and carried on running. I still felt very embarrassed about the other night especially as he never responded to my message. I must have come across as very needy. Now he was working on my parents house, it all felt a little bit mixed up.

I'd been running for about a minute when I realised my throat was on fire, blood was rushing in my ears and I was struggling to breath. I'm also pretty sure if I look back I would still be able to see my house. What an absolute loser I was. I stopped

under a street lamp and tried to get my breath back, sweat was pouring down my face and into my eyes, I decided to run, well hobble back the way I came, my feet also felt like they were on fire. James's trainers being too big for me had rubbed my heels and I was pretty sure I could feel blisters forming. My ankle that had felt much better earlier was throbbing painfully. It was probably better to build it up slowly and not force my body to do things before It was ready, although if I started any slower I probably wouldn't have have left my driveway.
As I reached my house Mike called out again. "Did you forget something Emily?" He said sounding confused. Yes Mike I forgot that I was kidding myself that I could run for a minute let alone a bloody mile... "Err yes, I forgot my water bottle...bye." And I let myself into my house really quickly, what a disaster that was. I slid down the door onto the floor trying to breath normally, Nicole was still standing in the same place where I'd left her and James appeared at the top of the stairs. "I thought you were going running?" said Nicole looking confused, as well she might. "I did, can't you tell?" Pant, pant, pant...the pain in my chest was excruciating, worse than labour pains in my opinion, maybe I was having a heart attack. "But you only just went!" Said James walking down the stairs now looking confused but happy I wasn't out there embarrassing him. "Well, now I'm back," I snapped at him. Running just isn't my thing. Maybe I should buy another fitness DVD?

Somebody knocked on the door. I managed somehow to pull myself up off the floor and open the door but it was a supreme effort on my part. Mike stood there, I looked up at him from my lowly position on my knees. "Here's a bottle of water," joked Mike, handing it to me, "when you didn't come back out I was concerned you couldn't find yours. I'd hate for you to miss out on your run," he laughed. I smiled back at him despite myself. "Very funny Mike, as you can clearly see running isn't my forte." I stood up as gracefully as possible. "The water bottle was just an excuse really, I got the impression you were being a bit off with me, I'm probably being paranoid but..." he trailed off. "I'm just embarrassed really," I said going a bit red. "Look, would you like to come in for a cuppa?" "Yes please that would be great as long as I'm not keeping you from anything important?" "Like embarrassing myself in front of my neighbours? No you're fine, come through." I smiled at him, beckoning him through to the kitchen, although I realised a second too late that the kitchen wasn't the place to take a neighbour who didn't know me very well.

"Wow!" Laughed Mike looking at me a bit oddly "that's a lot of vegetables you have here!" Shit. Shit. Shit! I'd forgotten that I'd bought the entire Tesco aisle of vegetables after my little talk with mum, you know, for my whole let's get this family healthy plan. I'd seen an extremely overweight lady and her two obese children in the frozen food aisle this morning, throwing pizzas and other processed crap into her trolley like she was panic buying for a snow day or something. I'm not ashamed to say I totally freaked out, visions of my own children getting bigger and bigger because of my fondness for convenience over slogging over a hot stove. Their lack of nutrient consumption resulting in health problems in the future. I practically ran to the fruit and veg section where I loaded up my trolley with good intentions and anything that looked remotely healthy. There were veggies everywhere in my kitchen, greens on every available surface, cabbages on the worktops, huge bags of potatoes on the floor. "Do you have a vegetable obsession?" he asked, only sounding like he was half joking. I'm sure I only imagined him scouring the room for a possible way out. "It's not what it looks like!" I exclaim, before wondering what it was I was actually worried about. At the end of the day it was some runner beans and carrots on the table not shotguns and balaclavas. "I went overboard on the whole 'healthy' bit! And apart from the obvious I have no idea what to do with them, I'm not much of an experimental cook." "Do you want some help? Put the kettle on and I'll do something with these vegetables." He said it very seriously but to me I'm sure I heard a double-entendre in there somewhere. "Really? You don't mind? I don't want to keep you from anything?" I said surprised he'd give up an entire evening for me. "I've got nothing planned, I love cooking, not much point when it's only me, although when Kimberly is at mine I cook a bit more. Do your kids like soup!" He asked grabbing a handful of root vegetables, a knife and a peeler of the draining board. "Yes. Tomato. Out of a tin." I felt embarrassed on their behalf. My poor malnourished kids, tinned tomato soup sounded very dietary poor compared to a homemade nutritious one. "Well they haven't tried my homemade soup yet, they'll love it." I privately doubted it, I thought but it was worth a shot. Otherwise they'd be a lot of wasted produce going into my composter, at least somebody was attempting to do something different with it. I watched as he peeled, chopped and pretty much worked his way around the chopping board as though he actually knew what he was doing. He added stock, cream and curry powder and whizzed the whole thing up in my food processor. I was actually more impressed with myself for owning a food processor in the first place, I'd had no idea it was in the cupboard when I'd been pretending to look for one and was going to use the excuse of lending it to Karen when there it was right in front of me. Never been taken out of the box. "I wore my last one out," I'd lied. He gave me a look as if to say I know you're clearly telling me fibs. I was mightily impressed with Mike, a sexy, macho builder, who could also cook and look good in a pinny. I wonder what else he could do with those big, strong hands? Stop it Emily, erase those dirty thoughts right now, this is all about vegetables, oh God that just made it sound even ruder in my head. This is totally innocent, one neighbour helping out another neighbour in a vegetable spree gone mad emergency!

"I can't believe what a coincidence it is that you're building my parents extension," I said. "Maybe it's fate Emily." He gave me a look that I returned, before remembering he didn't return my text. We chatted away like old friends, which we weren't, even though we'd been neighbours for a while. He told me about Kimberly, who was the light of his life and his ex wife who'd he remained on good terms with even though to me she sounded like an absolute witch. Of course, I would say that it, was a woman thing, we were programmed not to like ex-girlfriends/wives etc of men that we were interested in. Not that I was interested in Mike of course, well apart from as a soup making neighbour, oh shut up Emily you fool! He'd learned to cook for himself and his daughter after his wife Chrissy left him when Kimberly was only two, she remarried eighteen months later. An affair perhaps? He didn't say but she sounded positively ghastly to me. I decided to bring up the whole not texting me back elephant in the room. I mean, how awkward could it get? He practically invited himself in to make soup for us all it wasn't as though I'd forced him at knifepoint to cook for me and my family. It's not as though I was bunny boiler material for asking why he didn't respond. "So," I said "did you get my text the other night? Or were you ignoring me for a reason?" I tried to sound breezy but I just sounded petulant instead, I then laughed to make it sound like I wasn't being petulant, then I just sounded a bit confrontational. He looked at me in confusion. "You've not texted me." "I did! On the night you helped me out. Obviously I just thought you were on a date and I'd interrupted something..." " I winced as I said this, God I sounded pathetic and like I was fishing for personal

information. "Who said I was on a date? I haven't dated for years actually, I work hard, I spend every other weekend with my little girl and I fit my friends in around that. I've never found anyone I've been remotely interested in, yet."
Well that put paid to my ideas that he might take me roughly over the kitchen table, after enjoying root vegetable soup together. "I text you, about one in the morning, just to say thanks...I was a bit drunk actually..." "I give you my number and then not reply when you text? That doesn't make sense, you didn't text me Em!" He sounded a bit cross with me. "Well I definitely texted you, I looked the next morning it said Mi...NOOOOOOOO!" Realisation dawning horribly. Mike sat down at the table waiting for an explanation. "My ex is called Michael too, I've text him instead of you," I was aghast. "Was it terribly saucy then?" he laughed, " it's a genuine mistake I can't imagine that's it's caused too many problems." He looked surprised at my shocked reaction, probably because he's on such good terms with his ex he thinks all exes are all sane, understanding normal human beings. "You'd be surprised," thinking of what Nicole had told me the following morning after the text, about Tara's changed relationship status, "but hey, at least we know you didn't ignore me now." "I already knew that." he said quietly.

Then followed the first awkward silence of the evening to be broken by a child, specifically a child called James wanting to know what that smell was. It wasn't said in a way that made me think he was going to ask for seconds. He stood in the doorway wrinkling up his nose. I decided to stage an intervention before he said anything else that might sound hugely ungrateful or possibly hurtful about Mike's culinary skills. "James, this is our neighbour Mike, he's a very talented chef, and he's made us some very nice soup, come and taste it...now." I pointed to the soup, I now sounded like a nineteen fifties housewife. "Hi Mike," he said to Mike, to me he said, "he's not a chef he's a builder." Clearly couldn't get much past James. "Hey mate, you alright?" said Mike. "Just try it." I hissed at him through gritted teeth. Anyone would think I was trying to feed James a bowl of baby sick, the way he was carrying on, face screwed up, gagging noises, but eventually he managed to take a teaspoonful and was pleasantly surprised. "It's actually alright," he said nodding happily. I quickly poured him a bowlful before he changed his mind. I gave Mike the thumbs up and he winked back at me. I hadn't been winked at by a man for a while. I think permanently single Roger had been the last man to wink at me in the utility room and that had made me feel physically sick. Mike's wink however definitely had the opposite effect on me. What was happening here? In the end we all ended up having soup for dinner, it was absolutely delicious, I was suitably impressed with Mikes culinary skills. "I don't suppose you could whip up a loaf of bread?" I joked, scraping the bowl clean with my spoon. "Yeah sure no problem," he said, looking around, presumably for a bread maker, which I definitely knew would never be found in one of my cupboards. "I'm joking Mike, I have regular bread." He looked almost disappointed, like he actually wanted to make a loaf. He'd make someone a wonderful husband one day, although he'd been there and done that and failed miserably already of course.

Conversation flowed, and Mike then unbelievably whipped up an apple and berry crumble, which yes I know isn't at all healthy but it used up some of the many fruit punnets just sitting around my kitchen going soft. Nicole returned home and waded in with all the subtlety of an elephant in a china shop.

"Why does the house smell of a stale fart?" she called from the hall. Mike sniggered luckily. God my children were ungrateful. "Have you never cooked a vegetable in this house before?" he joked. I grinned but worried it was more of a grimace. "No just roadkill, for my nutrient-phobe children." Nicole didn't seem surprised to see a strange man sitting at the dinner table eating with us. Not sure what that implied about me, and the morals I'd instilled into her, but I introduced our neighbour. She pulled up a chair and also appeared to enjoy the healthy nutritious soup in front of her. We were just finishing up when Karen burst through the back door with a bottle of wine in her hand. I hardly recognised her, it had been so long. Yes, I was being unduly dramatic. "Fancy a glass...oh hi." She stopped still and took in the rather odd looking scene in front of her. Me and the kids eating homemade soup with a neighbour that wasn't her. Then she took in all the many different vegetables that were surrounding us. "Soooo, is this some kind of weird vegetable lovers gathering then that I've not been invited to? A vegetable cult perhaps? Or have I slipped into coma and woken up in a parallel universe?" She raised one eyebrow in quizzical amusement. I explained about my failed attempt at running, ignoring Karen's snort of mirth at this, and how Mike offered to make soup with my vegetables before they went rotten. Karen nodded along as if it all made perfect sense to her.

"And, Karen, remember I said I wasn't drinking midweek anymore?" I reminded her nodding towards the bottle in her hand feeling ungrateful and resentful as a glass of wine would be perfect about now.

She looked at me as if I were an idiot. "I know what you said and I respected that, so that's why I've brought round a rather disgusting bottle of non alcoholic wine, though they really shouldn't call this cats piss, wine." The kids then disappeared up to their rooms but not before I'd armed them with large bowls of fruit. "They are so going to have the shits tonight aren't they?" I observed wryly as they left, James stuffing strawberries into his mouth at an alarming rate. Mike got up to leave too. "I'll leave you two ladies to it then." Before I could say anything, Karen got in there first and told him to sit down. "Join us," she said grabbing three glasses. "If I have to suffer this vile shit, you can too. Sit." Mike looked surprised, as was I, but he did as he was told and sat back down. Once again, a situation that could potentially have been very awkward, actually was the complete opposite. We all winced at the first sip of "wine", fruity paint stripper would have been a more accurate description. We chatted away as if we were old friends, which two of us were but Mike was so easy to talk to. I kept sneaking looks at Karen. Something was up with her. She'd been absent all week. I'd seen her only once briefly in Tesco when I was buying sparkling water instead of wine. Stocktaking at work was her excuse. "So what were your first impressions of us?" Karen asked, if I didn't know better I'd have said she was flirting with our sexy neighbour. I wasn't sure I felt entirely comfortable with this. I was suddenly aware of what I looked like, frizzy hair from my ahem, 'running', loose tracksuit bottoms and a Cookie Monster top compared to Karen's smart trouser suit, perfect straight hair and even a distinct faint whiff of expensive perfume even after a long day of work. I just smelt of sweat and vegetables, not a great combination at the best of times. "Well, the day I moved in was one I'll never forget, I remember you Karen running out of your house, hair wrapped in a towel, in a dressing gown with a bottle of tomato sauce in your hands, and you pouring it all over a motorbike parked outside your house." He chuckled, "I was terrified! And wondered what the hell I was moving in to!" Karen grinned, "yes Paul my ex partner had turned up out of the blue, wanting an argument about nothing as usual. He'd parked his new motorbike outside the house while banging on about how poor I'd left him, I'd bought him out of his share of the house fair and square. Obviously I'd been a little bit miffed with him turning up again and went a little crazy!" "Miffed! That was an understatement, do you know what that ketchup could have done to the paintwork?" Laughed Mike. "Obviously, otherwise I wouldn't have done it," she giggled. "In hindsight I should have snuck over to his house and left it overnight. As it was, he wiped that ketchup off pretty damn quickly before it could do any lasting damage." She took a sip of vileness and pulled a face. "What about me?" I intervened, this was quickly becoming the Karen show. "What was your first memory of me?" I sounded like a sulky six year old. I knew I sounded like a sulky six year old and Karen also knew I sounded like a sulky six year old. Mike, thankfully, was oblivious to the big child in the room. Karen gave me a look, as if to say 'are you ok?' God I sounded so incredibly needy, I couldn't even use the excuse of being drunk, to blame how pathetic I sounded. Mike looked blank as he tried to rack his brains. "I can't remember actually Emily, I'm sure it was a good impression though." I felt my face flame. I felt embarrassed. I was rather hoping he'd say that he'd noticed my beautiful smile or my lovely long legs, shapely body, but ho hum, no, he had no first impression of me. At all. I was saved a slightly awkward few seconds then when somebody knocked loudly on the door. I waited just incase one of the kids came thundering down the stairs claiming it was for them but silence prevailed. "Look guys just because I'm not drinking doesn't mean you can't, there's a couple of beers in the fridge..." before I'd even finished my sentence Karen had jumped up and removed the beers from the fridge and opened them, with her teeth, only joking she'd never risk chipping those pearly whites. "Thought you'd never bloody say so!" she laughed. I smiled tightly at her and went to answer the door feeling a bit pissed off but not sure why. I opened the door to a big bunch of white roses standing there, my favourite. The roses moved away from the mystery face and then I had the shock of my life. Graham was standing there looking contrite, he looked me up and down taking in my baggy bottoms and cookie monster top and I could almost read his mind, 'look at her, she's let herself go to pot since I walked out on her, poor love'. He pulled a sad face at me. I sneered back at him.

"What are you doing here?" I ask puzzled, wondering if he was trying to collect what I "owed" him before I realised that he was carrying flowers and then I really hoped this wasn't in fact a booty call!

Retch, retch! "I'm here to offer my sincere apologies for my appalling behaviour the other night, I was a prick." Never a truer statement I privately agreed. "Right, well that's very grown up of you," I said patronisingly. "Thank you." I reach to take the roses but he moves them just out of my reach. "Was there something else?" I asked. Graham's face clouded over slightly. Maybe this wasn't going according to his plan. "Well, I was hoping to be invited in to discuss our relationship actually." He seemed annoyed that he had to point this fact out. "We aren't in a relationship anymore, remember?" Your parting words to me were 'you are a bitch!'" I sighed with the whole banality and pointlessness of this conversation. I thought the whole Graham debacle was already dead and buried, the situation that is, not Graham, mind you, that could be arranged if he didn't bugger off now. "Wow, you really are a piece of work Emily!" He was shaking his head in disgust. "How so?" Here we go again. How had I not realised the Graham was in actual fact a bit of a bipolar narcissist. "I come here out the goodness of my heart to offer you another chance, I even added a new line to my lottery numbers, your birthday, your house number..." "WHAT?" I splutter. "I don't want another chance, I've come to the conclusion I don't actually like you very much, goodbye." I try to shut the door on him but he puts his foot in the way to stop it closing, his face pushed scarily through the gap. I should feel more threatened but I know that Karen and Mike are just a stone's throw away from me, one yell and they'd both be there before I could say "Graham's a fucking weirdo'. "Moved on already have you? What a bitch you really are!" I shook my head sadly at him but Mike chose that precise moment to laugh out loud at something from the kitchen. Graham's face was a picture. I inwardly groaned now I'd never get rid of him until he'd had his rant. "You didn't waste much time did you, you whore. Is he laughing at me?" he puffed up his chest. "Just...just fuck off Graham I really can't be bothered with this and I kicked his foot out the way and slammed the door. My heart hammering away beneath the Cookie Monster. I sneakily watched him through the peephole to make sure he was definitely leaving. I watched him as he first threw the roses into my grey wheelie bin then marched to his car only to turn around and take the roses out of the bin and throw them on the back seat of his car, giving me the finger before wheel spinning away. I let out a breath I hadn't realised I'd been holding. What an absolute tool, mum was right. But all I could think about right now was what had Karen said to make Mike laugh out loud like that?

CHAPTER EIGHT

I woke up feeling agitated. Graham's late night visit had thrown me. An evening making soup with Mike had opened up something in me, a feeling of hope that I could have a normal relationship with a man. Karen appearing and highjacking the evening had, quite frankly pissed me right off. I rather unfairly took my frustrations out on the kids. Even though I believed at that moment in time, they deserved it. This morning a full blown row occurred over milk. Or the lack of it. Despite me buying six pints the day before. I looked around the kitchen hoping to spot it getting warm somewhere on the worktop. I didn't want an argument before I'd had a cup of tea. Only, for that to happen I needed milk. Black tea didn't count. It was disgusting. Nope. No milk. Then I spotted the empty carton next to the recycling bag, on the floor. Note that I said next to, not in. They couldn't even do that right. The only positive about this is that it wasn't back in the fridge, empty. I exploded. To my shame. "You didn't think to leave enough milk for me to have a single cup of tea? Are you that selfish? There was six bloody pints last night!" "Sorry," James mumbled, not sounding very sorry. He was glued to something on his mobile phone. Would it be considered abusive to swipe that phone out of his hand then beat him with the empty milk carton? Yes? So I threw it at him instead. "Ow, what was that for? You're bloody mental!" He clearly hadn't heard a word I'd said. I picked up the carton and threw it at him again. "Ow, I'm going to phone childline!" Then Nicole wandered in on the phone, drinking a glass of milk. I decided to leave for work before I phoned social services myself. I shouldn't have thrown the milk carton. At least, in my defence, it wasn't the kettle! I decided to walk to work this morning, to walk away my frustrations.

The first thing I did on arrival was make myself a mug of tea with lots of milk. I work on the front desk at a hotel in town. I'm part receptionist, part front of house, part toilet unblocker. It was the only hotel in town in fact. I loved working in the shabby but rustic surroundings. It had a great ambiance and was possibly haunted. The people I worked with however made me constantly feel like I was in a hilarious but surreal episode of Fawlty Towers, every day. There was never a dull moment. The White House Hotel was run by Logan, an eccentric gay man, who most of the time was a pleasure to work for. Slightly odd at times but a great boss. To look a,t he reminded me of an English gentleman actor, tall and distinguished, but with the essence of a cheerleader on speed. He was full of energy and hugely camp. He was in fact a retired dancer.

I worked alongside Michaela, my co receptionist, who was a right laugh. Unless she was off sick, which she was a lot. Or having one of her many cigarette breaks, which we aren't actually allowed to have. Michaela is what you'd call a tart with a heart. Twice married. Twice divorced. She was now currently single and on the prowl. Her words not mine. She had three children all with different fathers.
Yet she hadn't even hit the grand old age of thirty. She would make a great Eastenders character, a tragic but loveable minx, with a dark side and an aptitude for violence. She also had that rather sexy gravelly voice, caused by her horrendous smoking habit, and constantly sounded like a female version of Phil Mitchell. She also had the ability to fall out with anyone that looked at her. I think most of her insecurities stemmed from the fact she was ginger, falsely parading as a 'natural blonde'. Another rule at Hotel White House is that we are absolutely not allowed to use the phone to make or receive personal phone calls. Which is why my mum always rang

around eleven o'clock, while Michaela was on her fifth cigarette of the day. It's become a kind of ritual, even if she had nothing of great importance to say to me. It was like she just had to touch base, you know, just in case, I knew something that she didn't. There was no Spanish waiter running manically around the building causing mayhem a'la Fawlty Towers style. On the other hand, there was Maud from Witham, the odd job woman who clomped around with a face like a bulldog chewing a wasp. I don't think that she was intentionally miserable, she just had an ever present aura of a downtrodden woman about her. She looked about fifty when actually I think she was probably younger than me. She'd had a hard life.

She was also a little bit in love with Logan. I'm not sure she even realised he was gay. None of us had the heart to tell her. She hero worshiped him from afar. She was a kind soul underneath that miserable face. One day I was determined to give her a makeover. Once having overheard a rather moany guest complain about the lack of chocolates on her pillow, Maud in her great wisdom thought she'd help out by placing some rolos on her pillow. Unwrapped! Moany guest went to bed didn't see the chocolates and woke up to a caramel disaster on her head! It was the story of Maud's life 'it seemed like a good idea at the time'. I did sometimes wonder if she was a little backward.

So we might not be the most exclusive hotel in the area, but we still did a steady trade. Mostly dubious characters and businessmen, although sometimes it was difficult to tell them apart. We also had a lot of couples booking in under Mr and Mrs Smith, if you know what I mean. Also, the sad, lonely men who'd been kicked out by their wives. The White House was a safe haven for the unwanted. That should have been our advertising slogan.

At eleven o'clock, Michaela was grabbing some "fresh air". Logan had breezed in and declared he was having his ball-bags waxed. I was on my fourth cup of tea. Just because I could, there were no milk rations here. I'd just checked in a guy who I swear was on CrimeWatch the night before in connection with an armed robbery at a nearby service station. His balaclava certainly looked familiar anyway. Nicole text to say she had an upset stomach and wasn't going to work, lucky her I wish I had a bout of diarrhoea to get me out of work and maybe help me lose a pound or five. Mum phoned bang on cue, I could tell by her greeting that today she had important information to impart. This was not a boring routine call. I felt my excitement brewing. "Are you sitting down?" she said breathlessly. "Yes, what's up?" "It's your brother! He's only gone and split up with Cassia!" Well, I wasn't expecting that. "Who broke up with who?" I fired at back at her. This was news. "Well," mum then sounded a bit huffy "obviously I did ask that and Simon accused me of being nosy and insensitive. Can you believe that?"

Well yes, of course I could, because that's exactly what she was. Obviously I said "nooooo, what a grumpy pants. Should I phone him and offer my condolences? Send a card perhaps?" "No, I only found out seven minutes ago! I don't want him to think I've immediately got on the phone and told you." Neither of us say anything for a few seconds, because that's exactly what had happened. "Do you think there's someone else?" I break the silence. "For him or for her?" "Either or?" "Maybe!" We both pondered this new development in my brothers life. "How did you find this out?" I asked, knowing there was no way Simon would have voluntarily told her."Facebook!" Of course. "How's the building work going?" I asked nosily and out of context. "Not much has happened in the twenty four hours since you were last here, except possibly being down a hundred or more teabags," mum answered. "Although your friend Mike looks rather sexy in a pair of work shorts!" I felt decidedly sick, thinking that my own mother might be lusting over the man I was lusting over. Not that I was lusting over him, well maybe a bit. Luckily mum changed the subject. I tried not to linger on the image of Mike in shorts, as pleasant as it may be. "I'll find out what's going on and ring you back." she said before ringing off. I wondered if this had anything to do with Cassia being seen at my house that day, a mystery that had never been solved. Maybe she'd been after some relationship advice. Or maybe not. I decided to message her. I wasn't actually her friend on Facebook, well, because we didn't actually like each other very much, but I could send her a message.

SO SORRY TO HEAR ABOUT YOU AND SIMON. TAKE CARE OF YOURSELF. BY THE WAY JAMES SAID HE SAW YOU AT MY HOUSE THE OTHER DAY. DID YOU WANT TO TALK TO ME?

She replied two minutes later.

FUCK OFF EMILY. AND WHO'S JAMES?

Well that will teach me for being nice. Horrible cow.
The very familiar, heady mixture of cigarettes, mints and white musk indicated Michaela had returned to the vicinity. She looked pissed off, but there was nothing new there. "Bloody chef has called in sick again!" She declared in her gravelly voice and rather prophetically. "I've now got to go and start the bloody lunches." "But you can't cook," I said feeling worried for our guests potential health, well apart from the robber, he deserved a touch of salmonella. "I can do toast!" she said nonchalantly, as if serving toast at lunchtime was completely

normal. "Mmmm, but what if a guest wants something a bit more substantial than jam on toast?" I gently queried, not wanting to awaken the beast within. I had a feeling that today might be a day Logan had one of his rare but explosive hissy fits if he got wind of Michaela serving toast for lunch. "Then I'll send Maud out for some Tesco ready meals." And off she stomped before I could pour cold water on her rather stupid idea. I busied myself with a few loose ends and most of Michaela's jobs that she'd not done despite being here since eight o'clock this morning.

A cool draught indicated the main door had been opened and I looked up, with a welcoming smile plastered onto my face, ready to greet a guest but instead I saw my ex husband walking purposely toward me instead. My face dropped, my cheerful smile vanished. I hoped nothing had happened to one of the children, although why Michael would be the first point of contact would be a mystery. He'd been absent father of the year for the past eight years running. Then I checked myself, Nicole had literally just texted me asking if we had any more toilet rolls. So, unless she'd fallen down the toilet or had a fatal bum wiping accident then she was absolutely fine. James was at school as far as I was aware. "What are you doing here?" I whisper a snarl at him, hoping he wasn't about to tell me James wasn't at school and was currently hiding in a safe house because his mother had physically abused him with an empty milk carton this morning. "Do you speak to all your guests like that?" He answered sounding vaguely amused. "Only the ones I've been married too and what do you mean guest? Are you staying here?" I said aghast. So, him and Tara had split up. Interesting. Unless he was on a very sad bargain holiday, by himself in his hometown. "So it's true then, you and Tara are no more. I'm surprised you're not at your mums again." I tried not to sound smug or petty but failed, it's hard to feign sympathy when you feel none. "Well my timing was poor, mum decided that very morning to make the spare room into a gym, so unless I wanted to sleep on a weight bench..." he trailed off giving a fake laugh, I felt embarrassed for him. I wondered if he knew that his mum had lied and that he knew that I knew his mum had lied because she didn't want him in the spare room. Again. "Why this hotel though?" "It's the only hotel in town!" "There are other towns though Michael." I said deadpan. He just looked at me. "It's not for long. You'll hardly see me."Yes I've heard that somewhere before. "I hope your breakup had nothing to do with me," I said actually meaning it. "It appears I text you by accident. I can understand why it wouldn't be greatly received." Michael shrugged. "It didn't help matters no, but no, nothing to do with you. We were already in the process of breaking up, your text was the final nail." He looked sad. Oh well as long as it wasn't my fault. I felt absolved. "I let her believe that it wasn't a mistake though," he laughed then stopped abruptly when he saw the look on my face. "Great, so she thinks we..." I couldn't even finish the sentence, it was too awful a thing to contemplate. "Anyway," he said changing the subject before I started to strangle him. "I'm off for lunch, I'll try to keep out of your way." He sounded sincere. I acknowledged it grudgingly. I should feel bad for my gnarly behaviour but couldn't ever muster up that emotion where Michael was involved. Too many years had gone past. He'd not been as present in our children's lives as I hoped he'd be. I felt resentful. "Thanks. Enjoy lunch, I hear the chefs special of marmite on toast is a winner." Again he just looked at me. Was I joking? He could never tell where I was concerned. Ten minutes later Michaela strode back into the room and into her seat. "That was quick! Lunches done?" I exclaimed.

"Maud's doing it," she replied, logging onto Facebook on the hotel computer. I sighed.

"Is that wise?" Logan was going to go ape. Maybe I should make contact and let him know.
"It's all in the freezer, chef just microwaves it to order, I had no idea! I'm pretty sure Maud can't fuck that up!" I wasn't too sure, but let it go.

I got on with my backlog of paperwork while Michaela updated her Facebook status! Logan turned up, his balls all smooth and silky, apparently. "Do you want to feel them?" he wondered. I worried that he hadn't realised he'd said it out loud. "Gee, no thanks. But it's kind of you to offer nevertheless." He shrugged. "Your loss, lovelies." He sashayed in the direction of his office. The lunches had finished, with no obvious grievances reported. This was a huge win for Maud but Michaela was acting as though she was the saviour of the year, as if she'd single handedly cooked a banquet for a hundred people. I'd make sure Logan knew it was Maud that had saved the day. "Did you see that hunk of a man this morning?" Michaela asked me. I gathered she was talking about Mr crimestopper himself, he'd definitely be the type of guy she'd be attracted to. Trouble with a capital T. "I did," I answered distractedly. Michaela looked up sharply. "You're not interested are you?" she barked at me ominously. Just because I was single didn't mean I was on the lookout, especially with random guests checking into our rather shabby hotel. "No he's all yours, I'm not interested in anyone right now." A lie of course, I was very interested in Mike but this placated her, so I was safe from her wrath this time. I wouldn't want to be the woman to get in the way of Michaela and a shag. "By the way," Michaela said. "Your ex added me on Facebook, you don't mind do you?" "Michael?" Wasn't that a bit weird? "Who? No that curly haired dude!" "Graham? Why's he added you? You've only met him once before, briefly in Tesco." I asked not understanding why he'd do that. We'd

literally passed each other in the alcohol aisle and I introduced them in passing. "Well he added me," she shrugged. "Oh well," I had no idea why he'd do that. "Let me know if he says anything defamatory about me." "What does that mean?" She looked confused. "Things that aren't true." "Right...I'm guessing you don't actually fuck your own mum then? That kind of thing?" Yes. That kind of thing. What was Graham up to by adding Michaela?
Logan ran into reception at this point, pirouetted in front of the main desk, did the splits and gave us a cheeky, toothy smile, then pouted seductively. See I told you he was eccentric. Never a dull moment when Logan was about! Michaela then decided to tell Logan she was now ready to feel his smooth balls. Needless to say Logan disappeared pretty darn quickly and Michaela carried on checking her social media without fear of retribution.

When I arrived home Nicole was laying in a prone position on the sofa, pale as a ghost. I'll give her that at least. "I never want to see another vegetable again for as long as I live!" She declared weakly as I walked past her to the kitchen. I sniggered and bit back a retort of never being able to visit her father again. "Talking of your father, were you aware he was staying at my hotel?" I asked. "Ahh so you found out at last?" she said pulling a face. "Me and James were hoping you wouldn't find out."
"I work on the front desk of course I was going to find out! I'm not blind or stupid!" "Well does it really matter?" It's not like he's making your job harder by being there, he's been trying to avoid you if anything!" I tried not to take that too personally. Not that Michael was avoiding me but that Nicole was sticking up for him. "Would you like some toast?" I asked, thinking that might help her delicate stomach and a swift change of subject might be called for. "As long as it doesn't contain vegetables,"

she joked, well I think she was joking. I hoped she was joking. Her brains, if not, came from the other side of the family. "Well bummer," I said "I was just going to offer to do my specialty of brussel sprouts on toast!" She sniggered at my lame joke. "Uncle Simon phoned, he's on his way round!" "Why?" "Don't know, I said you weren't here but he didn't seem to mind, in fact I got the impression he was glad you weren't." "Right, well that's weird." Simon had only been to my house maybe twice in as many years, under duress I might add. I think he thought my neighbourhood beneath him. What was he up to?

Fifteen minutes later we found out. He pulled up on the drive in his brand new car, instantly making my three year old car look like an old shitter in comparison. He looked around suspiciously as he locked up. As if he if feared one of my dodgy neighbours may well try to steal his wipers or worse, approach and actually dare speak to the oracle that was him. His face dropped when I answered the door. "Oh. I didn't think you were going to be in!" Was his greeting. "Then why are you here?" Was mine.
He sighed. "Can I come in?" he said dejectedly, resigned to the fact he was going to have to deal with me and not Nicole for whatever reason. "I was sorry to hear about you and Cassia splitting up." I lied.
"Yeah well these things happen," he shrugged not appearing too bothered, but maybe he was putting on a brave face. Maybe he was dying inside, now he wouldn't be having lanky, hessian nappied babies with her. "It didn't take mum long to share my news...anyway, it's kind of why I'm here actually," he switching to his most winning smile. "Go on," I said feeling immediately suspicious. "Well, not to go into specifics but last week Cassia the dozy cow, despite knowing she was leaving, went and adopted a fucking cat!" He shook his head and rolled his eyes at her duplicity. Ahhh so he must have been the one

that had been dumped, that must have been galling for him. Dumped by a flake like Cassia. "Basically, I don't want a cat. Zero interest. It's ruining my furniture, so I was hoping you'd take it off my hands." He smiled again as he eyed up my ageing furniture. "So," I summarised, "you thought you'd come round and offload your unwanted cat on simple Nicole while I was at work?" I'd perfected the single eyebrow raise back in the day when having to deal with Michaels stupidity. "Hey I'm not simple!" protested Nicole. "I was hoping you'd help out," he counteracted. " Otherwise it'll be put down!" Wow. Hardball. "I'll even pay its insurance for the first year, and I have at least six months worth of food and cat litter in the car, please take it off my hands. I'm not a bad guy I don't want it's blood on my hand!" He pleaded. If I didn't know better I'd say he sounded sincere enough. I didn't even want to look at Nicole who I could see out the corner of my eye looking as though this would make her whole life complete. I sighed dramatically. "Girl or boy?" I asked. Simon looked like all his Christmases had come at once. "Is that a yes? I'll go and get Tonya."What? Who the hell is Tonya?

Not the cat? Surely! He came back with a cat carrier. Nicole kiddy with excitement! "Tonya?" I said again.He grimaced. "What can I say? "Cassia was a fuckwit!" I suggested. He opened the carrier and backed away from it as though letting out a man eating alligator, a fluffy ball of cuteness ran out instead. I heard Nicole gasp! "I love her already. We'll have to change her name. I can't have a cat called Tonya!" I watched as Tonya the kitten frolicked around my front room exploring her new home. What can I say, I'm a sucker. I glanced up at Simon just as he was checking his watch."Sorry are we keeping you from something?" I asked sarcastically but before he could answer I was distracted by a second, more timid ball of fluffy cuteness creeping from the carrier. "I've gotta go..." Simon started to creep out of the room. "TWO CATS?

SERIOUSLY?" I yelped as Nicole clapped her hands in glee. "Oh come on, it's practically the same as having just one cat!" I watched as Tonya clawed her way up the curtains and the other one took a shit on my living room carpet! Ace. "What's this one called?" asked Nicole, suddenly looking a whole lot better. Simon looked embarrassed. "Janis! Don't ask me why!" He exclaimed throwing his hands up. "By the way, did you know there was a man hiding in your bush earlier?" Simon said changing the subject as he practically ran away from my house. "What are you talking about?" I asked as I ran after him. "Maybe it was my imagination," he backtracked. "Maybe it was a dog!" "I can't believe you didn't mention this sooner," I said looking at the bush in question and hoping not to see a man shaped dent or indeed an actual man. My eye was suddenly drawn to across the road where Mike appeared to be cutting the grass. Shirtless. Again. Maybe he was poor and couldn't afford shirts. Or maybe it was for someone's benefit. Hopefully mine. Hopefully not Karen's!

I wondered briefly why he wasn't at my parents building their pointless extension. "Sorry, I forgot all about it when you answered the door, I wasn't expecting you was I?" "Oh it's my fault...never mind." I sighed. Simon looked relieved. "Maybe he was just looking for his wallet!" he suggested unhelpfully. "Yes, maybe he remembered he'd left it there the last time he'd sat in my bush! Does 'he' have a description I could give to the police?" "Not really, I was preoccupied." he mused. "Anyway, thanks again, you know for the cats." "That's ok, just two more hungry mouths to feed on my single mum wages." Simon looked aghast. Good I thought, something to think about when you're counting your millions, before putting him out of his misery. "It'll be fine, I've always wanted to be known as the stinky cat lady!" "Did you know that mum and dad were having an extension built?" Simon asked, pausing as he climbed into his car. "Yeah but only after I dropped by unexpectedly the other day, otherwise I'd be none the wiser. I can't understand it myself."

"Me either and I did the same. Mum started banging on about how contrary we both are. She doesn't see us from one month to the next then we both turn up unannounced in the same week." He laughed, his eyes still looking around as he spoke. He was acting very strangely. "I bet she was hoping that we'd rock up one day and not notice the extra turret sticking out of their house." Simon chuckled and waved. "Anyway see you later." Simon drove away as quickly as he could before I could change my mind about adopting his cats. I took a deep breath and wandered over the road to see Mike. I hadn't seen him since the the night he made soup. He'd then got drunk with Karen, while I sat there sipping the alcohol free crap. I felt a little awkward. He saw me coming and waved a hand in greeting, turning off his lawnmower. "You ok Em? That wasn't Mr Angry again was it?" Indicating my brothers car as it wheel spun away. "No, that was my little brother, offloading his poor dependants on me now he's split up with his girlfriend!" "His kids?" Mike looked shocked. "No, two kittens." He looked relieved. "How come you're not at my parents?" I asked trying not to sound like I was accusing him of being a typical slacker builder type. He grinned. "I'm not actually building the extension," he laughed. "I'm project manager, I arrange it all. Bricklayers, window fitters that kind of thing. I just pop up every now and again for cups of tea and your mums cakes." "So, you just boss people about then, you mean?" I laugh, glad he hasn't taken offence at my question. "Yeah, I boss people about." "A weird question maybe, but I don't suppose you've seen a man hanging around my bush?" I said it genuinely innocently, realising too late how rude it sounded. Mike looked at me, eyes wide before laughing his head off. "Sorry, I'm sorry, it just sounded..." and off he went again. God, me and my big mouth. "I'm being childish, ignore me." Cue more doubled up laughter. "My brother said he saw a man in my bush..." I carried on despite the fact Mike clearly wasn't listening to me. He was bent over in hysterics. Again. "I'm being serious Mike! Have you seen anyone hanging around?" Finally he pulls himself together. "God sorry, it sounded so funny. No I've not seen anyone hanging around. Is there a problem?" He looked genuinely concerned now. "My brother said he saw someone lurking about," I was determined not to mention bush again. After that night Graham turned up and acted like a escapee from an institution, I'd gone back into my kitchen a bit shaken up. Mike had jumped up and gone out after him but obviously he'd already disappeared. That was when I'd noticed the bottle of wine that had suddenly appeared on the table. Karen saw me looking. "I popped home for it, a single bottle of beer didn't quite cut it," she laughed. "Want one?" I remember shaking my head and feeling rather annoyed, that my wishes were not just being ignored but completely flouted. I hadn't seen Karen since. Not sure if she was avoiding me or if I was avoiding her. "I'll keep an eye out if you like," said Mike bringing me back to the here and now "are you worried?" "Not really, just don't like the idea of men lurking...in my bush." This set Mike off again and yes I admit it I did it in purpose for that very reason. "Do you fancy a cuppa?" I asked, it literally slipped out of my mouth. Mike looked pained. Oh God, he's probably wondering how to get out of it. "Look if you're busy..." "No it's not that it's just I promised Karen I'd put up a shelf for her, maybe after?" I like to think he said it hopefully but I'm sure he just said it to get him out of an awkward situation. What was Karen playing at? She didn't need help putting up shelves, she had her own tool box for heaven's sake. A pink one. I knew it, I knew she was flirting with Mike the other night. I felt stupid and cross at the same time. Not that I was jealous, of course not. "Not to worry," I said breezily, "I've got plans later, see you around."

And I scurried home, Mike calling out an equally breezy bye. He probably thought I was bipolar. I wondered if there really had been somebody lurking about in the bush or if Simon had just made it up to distract me?

CHAPTER NINE

Elaine popped in that evening under the pretence of catching up with me but really I knew it was to meet the cats. She was always a sucker for a baby animal, probably goes back to our sad Sylvanian family days. "Oh my God how cute are they?" She said soppily, watching as Tilly, formerly known as Tonya clawed the crap out of my sofa and Janis, now the sweeter named Lexus licked her private bits in front of us brazenly. Nicole and James were laying on the floor surrounded by bits of string and balls, wanting to play.m"If I'd have known it was this easy to tempt them out of their bedrooms I'd have got a couple of cats years ago. They haven't voluntarily sat in the living room since 2008!" I said so to Elaine as we walked through to the kitchen. To drink the wine she so thoughtfully brought with her despite me telling anyone who would listen I'M NOT DRINKING ALCOHOL DURING THE WEEK ANYMORE! Doesn't anyone ever listen to me? I was still feeling irritated after my conversation with Mike and had spent the last few hours waiting for the sounds of shelves being put up. I'd heard none. Despite having my ear pressed to the wall. "It doesn't really make sense," pondered Elaine. "Cassia goes to the trouble of getting and naming, albeit ridiculously, two cats. She buys a shit load of cat paraphernalia and then a week later leaves Simon! Doesn't add up." "She's a flakey hippy type, maybe the trees told her it was time to move on!" I said, tongue in cheek. "Maybe." Elaine said not buying it one bit. "Michael and Tara have also broken up," I announced, "not that it's any of my business, just gossip!" "Ahhh, that's sad," she said pulling a sad face. "Is it?" I said pulling a 'do we care' face. "Yes, eight years is a long time, thankfully no children this time." Taking a sip of wine. "Yes thank goodness, otherwise there'd be more children in the world for him to be a bad, absent father to!"

"The way you should look at it, is that Nicole and James are great kids, so that's all down to you. Take the positives, leave the negatives at home!" She said this just as Nicole called James a prick and James threw what sounded like one of the cats back at her! "Can I hit you with this wine bottle? For sounding like a self help - love yourself book !" I reply. "Sure why not. Anyway, what about you?" "What about me?""It's been eight years since your marriage broke up and you've not had a serious relationship since!" "Graham?" "Four months with a man who never met your parents and who was a bit of a drip!" "What about..." "Don't say Irish Benjamin!" She admonished. "I wasn't about to!" Damn! "It's hard being a single mother thrown back into dating again."

I can remember one occasion when the three of us had decided to give up on internet dating for a while and try other means of meeting a nice man. If there was a sure fire way to meet one that is.

Speed dating was mentioned, laughed at and then reluctantly settled upon. An event was coming up locally, how unlucky was that. It was in the same dingy hall as the fateful mother and toddler group. No amount of fairy lights and soft music could disguise the fact it was still a germ ridden hall of doom. Even the makeshift bar in the corner did nothing to lighten our spirits as we wandered in timidly. Same hard chairs, this time set out two to a table. Same rather damp, toddler smell lingering. I shuddered.

Chloe the slightly bouncy blonde in charge pounced on us before we had time to leave, issuing us with a name badge and leaving us fifteen pounds lighter. The women stood on one side of the hall sipping the lukewarm wine, the men, if you could call them that, on the other. Like a school disco when you were ten years old. "Look," Karen stage whispered at us. "That guy looks like he's been on the run for twenty years." I looked over to where he stood, eying up the talent slavishly, a disheveled, dirty looking man. He seemed rather familiar. Where had I seen that guy before? Possibly on the numerous dating sites I perused over the years. The men it had to be said had a better choice of date than us women did. There were eleven of each sex altogether, all between the ages of late twenties and early fifties. The women all attractive in our own way, clean looking and clearly literate, just more nervous. The men however wouldn't have looked out of place in a police line up for suspected park flashers. Most were overweight, not that this was a major problem I too was carrying extra baggage around the bum and stomach area but I like to think I hid it well. One mans jumper didn't fit and you

could see his hairy belly poking out the bottom. Yuck. Did he think his personality would carry him through?
Another guy was wearing a cardigan, that his mum had obviously knitted. Hang on was that his mum sitting in the corner waiting for him? God possibly, they both had the same serial killer expression on their face. They were probably here looking for their next victim. So the evening was an unmitigated disaster from start to finish, especially when Paul, Karen's ex walked in! Of all the bad luck. I then realised when sitting opposite the disheveled guy where I'd recognised him from, he was the single 'dad' from the mother and toddler group. So he probably had been on run for the last however many years. Thankfully he hadn't recognised me, but I could have looked like elephant man's uglier sister and he'd have still tried it on. Desperation seeped from his every pore. Sitting opposite Paul was rather cringeworthy too, remembering how much he detested me back then. But it wasn't as terrible as when Karen had to sit opposite Paul and they then had a stand up row about a credit card that he was supposed to have paid off and hadn't, leaving Karen with the debt. Awkward indeed!
Especially when we were then escorted unceremoniously out of the building, giggling because the wine, although cheap was potent and had gone to our heads. Chloe was crying about the disaster of an evening, especially when the men who wanted their fee back, started harassing her. "I'm never coming back here again," sobbed Chloe dishing out the cash to the men who felt they'd been diddled out of a date. No, the fact they were overweight and had no personality to speak off were the reasons they were leaving dateless. I patted Chloe on the arm as we left. "I said that once and look what happened." She cried harder, not understanding. We had a great night in the end. Karen met a dishy (oh dear God, I just heard my mother come out of my mouth. Dishy?) man who

she dated for a few happy months until she discarded him when he wanted more. I bumped into an old male school friend and we spent the rest of the evening reminiscing about old times, even getting a sneaky snog at the end of the night. Poor old Elaine was comforting Chloe who had turned up pissed, crying that her business idea of speed dating was shit! Agreed!

"You've had eight years to practise, seriously! I mean there was married Dean..." said Elaine oblivious to my not wanting to rehash the who's who of crap I'd dated, although dating was a word used lightly.
"I didn't know he was married!" I exclaim, I still feel the shame of that particular fling and the horror of finding out he had a wife and child. "Then there was long distance Pete..." "That would have worked out if he was local, an eight hour commute both ways just have dinner and just one full day together was extreme! Bloody internet dating!" I said. Pete was a nice guy."Then there was flash Harry who..."
Luckily the phone rang. Saved by the bell. The landline. This meant one thing only. Mother. Maybe I'll ignore it and let Elaine carry on. "Hi mum," I said sweetly rolling my eyes at Elaine who missed it as she'd already whipped out her mobile and was scanning it in case she'd missed something important in the last half an hour she'd been with me. "Hello Emily, I've been waiting for a phone call," she said sounding serious. "From?" "You, you daft girl. I hear Simon was at your house today!" There was an accusation there somewhere. But I couldn't be bothered to look for it. "Ah mum, have you been playing with your car tracker device again?" Elaine dragged herself from her phone long enough to snigger at this comment. "Well? Did you find out anything?" "She broke up with him, apparently," I said, sipping my wine as quietly as I could so mum didn't hear it. I'd also made the mistake of

telling her I was giving up the alcohol, she wouldn't believe I was drinking just squash. "NO! How dare she?" Mum sounded furious. "Mum, remember we didn't like her, so it's all worked out ok," I reminded her.

"Yes well I suppose so. How are the cats settling in?" "Have you installed cctv in my house without me knowing?" "I saw it on Facebook actually. Not from you of course as you still haven't accepted me as a friend, but Nicole and James have put lots of photos up. It looks like your skirting boards need repainting Emily." I start to count to ten but only make it to three. After I promise to let her know if I find out more about Simon, I manage to get her off the phone. I down my wine and ask for a refill.

While I was an the phone, Elaine had been rooting around in my cardboard boxes. "Oh my God," she exclaimed pulling out my Take That scrapbook. "You kept this pile of crap?" A bit cheeky I thought as she had one too, in fact it had been her idea. "Nooo, my mum did, anyway it's not crap! Its memorabilia of my adolescence." Cringing at the sexual references I innocently scrawled all over it when I was fourteen years old. 'Give good feeling to me' being one of them. "OH MY GOD!!" Exclaimed Elaine suddenly, "Is this what I think it is?" She pulled out a VHS video from the heap of crap that was my memories. I shrugged. She showed me the carefully printed title. TALENT SHOW 1989. "Nooooo," I exclaimed in shock. " I thought that had been destroyed, mum said she'd thrown it away!" In fact my judas of a mother had promised me the video had been destroyed after I'd almost killed Simon for watching this daily in order to wind me up! She'd lied. "We have to watch this!" said Elaine clearly in her element. "Do you have a video recorder anywhere?" Do I have a video recorder anywhere? Does anyone have a video anymore? So ok, I have one in the cupboard, in my cupboard of crap. Doesn't everyone have a cupboard or drawer of crap?

I dutifully pull it out, moving the giant packets of sugar puffs out of the way huffing and puffing as I do. Suffocating in the dust clouds it's produced. The cats getting in the way. I set it up just so Elaine could relive our, sad, misspent youth and honestly the most embarrassing moment of my life. There have been many more in my life since, but none that rival this.

Picture the scene. Five eleven year old girls. Going through puberty. In their last year of primary school. Top dogs if you like. Myself, Elaine and three girls that meant the world to us back then whose names I can't even remember right now. Dressed in denim shorts, vest tops and bandanas. All wearing plastic dummies around our necks. That's right, tonight Matthew we are going to be Take That!! What were we thinking? We'd choreographed a dance routine to Relight my fire. We thought It was the bollocks, it certainly was bollocks. I watched the grainy images through my fingers, cringing away as Elaine whooped and laughed uproariously throughout. "You do realise that that's you, dressed there as Jason Orange?" I said. As she pranced around on stage like a fool. She shhhed me, actually shhhed me. The problem being, that instead of Relight my fire, the theme tune to Postman Pat was playing. And instead of halting the performance to admit this mistake, we carried on regardless. The moves that would have looked amazing (a bit of an overstatement) to a funky beat, looked ridiculous when singing about a black and white cat. Nicole and James turned up to witness this dance of shame. Despite me ordering them to leave. Holding each other as they cried at my most embarrassing moment. At one point an energetic move caused the plastic dummy to whack me in the face and I fell to the floor. A head injury being preferable to carrying on with the farce that was our dance routine, I didn't get up again. The others danced around me, Donna I think her name was tripped over me. The others carried on regardless. One girl, I

think her name was Claire was crying, huge heaving sobs and she danced around the stage. Shimmying away. Why didn't we stop this and say, the tapes had been mixed up? Because we were kids, and the audience was waiting to be entertained. And entertained they certainly were. It was only after I spotted Simon and his annoying mate in the front row that I realised he was behind this. They were wetting themselves. He'd swapped cassette tapes. He'd done this on purpose. Without thinking I'd yanked off my dummy and thrown it at him. Missing him and hitting the headmaster's wife. It was a humiliating experience. Made worse when my parents actually bought the tape for prosperity. According to them it was purely to raise funds for the school of course. I heard that it was the most popular talent contest ever, raising the most funds through video alone. Editing clearly not a thing back In the late eighties.
"But why didn't you just say the music was wrong and wait for the correct track?" asked Nicole.
"Hindsight is a wonderful thing." I replied. "So's keeping your dignity!" She shot back with.
"Is this your digital camera from your childhood!" asked James, holding up a camera that was definitely not from our childhood. It came from one of the boxes. "No darling, the cameras we had were about as big as a shoe box, we had to wind them on and if we were lucky we'd get our photos through the post three weeks later.." "Only to find they all had under exposed stickers on them and they were crap." finished Elaine. "It must be mums, put in the box by accident." I said taking it and having a look, hoping not to find anything too embarrassing on it. Just grainy images taken in the dark. Then a house, hang on, it was my bloody house, lots of photos of my house in the dark. Followed by photos of me and Karen, so grainy I couldn't work out where we were. The hairs on my

arm stood up on end, I passed it to Elaine. Who shook her head as if to say 'what the hell'.
The kids had lost interest at this point and wandered off. "There's an innocent explanation for this, you'll see," said Elaine looking nervous. "Yes, I often take pictures of people's houses in the dark, and spy on people unawares. Then lose my camera and have the person who I'm spying on find it, just to freak them out!" We decided to drink more wine, while we tried not to think about the creepy camera. I text mum to ask if she's lost her camera.

MY CAMERA IS LOCKED IN OUR SAFE WITH THE REST OF OUR VALUABLES. WHILE THE BUILDING WORKING IS GOING ON. WHY? X

NO REASON. HAD ANYBODY YOU KNOW LOST A CAMERA? X

NO. WHY ARE YOU ASKING? X

I ignored this text and sipped my wine thoughtfully. I knew she would eventually end up phoning so I turned the ringer down. Graham popped into my head. Had he been in my house and placed the camera there? Or had it been put there whilst still at my parents house? Is that where the rumours about a man hovering in the bushes had originated from? It made sense. The whole let's watch us humiliate ourselves on video was a clear diversion by Elaine to stop me asking her about her own love life, so obviously I asked her about her own love life. "So what about you?" I ask before we can get back onto the subject of my non existent love life. "How's your man?" Elaine looked shifty. "I really don't want to talk about it yet, don't want to jinx it." "I'm your best friend, what's the problem?" "I've never had what you've had!" "A non existent love life?" I ask confused. "No, a marriage and children. I thought by now I'd at least have something resembling a long term commitment. I go from one disastrous relationship to another. Mostly my own doing, I'll grant you. I get so clingy and desperate, but this is different and I want it to work!" She looked a bit teary. I squeeze her hand. "When you're ready let me know." "Thank you." She looks mightily relieved. I feel I have let her off the hook too easily. Maybe the tears were cat allergy and not emotional ones. "So how about your mum and not so single Roger? Still rogering?" "God don't be disgusting, I walked in on them holding hands in the kitchen the other day." "Those sick bastards!" I joke, Elaine smiled reluctantly. "Your mum needs this, try and be happy and if you can't be happy, then just ignore their blatant displays of affection. Hand holding, yuck!" "So, back to you..." "Nooooo!" Head in hand, wine glass to mouth. "Let me set you up with a friend of mine, he's lovely?" "I know all your friends, and if he's so lovely why is he single?" "You're lovely and still single." Touché. "His name is William and he's a really nice chap." "Nice chap? How old is he? Seventy?" "He's a work colleague and in his forties, divorced no kids. Go on give him a chance?" "Do you have a photo?" I ask hopefully. "No, it's not about appearance it's about personality!" "No it's not," I laugh. "He's ugly then?" "No, will you give him a go?" "Do I have to?" "Yes. I'll set it up." Great, what have I let myself in for. Anyway, why not? Mike was "putting up shelves" for Karen maybe this William guy could "put up shelves" for me.

When I arrived at work the following morning, I found Logan doing the foxtrot with elderly Ethel in the lobby. As you do. Ethel was our permanent guest. She'd lived here now three years. I kid you not. She said it's cheaper to stay here than pay to go into a nursing home. She had a point there. She sold her house much to her children's disgust and moved in for the foreseeable. I skirted around the edge of the room as to not interrupt them in full flow. Mainly so I didn't get dragged into anything resembling a dance. I wouldn't put it past him. It had happened on numerous occasions. It was as I was trying to get to my post unnoticed that I had the horrible sensation of being watched. I scanned the vicinity with a rising sense of panic, only to find Maud hiding in the shadows videoing Logan. I'm not sure Logan knew she was there, let alone filming him. I didn't even want to know anymore. My biggest shock however was finding Michaela at her desk, looking like she was actually working for a change.

Blimey! "Everything ok?" I query as I approach. She looked up all bleary eyes, she was either stoned or tired.
"I'm fine, just tired," she smiled "I hooked up with that hunky guest last night!" She confided in me. I suppressed a groan. "Good, that's nice." I said as sincere as I could muster. "I think he really likes me," she gushed. "He had me in the shower!" "Good, that's nice, he must really like you." I only hoped it was as a shag that he liked her for and not as an accomplice or an alibi for his next crime. "I'm just going to grab a tea, want one?" Michaela ignored me, submersed in a dodgy daydream with her hunk.

I'm pretty sure it was against hotel rules for employees to shag guests in the shower, or indeed anywhere on hotel grounds. It wouldn't be me enforcing that particular rule. As I entered the dining room I spotted Michael sitting eating a cooked breakfast. He looked up, his eyes widened and he started shovelling it in his mouth, he looked like he was about to choke. "What are you doing?" I hissed at him. He took about five minutes to chew the vast amount of food in his mouth. "Sorry," he said eventually "I said I'd stay out of your way so I was hurrying up." "Yes, a great way to stay out of my way is to choke on a sausage and have me perform first aid on you. Genius!" I rolled my eyes at him. "Finish your sad little breakfast, I'm just passing through." "How's Nicole?" He called out. I narrowed my eyes at him. "What do you mean? Are you implying I'm not looking after her?" I snarl. Forgetting that she was indeed a nineteen year old woman and unlikely to be of any interest of social services. "Noooo, she had an upset tummy yesterday, I was just asking after her." He seemed genuinely confused by my sudden venom. I must control myself when in Michaels company, I wouldn't put it past him to tell people that I was unhinged. "Ah, yes she's fine now thank you for asking." I adjusted my attitude. "I hear you've got two cats?" Michael laughed. "You hate cats!" "No I don't, I love them. Anyway, carry on with your breakfast, don't die from a heart attack" I mutter the last bit under my breath as I walked away. When I returned to the front desk Michaela looked up. "Graham was here just now, looking for you!" "What did he want?" I asked aghast. Bloody Graham, turning up like a bad smell again, I thought I'd seen the last of him. "He didn't say." "Are you sure it was me he was after then? And not you? His new Facebook buddy." I mocked. "Yes he asked for you, Emily. Although he did compliment me on my new profile picture," I rolled my eyes. "He asked if you were working today, I said yes. And then he left!" "That didn't strike you as odd?" She shrugged. She was already bored with this conversation. It was only after I seethed inwardly for ten minutes about what a pain in the arse he was that it occurred to me. Was he trying to see if the coast was clear at home? Was he planning on breaking in? Why else would he check my whereabouts? Did I in actual fact have a bloody stalker in the shape of Ghastly Graham? Was I in fact losing my bloody mind? Was he the man in my bush? "Did he not give any indication about what he wanted?" I asked. Michaela shrugged again, she'd already moved on. She was redoing her lipstick. She was on the prowl for her man. Good luck I thought I'd just seen him leaving the hotel ten minutes ago. I decided to text him. Not that I wanted to reopen the lines of communication with Graham but needs must.

MICHAELA SAID YOU WERE LOOKING FOR ME. WHAT DID YOU WANT?

He replied straight away.

I'VE LOST MY WATCH. I WONDERED IF I'D LEFT IT AT YOUR HOUSE?

NOPE. WHY DID YOU RUN OFF?

I DIDN'T THINK YOU'D WANT TO SEE ME. THE WATCH WAS AN EXCUSE. I MISS YOU.

Oh dear, I could do without this. I decided to turn it round.

LOOK I UNDERSTAND WHAT'S HAPPENING HERE. IT WAS AN EXCUSE TO COME AND SEE MICHAELA. YOU OBVIOUSLY LIKE HER. DON'T WORRY YOU HAVE MY BLESSING!

I waited for an angry reply back but none was forthcoming. Maybe I had hit the nail on the head after all. I was still not convinced he hadn't been trying to see if I was out of the way. Both kids were at school, luckily. Although that did leave two very vulnerable kittens home alone. I did not want to return home to kidnapped cats or worse, boiled cats, like that film about a rabbit. Maybe he was after the camera? That's got to be it! But how did it get in the box in the first place? I knew Karen was at home, she didn't work on a Wednesday. I was going to have to swallow my pride, or whatever it was that had been keeping me from contacting her this last week to get in touch and ask her to keep an eye out for curly haired wankers. Fuck it. I bit the bullet and rang her number, preying there wouldn't be any awkwardness. "Hey stranger," she answered but not in a way that made me feel uncomfortable. Maybe the problem was all in my head. "Karen, this might seem odd but..." I explained about Graham and my misgivings. This was met with silence. "Well, you know my feelings about him, but are you sure he didn't just pop in to talk to you then get cold feet? He is a flakey wuss after all." True. And highly probable. I'd prefer to believe that of him than him breaking into my house and boiling my kittens! "If you are that concerned I'll use my key and pop in and sit with them for a while if you like? I haven't met them yet." Did I detect a slight tone of something there? I chose to ignore it and be grateful instead. "Shall I pop around later with wine? Or if you're still being boring, tea?" She asked. "I'd like nothing better," I answered "but I have a date tonight. How about tomorrow?" This was met with silence. "A date?" She repeated. She made it sound like I'd just admitted to going on a killing spree tonight instead. "With who?" "Elaine has set me up with a 'chap'" I laughed, Karen didn't laugh with me. "Didn't realise you were on the market for dating?" "I'm not really, but I thought why not?" "Mmm, well hope it goes well." She blatantly lied, it was obvious she hoped anything but, but I had no idea why. Maybe Karen wanted to date me instead. Maybe Karen was a secret lesbian and wanted me all to herself. Maybe that was why she was thwarting a possible budding relationship between me and Mike. Yep, I know I'm an absolute idiot! "How are your new shelves?" I asked, it just slipped out. I hadn't meant to ask. Karen only hesitated for a slight second.

"They're great thanks, look great in my bedroom!" She rang off. She said bedroom rather pointedly. What did that mean? The rest of the day passed without incidence. Michaela flagged at lunchtime and by that I mean returned to her usual lazy ways of not working and taking a lot of 'fresh air' breaks. She probably had the hump that she couldn't find her man. Karen kept me updated by text. No sign of Ghastly Graham but Lexus had shit on the sofa. And did I know that Tilly was trapped in a cupboard? Poor love, it must have happened when I was putting the video recorder back. Deep joy. By the time I got home, the thought of going out on a blind date with Elaine's friend William did not excite me at all. I just wanted to crawl under a blanket in my lounge pants and watch telly with the cats. Still, I'd promised. So I fluffed up my hair, put on a sparkly top and added some lip gloss. I'd do. I guess. "Where are you going?" Asked Nicole. "On a blind date," I'd replied without enthusiasm. She looked at me blankly. "By that do you mean he is blind?" "What? No of course not!" I said pulling a face.

"Right because you've hardly made an effort mum. It might be a chore for you by going on this date but it might mean a lot to him! No offence, but it's obvious you have not made an effort!" she said looking rather cross. I felt suitably ashamed. Who was the adult here? "That top looks like something Grandma might wear, go and change into your going out clothes, you normally look so lovely." she admonished. What a sweet but slightly offensive thing to say. My mother would never wear such a funky, shiny, glittery top...yep Nicole was right, a change of outfit was needed. "And mum?" I turned to look back at her. "Please bring me back a new daddy!" she asked sweetly. I told her to piss off and I went to get ready. Again. Nicole was of course right. It was not Williams fault that I didn't want to go.

An hour later I was standing in our designated meeting place, a busy bar on the high street. I bought myself a glass of wine and took to a high stool by the door. I realised then at that precise moment that I'd left my mobile phone at home.

Bugger. Now I couldn't even distract myself with Facebook while I waited for my date to arrive who I didn't actually want to date. After ten minutes an extremely attractive man appeared at the door and looked around the room as if looking for someone. I hoped that someone was me. He made eye contact and smiled. I smiled back. He walked towards me, I went to stand up to greet him but he sailed on past me and he greeted an equally attractive blonde woman on the table behind me. I felt myself redden. I hoped nobody had noticed. I knew it had been too good to be true. This happened a couple more times. But the man in question got less and less attractive every time. I wasn't so much a gooseberry amongst all these dating couples but more of a tomato. I was about to neck my glass of wine and leave sharply as my 'date' was now ten minutes late, when the door flung open and an incredibly short man with a bald head entered. He stood there looking around as if looking for someone. I really hoped that someone wasn't me. I tried to hide behind the drinks menu. Unsuccessfully. But yes, yes it was. Of course he was looking for me. The disappointment was crushing. "Emily I presume," he said rushing straight over to me. "I am so sorry about my tardiness, bloody taxi was late." He attempted to kiss me in greeting but couldn't quite reach up to me on my high stool. I had to practically bend myself in half to make this happen. He smelt nice, I'd give him that. "You look exactly like your photograph, you never can tell these days can you?" He laughed. Nice smiley eyes, big forehead though, head slightly coned. I hoped he wasn't doing the same to me. Nice smile, but big bingo winged arms! So Elaine had shown him a photo of me but neglected to offer me the same courtesy, not that I'd mention that to him. It seemed offensive somehow. "That's a relief, you too." I said necking my wine anyway. "Another?" He gestured towards my glass, didn't wait for a reply and went to get me one anyway. He came back with a bottle, and then struggled to climb up on the high stool. Would it be bad first dating etiquette to offer him a leg up?

Luckily he made it up on it before I had chance to offend him. He was red in the face though and breathing hard. It was was off putting. I imagined it was what his sex face would look like. Yuck.

"So, tell me all about you," he said. There was a film of sweat covering his face due to his physical exertion of getting on the chair. He pulled out a hanky, a clean one thank goodness and mopped his brow. "I, err, am thirty eight, divorced, two teenage children and two cats. I work in a hotel and I like wine." I tried to sound quirky but ended up sounding like an alcoholic bore. I took a sip of my wine as if to confirm my sad statement was true, even to my own ears it seemed pretty lame. He reacted as though I were the most interesting person he had ever met, a true gentleman. "Tell me about you," I asked. Which he did. He was forty four, also divorced. He also liked cats and wine. He worked in insurance (yawn). So quite similar to me then, I thought privately. "I have an open topped sports car," he gushed. "I love to feel the wind in my hair," He laughed at himself as he rubbed his shiny head.

Two dullards together. And the sports car was obviously a sign of his impending midlife crisis. However, he then launched into his many hobbies. Extreme sports, skydiving, snowboarding, jet skiing, anything that posed a life threatening risk by the sounds of it! He liked mountain climbing, cycling, walking, running and anything that caused me to break out in a sweat just thinking about it. Or make me want to reach for the biscuits and flop on the sofa. He wasn't finished yet, he liked to travel too. America, India, Japan, Italy, Cuba, Jamaica, the list went on. I wondered if his real name was in fact Phileas Fogg? "How about you?" He asked. "Do you Travel?" Only to work and back I wanted to joke but thought better of it. "Well, I went to Spain when I was fourteen." He nodded in encouragement, but I noticed his eyes dulled slightly. "I've been to Turkey a few times. But tell me about Cuba, I've always wanted to go." I thought it best to change the subject. My jaunts to Turkey were miserable family holidays with Michael when then the kids were young and almost always ended in disaster. Sunburn, mosquito bites turning septic, deflated lilos and no sexual offerings in the sun.

After a few minutes of chatting, about all the extreme sports Cuba had to offer, William lent in closer to me. I instinctively backed off thinking he was about to kiss me, a look of horror on my face. The embarrassing thing was that he wasn't trying to kiss me at all, but he now knew that I thought that was what he was trying to do. I could also tell by his face that he had no intention of wanting to kiss me either. "I was just going to say that there's a man over there who has been staring at you for the last few minutes, he doesn't look happy," he patted my hand, the way an elderly uncle might, before checking his watch in a sneaky gesture that I caught just as I went to turn around to see this man who'd been staring. This made my face flame. I'd come on this date thinking I was superior to him, especially after seeing him when actually he was just as disappointed with me, not with my appearance I doubted, but with my personality. This felt much, much worse.

I fully expected to find Graham sitting behind me like the stalker I believed he'd become, so imagine my shock to find Mike instead. We just stared at each other, he downed his pint giving me a curt nod of the head. I turned back to William to explain I just wanted to pop over and say hi to my neighbour but William gave me look filled with pity. "He's already gone I'm afraid love." It was true, he had certainly high tailed it out of there. "I'm off too I'm afraid, it's been lovely meeting you. Take care." He practically threw himself off his stool in his haste to get away from me. I'm only surprised he didn't commando roll out the door. Maybe he could list that as one of his extreme sports on his next date. He already had his mobile phone out and in his hand as he left the bar, probably texting Elaine to berate her for setting him up on a date with a boring loser! The entire date had taken just twenty minutes. Epic fail.

CHAPTER TEN

I knew, as soon as the taxi pulled up in front of my house something was amiss. The entire street was in darkness, indicating a possible power cut. There was an unidentified car parked on my driveway, it looked out of place. It was also blocking my car in. This seemed rather sinister to me in my drunken and agitated state. "Is everything ok?" I called out, frantically, as I rushed through the door, treading on a poor kitten in my haste to get in. "Mum? What are you doing back?" Nicole appeared in the doorway with her phone on torch setting, almost blinding me. "I take it the date didn't go well?" she whispered, pulling a sad face. "I don't want to talk about it, it's really not that big a deal." I said in a rush. "Who's car is that on the driveway?" This was met with a few seconds silence before someone cleared their throat. A man. My eyes widened in surprise. Did Nicole have a secret boyfriend that she invited round as soon as I left the house? "That would be mine," said a voice sounding suspiciously like my ex husbands. Really? Not again? "What are you doing here? It's been eight years. Just because you've split up with Tara doesn't mean..." I rant, as Michael appeared sheepishly in the doorway armed with his phone torch too. Blinding me again for a second time. "Don't blame dad," called out James, defensively, from behind them. "I called him, the power went off and we didn't know what to do. The landline kept ringing but there was no one on the other end and then Nicole thought she saw someone looking through the window!" It all came out in a rush, he sounded ever so tearful. No sign of the normal teenage bravado present. I sighed, putting my own feelings aside. I plastered a look on my face in what I believed to a smile but I'm pretty sure It just looked like I was baring my teeth at him. "Well, thank you for coming to your children's aid, it's much appreciated but I'm home now, so if you'll be on your way..." "No!" Shouted Nicole, making us all jump. "I swear there was someone looking at us through the window! Dad said he saw someone outside the house acting suspiciously when he arrived." I looked in dismay at Michael. "Mum, please let dad sleep on the sofa, we'd feel safer if he did." James nodded in agreement. Michael just looked embarrassed. Nicole and James looked at me hopefully. I wanted to ask what puny Michael would do in the event of an intruder emergency but resisted the urge to ridicule him in front of his children. He did that well enough by himself. God, what was I supposed to do? I wanted to kick him out on his rear but I suppose that wouldn't be in the children's best interests so I grudgingly agreed. "What did the face look like?" I asked, it suddenly hitting me that someone had been staring at my children through the window. My blood ran a little colder at the thought. Who kept hanging around the house? Were we in danger? "It just looked like a face!" said Nicole vaguely. "It was dark." "Are you sure it wasn't just your own reflection?" I pondered out loud. "Are you saying I'm lying?" Her voice going all shrill and high pitched. "Are you saying I don't recognise my own face!" She asked incredulously. "No," I soothed "of course not." Although you are your fathers daughter, I thought privately and then immediately felt ashamed. "I'm just trying to establish what you saw darling. Was it a dirty pervert? Or was it someone walking past the window?" Was it somebody looking for a camera?

I made a mental note to myself that we must start shutting the curtains in future. Michael meanwhile looked rather uncomfortable standing about waiting to be told to make himself at home. Lexus kept trying to claw his way up his trouser leg, he kept trying to shake her off but she clung on for dear life, like it was a game. It obviously hurt. I tried not to smile, until I saw that somebody had lit my expensive, purely decorative, Jo Malone candles on the mantelpiece. I couldn't even be angry could I? They were kids. They saw candles. There was a power cut, so they lit the candles. The forty-five pound each bloody candles! I bit back my utter frustration at the situation. "Did you check 1471?" I directed this waspishly at Michael, as the kids wouldn't have a clue what that meant. I'm only surprised they even knew that we had a 'landline'! They were so dependent on their many handheld devices that didn't require a cord. "I didn't think it was my place to start playing about with your stuff." He said piously. Ahh fair point actually. "I'll do it then." As if I had to do everything. Poor

Michael he couldn't win whatever he decided. Poor sod. Number withheld. Of course it was. No clever stalker would be rookie enough to leave a recognisable number behind. So it obviously wasn't Graham then.
"Right well, I'll leave you two to entertain your dad then. I'm off to bed." Both kids looked a little shell shocked at this. Michael too looked a little worried about being left alone with his children. "Oh," said James "I was going to go back upstairs to play on my PlayStation." He looked pained at missing out on precious FIFA time. "There's no electricity James, so unless you have a secret generator hidden in your bedroom there will be no further FIFA action tonight!" "I meant I was going to read, a book." he lied. Nicole also looked a little put out. "What would we do?" she asked, looking worriedly at her brother then her dad. It was like I was leaving her alone in a room with a couple of sex offenders. "Play a game? Chat about your day? Discuss your hopes and dreams for the future? I'll grab you a spare sheet from the airing cupboard Michael." "Gee, thanks," he said a little waspishly himself for someone who was about to be offered my hospitality for the night. Enjoying the expensive scents wafting around the room for free. The kids sat down on the sofa and all three of them stared at each other in silence, in the gloomy, but exotic candle light as if unsure what to say to each other next.
"Night then," I called, grinning as I grabbed my kittens and disappeared to the relative sanctity of my bedroom, but not before I'd checked every window and double locked both doors. My phone was right beside my bed where I'd left it charging earlier. Three text messages awaited me. Two from Elaine. First one at 7.50 wishing me luck on my date. The second one at 8.30 saying never mind plenty more fish in the sea. I suddenly felt extraordinarily angry at her for setting me up on a blind date with somebody who so obviously wasn't going to be a good match for me. I wanted to cry. Not because

I was upset by the badness of the date, I was used to that. All I ever seemed to have was dating disasters, none quite so bad as ending up with an ex husband sleeping on my sofa though! I felt saddened by the whole horribleness of having a possible stalker in my midst, terrifying my children and forcing them to call their father for assistance.

Then I remembered Mike's face, the look of blankness when I caught him looking at me tonight. Why hadn't he said hello? Why did he disappear so quickly? I put this out of my mind for now and turned my attention back to my phone. The third text was from mum declaring she had news about my brother, phone when I can. I found that I didn't actually care about Simon and his shenanigans right now.

I woke the next morning to Tilly tapping me on the nose wanting her breakfast and the strong smell of coffee in the air. I sat up hurriedly in bed expecting Michael to be standing at the foot of it with a cup of coffee in hand. Thankfully not. I would have had to kill him otherwise. I got myself dressed, something I would never normally entertain this early on a Saturday morning but not wanting to go downstairs in a state of undress in front of the ex husband. I wouldn't want him to be driven wild with longing at my sexy body. I am of course joking. I found him in the kitchen drinking coffee. "Sleep well?" I asked mainly to make conversation. Not because I actually cared. "Your sofa is more comfortable than the beds at the hotel," he admitted. "But the electric came back at two thirty this morning and the telly blasted back on scaring the life out of me. The sickly smell of the candles made me feel slightly nauseous too. The sheet was pretty scratchy and smelt of wee but other than that, yeah I slept great!" He appeared to be stretching his back, wincing as he did so. "That's good." I answered, not really listening to him. "And the kids? Did you spent some quality time together?" "Yes, it was great!" Unfortunately he hesitated a moment too long. "You all just sat and stared at your phones for an hour didn't you?" I said crossly. "Yeah, well none of us knew what to say to each other," he protested. "Teenagers are so difficult to communicate with." he added defensively. "Oh please, that's such a cliche!" I said sharply. "You sit and chat all night every night with them do you? Please give me some tips oh wise teenage whisperer you." sarcasm dropped off his tongue. I couldn't let him know that I sometimes went days without actually saying a word to the children, not because I had nothing to say. I always had plenty to say but because we were like ships passing in the night sometimes. And you know, James would rather shout at his friends on the PlayStation than communicate with his mother. Nicole was either at work, the gym or out. When she was at home she always had her head buried in her phone. I decided to change the subject. "Coffee ok?" It turned out this was the wrong subject to switch to. "Really good actually." he enthused. "Nice coffee maker. Expensive?" "Err, not really." Shit. Awkward territory here. It was in actual fact his coffee maker that I'd lied and said was broken when he asked for it back eight years ago. I was on dangerous ground now. It had been a birthday present from his mum. I don't know why I'd kept it, apart from the fact I wanted to be petty and awkward back then, to get back at him for being petty and awkward. Plus it looked good on my worktop. "Do you even like coffee?" he asked, already knowing the answer was no. He sipped his coffee pulling an appreciative face. "Sometimes I fancy a coffee," I lied. "I'm pretty sure this is the same make and model of the one my mum bought me, you know, for my thirtieth birthday. You know, the one I asked for when I moved in with Tara, the one that had never been used but had mysteriously been damaged somehow!" There was no way in the world he would ever be able to prove that my coffee machine was the same one his mother had brought him for his birthday. It was all purely circumstantial evidence. I was confident that I would not get found out in my lie, hang on what was he now doing? Michael had moved over to the coffee machine and was turning it round. What on earth? "Mum told me afterwards they were doing a deal in store that day, engraving for free on appliances costing over a hundred pounds, and as it was a special birthday she'd had it engraved for me." Oh dear God no! Please let him be winding me up. Why had I never noticed that bloody engraving? Oh that's right, because once I'd unpacked it in anger eight years ago I'd never used it once. Since I hated coffee with a vengeance. "To my darling son Michael, happy 30th birthday. Love from mummy..." he read out. I'd forgotten the ex mother in laws annoying habit of calling herself mummy. "Well, I don't know what to say!" I exclaimed, thinking quickly. "But what an amazing coincidence!" "What?" he scoffed. "I did lie, I'm sorry," I made myself sound sincere. "I, as you know don't like coffee and I gave it away after we split up and then panicked when you asked for it back. So I told you it was broken." I hung my head in mock shame, trying to sneak a look at him to see if he was buying it. "Two years later, unbelievably it would seem, I won this coffee machine in a raffle at work! What are the chances of this happening? The same machine!" "I'll be taking my coffee machine Emily!" He was not buying my story at all then! "Yes, of course you must." I agreed feeling rather shamefaced. "That mystery figure you saw hanging outside the house last night, are you able to describe them?" I remembered to ask him. "Not really, it was dark! Tall, wrapped in a big coat." "Sitting in the bush?" I volunteered. "No," giving me a weird look, as he might. " Just standing there, obviously I turned up and they walked off." The phone rang then. Landline. Obviously it would be mum phoning to find out why I hadn't I immediately phoned her back last night. "Hi mum," I answered, guessing correctly. I watched Michael struggle as he carried the coffee machine out of my kitchen to his car. "Emily, did you not get my message?" She sounded a bit put out. "Yes, but not until quite late mum," I lied. "My phone showed that you read it at 8.50! That's not late in my book." Damn my mother and her new found love of new technology. She shouldn't even have an iPhone at her age, she should still be carrying her house brick sized phone around with her. "I tried the landline a few times too, I heard Nicole answer but she couldn't hear me. Is your line out?" "We had a power cut last night...oh, hang on..." It then all became crystal clear! They had been no scary phone calls, just my mum trying to phone the landline and our phone ridiculously, in this day and age didn't work if there was no electricity! "I don't suppose you also popped round and stared through the living room window, scaring the living daylights out of the kids and then just vanished off into the night, did you?" I asked hopefully.

"Of course not." She sounded highly offended as one might if being accused of being a peeping Tom, especially against one's own family. Nope. Of course not. That particular mystery still currently unsolved then. "Anyway back to your brother, or are you not bothered anymore?" She accused.

"Well not really..." I started to say before she interrupted me with what she'd found out. It turned out naughty Simon had been cheating on Cassia. "But why?" I'd argued after hearing how he'd been 'seeing' someone else. Behind her back. "Surely he'd have been better off just to end it then he could shag whoever he wanted!" Mum gasped at the word shag! I sighed I could really do without this right now. Michael hadn't come back, I looked out of the window and the car had gone. Oh dear I think he might actually be very angry with me.

The man was currently homeless, with only the clothes on his back. At least now he had a coffee machine he could not use.

Idiot. I wondered what to put in the big space the coffee machine had left behind. "How did you find out?" I asked distractedly. "Cassia turned up on the doorstep in a right state, she was trying to track down the kittens," I gasped at what this might mean for me. "Don't worry I didn't reveal their whereabouts, I led a false trail, but she filled me in on Simon's duplicity. I'm very angry with him." she added. "Yes, he's been a twat." I agreed. "So is it just one woman or lots?" I wondered. "Just one apparently, Cassia became suspicious about his behaviour and checked his phone. Her name is Kay apparently!" mum said huffily. "I tried to phone him last night but he said he was out and would call me back. He didn't." "I'm confused mum, did Cassia communicate this to you in sign language or in a letter? She normally doesn't talk!" I snorted finding myself very funny. "Very funny Emily," said mum in a way that meant she didn't think I was very funny at all. "I think she's just misunderstood. Maybe we just intimidated her." We talked, well mum talked some more about how cross she was with Simon and how she couldn't get rid of Cassia now, she'd become a permanent fixture at their house. "It was my turn to host the coffee morning and she turned up blubbering away. She spoke more in that half hour than she's said in a whole six months! Quite a sweet girl really, shame she didn't show her sensitive side more often, maybe Simon wouldn't have found solace elsewhere with a woman called Kay! Now she keeps texting me and wanting to meet to talk about it."

"It's a shame she wore such horrible dresses made out of wood, maybe Simon was fed up of getting splinters every time he touched her." We both chuckled at this. "Also," said mum "just so you know Roger and Sandra have got engaged! Can you believe it? It's so quick. Elaine doesn't know yet but I can't imagine she'll be too happy, just to give you fair warning." said mum in a hushed voice. There was some disturbance in the background. "I have to go your father's calling for a bacon sandwich and a coffee. Bye."

I decided as I was already dressed I might as well pop in and visit Karen. I could fill her in on my terrible date and maybe even arrange to go out later and do something fun, like drown my sorrows in a cool bar and dance the night away, it sounded like the lyrics of a cheesy pop song. I locked up the house and jumped over the fence, a quick rap on the door before going in to find Karen and Mike at it on the kitchen table! I'm not sure who looked more surprised. By 'at it' I meant sitting at the table drinking tea, but they might just of well have been 'at it' that's how surprised I was to see him there. He was surprised to see me too, by the look on his face. "Shall I come back?" I asked feeling uncomfortable in their presence. They both just stared at me. Karen recovered first. Mike looked like rather miserable. "Don't be stupid, pull up a chair I'll put the kettle back on." "Hi Emily," said Mike quietly. He pushed his chair back. "I'm off anyway, thanks for the chat Karen, see you around Emily." He didn't even look at me as he said this. Where had the easy banter the two of us had disappeared to? I debated shouting 'bush' at him to see if it raised a laugh, but decided against making a fool of myself, again. Karen walked him to the front door. I heard hushed voices then the door shutting. "Sorry I didn't mean to interrupt anything," I said not meaning it at all. I was glad I had. I was not glad I hadn't made more of an effort though, of my hair and face mainly. "You didn't." was her answer. "How was your date?" "Completely rubbish!" Karen pulled a dubious face."What?" "Mike saw you, he said you looked pretty cosy." she pulled a face. "Well maybe if Mike hadn't disappeared so quickly after spotting me, he'd have seen that the date ended two minutes after that and the date started half hour before that, so yeah pretty bloody crap!" "What about the car on the drive overnight?" Karen asked quizzically. "Michaels car. The kids got freaked out during the power cut, they called their dad and he stayed on the sofa at their request." I told her about the peeping tom at the window and the dodgy phone calls. I neglected to mention that mum had turned out to be the accidental culprit. I wanted to dramatise as much as possible. Karen looked shocked. "There was also a strange person hanging about outside the house again." I threw in for good measure. "I had no idea," she said shaking her head. " I was out last night, I didn't realise we'd had a power cut."

I wondered where she was. I wasn't going to ask, she clearly wasn't going to tell me either. Still, at least she wasn't with Mike, unless she met up with him later! We just looked at each other, not knowing what to say. Too many unanswered questions. Maybe I should ask a few. "Mike looked..." how to finish that sentence? "fed up!" Seemed the least rude. A miserable bastard would be more accurate. "Yeah, a case of mixed messages it would seem." She didn't elaborate. We stared at each other, there was definitely tension. Maybe Mike fancied Karen and tried it on and she'd knocked him back! That would explain the mixed messages comment. "So are you and Mike...? I trailed off, it sounded juvenile to my own ears. "No of course not!" she replied. "Are you really that dense?" "I'm not dense." I proclaimed feeling hurt. "Yes you are." "Is it too early for wine?" I wondered out loud. Karen just looked at me. "I guess it is then." "Look, sit down for God's sake, standing there like a sap! I'll make a cuppa and tell you what's going on shall I?" I sat down. Karen put a mug of hot tea in front of me.

"Mike, for some unknown reason really likes you. He didn't want me to say anything, but I'm getting the impression that

things are getting weird between us and I don't want that." "Me?" I squealed.
"I know I couldn't believe it either." She said dryly. "I'm joking, dickhead." She said when my face dropped. "I thought it was you he liked." I admitted. "And that you liked him back." Karen laughed uproariously at this. "No, Emily. He's not my type at all." "So why is Mike ignoring me and looking like he's been given a permanent wedgie in life?" "Duh, are you really that stupid? Don't answer, obviously you are. He saw you on a date last night, looking pretty cosy and then a mysterious car was parked on your drive overnight! He put two and two together and got it wrong but in his eyes it looked how it looked. Like you'd hooked up." "Yeah I guess so. So he likes me?" I tried to not smile but it was difficult. Mike was my secret crush and he liked me, this almost never happened. "Yes, but the question is? Do you like him?" That certainly is a question. Do I? Well, yes I like him obviously. Thing is, do I like, like him? He's good looking definitely, that's why we call him Mike the sexy builder and not the butt ugly builder. He's funny, he's kind and he can make soup. "I think so," I admit. "I wish he'd have come to me and asked me on a date instead of muddying the waters by involving you. I feel like I'm in high school again. 'My mate fancies you, do you fancy her?'" "Well, in an ideal world perhaps, but you have ghastly Graham turning up being a twat every other day also muddying the waters too. I don't blame him for asking for advice. For the record I said I suspected that you were interested in him but it would be a good idea to ask you himself. That's when he then saw you on a date with the hobbit." "What about your shelves, in your bedroom?" I pouted. "What was that about?" "There were no shelves, that was an excuse to get him round. I said bedroom because otherwise you'd see there were no shelves and become all suspicious. I was covering my back." "An excuse?" "Yeah, I wanted to ask him for some advice, I..." My

phone rang at this point. It was Elaine again. She'd already phoned three times this morning. I was, of course, ignoring her. I was still angry with her for setting me up with a totally unsuitable person. It rang off only to ring again. "Is that your mum?" asked Karen understandably getting the wrong end of the stick. "No not this time, bloody Elaine. She's probably phoning to moan about her mum and Roger getting engaged and berate me for it. Even though the whole thing is her fault." "Elaine needs to grow up. She disappears leaving her mum frantically worried about her, turns up again and then has the cheek to complain that her mums met a man and is actually happy for a change." said Karen. "I'm sure Roger is a nice guy." I nod, because it's true. "I just don't understand all the secrecy..." I trailed off, thinking. Karen turned around to look at me.

"What is it?" "Elaine and Simon. It all makes sense. Simons been shagging around behind Cassias back according to the gospel that is my mother. Elaine is with a guy that has to be kept a big fucking secret for no reason whatsoever as far as I can see! Elaine and Simon!" I sit there mouth wide open. It makes sense. I can't believe it. Karen busies herself at the sink. "I can't see Elaine and your brother as a couple to be honest, can you?" Well not really. We all grew up together. It would feel a little like incest. "Anyway, didn't you say your brother was at the Easter dinner at your mums whilst Elaine was still AWOL?"

Yes good point. Damn, it all seemed to fit so well, but maybe Simon being at the meal was a red herring. Was I reading to much into this. I decided to tell Karen about the camera, she was suitably stumped too but looked a bit wary when I said there were photos of the two of us on there. "But how did it get into your memory box?" "That is the real mystery," I shrugged wishing I could solve it.

My phone rang again. This time it was Graham. "Just ignore it Emily, the guy is a bloody dick!"
"No I better answer it, I'm still convinced it was him that was stating through the window last night." Karen stayed silent. "What do you want Graham?" I asked warily. "I just want to talk to you, that's all. It won't take long. I'm outside." I sighed and agreed. Karen pulled a face as I walked out. "Just remember he is a nut job."

I wandered outside and saw him standing on my drive. I approached cautiously in case he turned a gun on me and shot me dead. You read about these things all the time. Yep I've still been watching too many Murder she Wrote on Gold. I also took a sneaky glance over to Mike's place in case he was watching me. His van was parked on the drive but there was no sign of Mike. I kept a suitable distance away from Graham. I didn't want Mike to see me out the window and think I was having a clandestine meeting with my ex in full view of him, rubbing his nose in it so to speak. Not that he knew that I knew that he liked me. Why was everything so complicated? "What do you want?" I repeated. Graham looked different, the wild angry look had gone. Today he looked almost normal. Nice. "To apologise to you, I took our breakup badly. It was rather ridiculous of me to be honest. We'd only been dating a few months it wasn't like we were married or anything!" He laughed even though it wasn't funny. I smiled and nodded. Precisely, I thought. "You were right, I do like Michaela, I'm thinking of asking her out. Are you sure you wouldn't mind?" He peered at me as though waiting for a jealous reaction of sorts. "That's complete fine, good luck and thanks for the apology. Take care Graham." Should I shake his hand? No obviously not. I went to walk off giving him a small smile. Phew that was easy. "Is that it?" He called after me incredulously. I turned around to face him. "You came to say sorry, you did so. You asked if it was ok to date an acquaintance of mine I said I didn't mind. What's the problem?" I shrugged my shoulders to indicate my confusion. Graham really was worse than a woman. He started to go red, his eyes a little wide. Here we go again. I sighed. I wasn't sure what he actually wanted. For me to spend half an hour accepting his apology for old times sake. "Graham I've had enough. We dated. It didn't work out. You've apologised. I've accepted. Many times. You want to date Michaela then fucking date her. I COULDN'T GIVE A FLYING FUCK. There's no need to keep rehashing this. You know I'm still convinced you were trying to make sure I was out of the way the other day. Looking for your camera by any chance?" Oh why, oh why did I just say that? Graham's face started to go redder, his eyes all bulging with suppressed rage. Or not so suppressed rage as the case may be. Obvious rage. "What? You thought I was going to break into your house and go through your knickers or boil one of your ridiculous kittens?" He erupted, a little bit of spit flew from his mouth and landed on me. Not bad considering the rather large gap between us. I looked over to Mike's house, hoping he was now watching and could sense the situation. Still no sign. Yes that's exactly what I thought he might have done that day. Hang on..."How do you know about my kittens?" I ask, knowing full well I'd never told him I had acquired them. Unless, oh my goodness. "It was you!" I declare. "You were staring at my children through the window last night and saw the kittens?" His face was a picture. Not a nice one an angry incredulous one. "How dare you!" He spluttered. "Accusing me of being a pervert now are we?" "Well if the cap fits, you peeping tom you!" This was quickly escalating at an alarming rate. Then he did a surprising thing. He stopped looking angry and smiled, a horrible 'I'm going to fuck you right up smile'. "Last night you say, mmm, I have a rock solid alibi for last night actually." "Really?" "Ask your friend Karen. She'll be able to confirm my whereabouts. You have my number when you're ready to apologise for calling me a peeping tom. That's actually slander maybe I should report you..." he then wandered back to his car and laughing to himself as he did so.

What the hell was going on? How could Karen of all people alibi him. Who was the mysterious person hanging around my house. I was starting to realise it might not be Graham at all.

CHAPTER ELEVEN

Michaela was in the foulest of moods. The hunk had stood her up on Friday, a pathetic excuse about his ex. So she was angrier than normal, stomping around the hotel, a meat cleaver in one hand a cigarette in the other. Spoiling for a fight with anybody who so much as looked at her in the wrong way. Even Logan had, for the foreseeable future, retreated to the relative safety of his office and deadlocked the door from the inside. Maud ran in the opposite direction if she so much as caught sight of her, wailing pathetically I was joking about the meat cleaver, obviously. I just wanted to establish the scale of Michaela's anger. I however, simply ignored her ranting and her over dramatics. I had my own problems. The inside of my head was like a rubbish television drama. It was giving me brain-ache. I just wanted to switch it off. There was the possible stalker element with Graham swanning about telling me that my best friend could alibi him! I mean, what was that about? Was he the face at my window? If not, who? Then there was my other so called friend setting me up with totally unsuitable, adrenaline junkie midgets. Keeping secrets about her own love life. Bitching about her poor lonely mother finally finding love with randy Roger. She was bloody selfish and I was fed up with her. There was Mike who apparently liked me, but was using Karen as a sounding board, it was all a bit juvenile for me. Despite that I kind of liked him too. My oh so perfect brother had been cheating on his weirdo girlfriend, with somebody called Kay. Which mum had become obsessed about and was bombarding me with phone calls at all times of the day and night. Now Michael had discovered I lied about the stupid coffee machine. Trivial I know, but after years of playing the hard done by martyr card, it pained me to get caught out in such a stupid lie. Oh and last but not least my son had a cigarette habit! I decided to do something I'd never done before and feign illness to go home and tie up some loose ends. The problem was I wasn't a very good actress. I knocked on Logan's door, I coughed loudly getting into character of a poorly employee. Silence. "Logan it's Emily," I called out throatily, you know, just in case he thought it was psycho Michaela wielding her meat cleaver.

"Oh thank God." I heard him exclaim. He unlocked the door and pulled me in, then locked it again. "I've been sat under the table for the last hour. I've got bloody leg cramps now!" "Isn't that something you do in an earthquake? Why under the table?" I asked intrigued. "I wasn't thinking straight, she terrifies me, blasted woman is a liability, but I'm scared to let her go in case she chops off my smooth bits in revenge and serves them up for breakfast." "Sorry Logan," I coughed again and massaged my head wearily. "I'm feeling rather under the weather, would you mind if I bailed out early and went home, to rest? I'll make up my hours over the rest of the week." I did indeed sound pathetic and rather rehearsed. I coughed again for clarity. He looked at me in concern, no suspicion in his eyes. I felt wretched at my duplicity. "Of course, no problem at all dear girl, although this does mean I'll have to put myself in the line of fire." He gulped dramatically. "But no worries, go, go and come back when you're better. You've looked bloody awful for over a week now love, shoo off you go!" Gee, great, not great for the old self esteem. I'd only been acting for five minutes so clearly looking rough just came natural to me. I hightailed it out of there before Logan could change his mind. I remembered to hightail it with a hint of lethargy, you know just in case he was watching me. I got to my car and noticed The Hunk, the object of Michaela's affections loading his case in the back of his car. I hoped he'd said his goodbyes to her or at least passed on a phone number, even if it was just a fake one. I decided to be brave and see. "Excuse me," I called over to him. He looked up giving me a dirty look. "Have you said goodbye to Michaela? She's already annoyed about you standing her up Friday, this might send her over the edge." He looked blankly at me. I realised he was a possible bank robber and I was telling him off. I should be careful as he might have a sawn off shotgun on him. "Who the fuck is Michaela?" He gave me another look before climbing into his car and racing off. Ahhh, he was probably married, that would explain it. Poor Michaela, no, scrap that, poor bloody us, she would be a cow now for days.

I decided to give her a heads up on the situation. I typed out a text and sent it to her, hopefully any vengeful, angry behaviour would be over and done with by the time I returned to work. I also mentioned the fact Graham had a soft spot for her.

Karen was my first port of call. I needed to check out Graham's alibi. I only hoped it was another figment of deluded Graham's imagination. She was laughing at something somebody was saying on the phone when I tapped on her back door. She turned around in surprise and her face fell, just for a second, she adjusted it quickly and gestured for me to come in whilst saying goodbye quickly to her caller. "Everything ok?" she asked. "Tea?" She had her back to me. I nodded. Then realised she didn't have eyes in the back of her head. "Yes please." Here goes nothing. "Graham said you could give him an alibi for the night of the power-cut. Is this true? Are you seeing him?" No point beating around the bush, might as well bash up the bush. Karen turned slowly and looked at me in shock. Eyes wide in disbelief. Mouth open. Oh God it was true. Then I noticed her mouth start to twitch, she covered it with her hands and started to make a weird noise. Her eyes started streaming. She was bent double. What the fuck? Oh God she was having a nervous breakdown, what had I started? "Karen don't..." I began to backtrack, but then realised she wasn't crying or upset she was laughing, bloody laughing at me. "You think...you think I'm seeing...that curly haired wanker!!" The noises got louder, she grabbed onto the worktop to steady herself. Tear of great mirth running down her face. "It's not that funny." I mumbled while she gathered herself together again. "No, of course not but it's just the idea of me and...him." That set her off again. I waited patiently for her to finish. Did she not realise she was offending me greatly here? I know he wasn't the love of my life but I had chosen to date him you know. I realise Graham was no first prize, but he was a decent enough man, not too bad to look at. He saved me from a mugger once, but then went on to possibly stalk me...Hmmmm. "Sorry, sorry about that." Karen appeared to have composed herself. "He said you could give him an alibi?" I repeated.

"Yes, that much is true I suppose." "Explain please." Karen abandoned the kettle and pulled a bottle of wine from the fridge, without waiting for an affirmative poured a couple of large ones. "There's not much to tell actually, I wasn't aware that he'd seen me," she pulled a worried face. "I'd seen him though, I was having dinner..with a friend..at that new Indian restaurant in town. He walked in with a woman. He sat with his back to me, but he was there the entire time I was, so yes, I can alibi him the time you think someone was peeping in your window."

My phone beeped indicating a text message. I used this as an excuse to think about my next move. I should really apologise to Karen for ever thinking she'd go behind my back and date the odious Graham. What a shitbag for trying to cause problems and insinuating more to his alibi story, especially as he was on a date himself. I must find out who this poor woman was and warn her! The message was from Michaela.

WHAT ARE YOU TALKING ABOUT? I'M SITTING HERE HAVING LUNCH WITH HIM NOW.

Followed by several winky faces. There was a photo attached also but I'd look at that later. Maybe he'd turned his car around after our conversation. Karen was quietly sipping her wine, deep in thought. My phone beeped again.

I KNOW ABOUT GRAHAM. HE TOOK ME OUT FRIDAY AFTER HUNK STOOD ME UP. KEEPING MY OPTIONS OPEN LOL

She was unbelievable.

"Did he say anything else?" Karen asked. I shook my head. I wondered who she was actually having dinner with but resisted the urge to ask. What had happened to us? We used to share everything. "I don't know what to say apart from sorry for thinking that you'd ever..." I started to say. She held her hand up to stop me from talking. "Don't say it, you'll only start me off again. Anyway...I don't deserve your apology, I've not been entirely honest with you. I need you to trust me. Can you do that?" I gulped my wine, what bloody now? I nodded despite not really knowing what I was nodding about.
"I'll explain all later. Are you free this evening? Say, half seven here for dinner?" I nodded again. I felt like Churchill the nodding sodding dog on the adverts. "I'm worried," I say biting my lip. "Can't you tell me now?" "It involves more than just me I'm afraid, a few hours that's all I need."
I nod again. "I guess it's the least I can do after accusing you of knobbing ghastly Graham." I attempted a joke. We smiled at each other, a truce as such. I wondered what the bloody hell she was going to tell me though. And I hoped fervently it had nothing to do with her knobbing Mike. "You're not my window peeper are you?" I joked. "No but I think I know who is?"

Next loose end to tie up was my mother! I liked a bit of gossip as much as the next person but my mother had now taken my brothers business and made it her full time job! It was ridiculous and unfair.
Who my brother was shagging was nothing to do with her, me or indeed Cassia. Mum needed to cut her newly formed ties with Cassia and tell her to do one. I enjoy a bit of family gossip as much as the next person but this was getting out of control. She answered on the first ring! "It's only taken you four hours and twenty nine minutes to return my call!" Was her greeting. "I even phoned you at work only to be told by that transvestite you'd gone home sick!" Transvestite? "Mum, Logan is gay!

Not a transvestite. You really need to work on your terminologies, it'll get you into trouble one day!" This was met with silence. "I'm well aware that your boss is gay! I was taking about that 'woman' you work with, who sounds like Phil Mitchell off of Eastenders!" Pah ha ha, she meant Michaela, that was actually quite funny. I didn't put her right. Maybe mum would meet her match in Michaela if she ever let that one slip out in her ear shot. "What's wrong with you?" She demanded. "I'm just run down mum, nothing serious." "Have you found out anything about this Kay?" She asked me impatiently changing the subject. I let out a slow rush of air. "Mum it's nothing to do with us, you need to back off. If Simon wants us to know, he'll tell us in his own time. You've never shown this much interest in my love life why is Simon's so fascinating?" "What love life?" mum exclaimed rudely. "There's been no one since that bloody Michael. Your father and I have wondered over the years if you're still pining over him..."

I didn't let her finish. "WHAT?" Are you serious? Actually I have dated, lots, but never found anyone I liked to have a serious relationship with!" "Well what about this Graham? I had high hopes for him but he disappeared without a trace too!"she said sulkily. I was livid. "You need to back off. We love you but you'll push Simon away if you continue. And me." I kept my voice as calm as possible. Inside though I was furious. "It's none of our business." I repeated. "Yes, well that's what he said when he phoned me up earlier." she said huffily. "So he knows you've been trying to find out his private business then?" "Well, he may have seen me sitting in my car outside his office earlier." "He may have? Or he did?" I ask, dumbfounded at the lengths my mother would go to to find out who Simons new girlfriend was. "He did." She acknowledged in a small voice. "He was then very underhand and phoned your father and told him what I'd been doing. Daddy wasn't very happy with me." It must be quite galling to be the one in the doghouse for once instead of the other way round. "Although at least it explained why his dinner hadn't been on the table when he got in from work for the last week. He thought.." she giggled girlishly "..that I'd been having an affair!" Yuck! Too gross to think about! "Yet you're still phoning me asking if I know anything?" I accuse. "There's no harm in that is there, but I'll stop that too! I may as well be chained to the kitchen sink, now that I'm not allowed to do anything." she said, full of self pity. "Or get yourself a hobby that doesn't involve poking your nose into others business." I was still smarting from the no love life comment, true or otherwise. No one wanted to hear that their parents thought you were sad lonely spinster. Still hung up on the rubbish ex husband, that I'd dumped years ago! "By the way Cassia knows that you have her kittens, she wants them back! I never confirmed it but she does know. I tried to throw her off the scent by telling her you had two dogs instead but she didn't believe me." "Well she can't have them back! How does she know?" "No idea, but I won't be talking to Cassia again, your father has banned her from the house. After she smashed the graduation photograph of your brother during one of her rages. Your father is being rather masterful just lately. I like it." Errr, double yuck. Now I felt sick! "Cassia has rages?" I asked. "I don't think in the entire time she was dating Simon I ever heard her speak?"

"She gets very cross, very quickly. It was when I suggested she might need anger management classes that she smashed my photo! Strange girl." So Cassia knew that I had her kittens, what would this mean? They were mine now and I wouldn't give them up. We had no social media connections, no mutual friends apart from Simon and he wouldn't have told her. There was no way she'd know they were here unless mum had accidentally slipped up in conversation. I sighed. Could things get any worse? The answer to that was obviously an astounding yes.

Next loose end was Mike. I looked out of the window. His truck was on the driveway. Did he ever go to work? I popped a mint in my mouth aware that I stunk of wine. And marched right over to his house before I could change my mind. I think my mothers comments about the lack of any love in my life had left me feeling frazzled. Mainly because it was true. There'd been no one really since Michael. Even Michael was hardly the greatest affair of my life. I'd never met anyone I actually wanted to spend any length of time with. Anyone I might have wanted to have a relationship with ended up being either, married, a liar or lived a million miles away. Then came Mike whose location was pretty perfect. He was good looking, funny, could cook and best of all he appeared to like me back despite all the crossed wires. I only hoped Karen hadn't got it wrong otherwise I was going to make a huge tit of myself. I knocked on the door. He didn't answer. I knocked again. Louder. Still nothing. There was definitely someone in there though I heard someone moving. Maybe he was still smarting from seeing me on my 'date'. Maybe this was better this way. I decided to talk to him through the letterbox instead. I blame the glass of wine for this ridiculous decision. "Mike?" I call " it's me Emily!" I immediately heard him shuffling around. "No don't get up, just listen!" Movement then stopped. "It's just this might be easier this way. I like you. Karen implied you liked me too. I know it must have been strange seeing me on a date with a midget the other night, but that was a mistake. I was set up by a friend. I understand why you'd have got the hump. I did when I thought that you and Karen were seeing each other. I was so jealous. So do you think we could maybe go out on a date? A real one? I'm not normally this forward but my parents think I'm a sad, sex starved spinster and maybe they've got a point! So I'm putting myself out there. For you. What do you reckon? Shall we bite the bullet? Shall we go out and see where it leads to." I manage to pull myself off the ground, I could see Mikes silhouette walking closer to the front door, hearing the footsteps padding nearer. Oh God here we go. I smooth down my hair and plaster what I hope is a sexy smile on my now red face. The door opens and...what the fuck have I done. There stands a woman in the open door of Mike's house, an attractive woman a look of pure amusement etched on her face. But the worst part of it all is that she was wearing just one of Mikes T-shirts, and nothing else. She just stared at me. Unfortunately I couldn't see much else as tears of mortification were running down my face, I just turned and ran. She called out something after me but I didn't hear her. I ran into my house, ran up to my bedroom and cried and cried and cried some more. Oh the absolute shame of it.

CHAPTER TWELVE

Three hours of deep, sleep later, a hot shower and a can of gin and tonic, I felt, well, a lot worse actually. I still felt horrifically embarrassed. My skin prickled when I thought about what I'd done. We'd have to move house now, I suppose. I couldn't ever face Mike again. I'd have to adopt a disguise every time I left the house in the meantime. Or leave through the back door, climb over the back fence and leave my car in the neighbouring street in order to avoid contact with him. No, moving house would be the easiest option here. For now though, I couldn't wallow in my bedroom as I'd have liked to, as I had dinner plans. Although I was sure Karen would understand once she'd heard what I'd done. I'd made a pasta bake for Nicole and James, threw in some random vegetables that I was sure would just get picked out and left on the side. I'd had a dozen missed calls and texts from Elaine whilst I was in my mortification induced coma. I was still ignoring her. I was still as mad as hell at her. I'm five foot ten and a half why would you set someone up on a date with someone barely over five foot? It was cruel.

I NEED TO SPK TO YOU EMILY X

PLEASE CALL ME ASAP X

I WANT TO EXPLAIN TO YOU BEFORE YOU HEAR IT FROM SOMEONE ELSE. X

It shows how mad I still was that those texts didn't make me immediately call her back. The last text was intriguing but I had my own issues at the moment. Hers would have to wait. It was probably more bullshit about her mums engagement to Roger. "Mum, Mike knocked on the door an hour ago. He was desperate to talk to you." Nicole, true to form, was picking out the peas and broccoli from her dinner and leaving them on the worktop. Both kittens, despite not being allowed on the worktop, were on the worktop playing with the discarded vegetables. Batting them off the surface and onto the floor. Enjoying their new game. "I told him you were asleep." "From now on I'm always asleep when he knocks." I replied, feeling my face flame up again. "Won't he think that's weird?" "Yep, maybe!" Not caring. Him thinking I had a chronic sleep issue was preferable to what that woman would have relayed to him and she obviously had considering he'd already called by. "Have you had an argument with Mike?" she probed. "Where's James?" I said, ignoring her. "Make sure you pick all those vegetables up." "Not sure mum, I'm not his keeper." "Helpful, thanks. I'm off to Karen's. If Mike knocks again, not that he will I suppose, but tell him I've moved to America or something." "Ok, or I'll just tell him you're asleep!" "Whatever." My phone rang again. Elaine. Ignore. "I'm leaving my phone here too, I'm at Karen's if you need me."

Karen looked nervous when I turned up, a bit jittery. "I didn't have any wine at home, but I found these in the back of the fridge." I handed her two cans of gin and tonic. She looked at them and we both laughed. It broke the tension. "Shall we?" she asked. We cracked them open and downed them in one

straight from the can. "We are two classy birds." She commented. "What's for dinner? Something smells nice." I say, my eyes wandering around the her kitchen. "Tapas, olives, warm breads and oils."
"Oh lovely, my favourites." "We just have to wait for someone else first, shouldn't be long though." I raised my eyebrow, Karen ignored it. I had a sudden horrible thought. "It's not Mike is it?" I asked aghast. No, I'd have to leave if it was. It would be too awful for words. Karen looked puzzled. "No, not Mike. Why would it be a problem though? You get on, I thought we'd talked about this, he likes you, you like him." To spill or not to spill that was the question? I decided to spill, much to Karen's absolute amusement. "That is so funny, not obviously the part about him having another woman in his bed, but you know the midget admission and the sex starved bit!" My face blushed furious red again, but I could kind of see the funny side of it looking at it from someone else's view. If it had happened to a friend I'd be wetting myself at their expense.

Who was the woman? A random he'd picked up in a bar? Someone he'd been seeing for a while. It doesn't make sense. Unless it was because he'd thought I'd pulled the other night. A revenge shag to get back at me, although how did he know I'd knock on his door and see her in her undressed state.

The doorbell rang, Karen took a deep breath. I waited patiently for the surprise guest to appear, helping myself to an olive in the meantime. I heard muffled voices in the hallway. A voice I recognised actually. What the… In burst Elaine. Looking completely flustered and out of breath. "Why have you been ignoring me?" she wailed. Karen looked nervous and rather bewildered at the same time.

"Look Elaine, I was ignoring you for a reason, I'm busy right now." I popped another olive in my mouth. Not trusting myself to speak. I still had the hump with her, not even her sad little tear stained face could sway me right now. And she did look rather sad. No, I won't be swayed. "It's so important, I can't risk you finding out any other way, it has to come from me!" She gave Karen a funny look and Karen looked rather scared. She touched her arm as if to warn her to calm down, but Elaine shook her off crossly. What the hell was going on here. "Well spit it out then, seriously it can't be that bad!" Both Karen and Elaine spoke at the same time."I'm a lesbian!""I'm dating your brother!" I looked at them both in shock!

They both looked at each other, wide eyed! Karen obviously wasn't expecting that and looked furious with herself. "I thought you were here to tell her my news!" she said, looking shocked. "Emily I'm so sorry I shouldn't have shouted it out like that, I was waiting for Simon to turn up, we were going to tell you together." I just stared at her. "That's your big secret? That you're shagging my brother, oh my God I was imagining all sorts!" I burst out laughing. Karen still looked worried. "It's not just shagging!" She said humpily. "I love him." Turning red. What? Love? I couldn't process it especially with the other bombshell that had just been dropped. Elaine was slumped against the doorframe, tears in her eyes looking completely defeated. "You're gay?" I ventured tentatively. "I've only just found out. Well I guess I've always known really but never wanted to admit it. It's probably why I've dated so many men but never made it beyond a third date." She took a deep breath. I smiled encouragingly at her to continue. I hadn't expected that .Karen passed her a glass of wine, Elaine took it gladly and downed it in one. Karen passed me one too but I decided to wait until I'd heard the whole story before getting drunk, sorry drunker.

"I came out to mum tonight," she gulped back sobs. "she was amazing! Really supportive, actually her and Roger thought it was you that was gay, no idea why, but she was great. I felt dreadful especially how badly I've treated her and Rodger the last few weeks." "I'm sure she understands," I lied. I personally thought Elaine had acted like a spoiled brat when it came to her mother's relationship with Roger but this wasn't the time to bring that up. They probably thought I was gay due to me telling Roger I was when I was rejecting his advances that time in the utility room. Elaine gay? Had I ever wondered? Nope I could honestly say not. I just thought she was a bit of a slapper for the amount of men she'd gone through over the years. Had she ever made it obvious that she preferred the female of the species? Nope, not really. It was certainly a surprise, but oddly at the same time it sort of made sense. Elaine was so perfect in so many ways, her dating disasters never really made much sense. She was the sort of person who should have settled down at twelve years old and stayed gloriously happy forever. "And just so you know, all those times we had sleepovers when we were younger or went swimming I didn't look at you that way, I mean you're not my type at all. I just don't want you to feel uncomfortable around me." She said all in a rush. To be honest It never entered my head that she might have lusted after me, now it had though. Was she protesting too much. Strangely I still didn't feel uncomfortable. Elaine was just Elaine. Just because she'd come out wouldn't make her any the less annoying. "It's fine, I'm glad you've told me, well us." "You don't mind?" She asked, looking pathetically grateful, first at me then at Karen. "I wouldn't be much of a friend if I did. I'm guessing you've met somebody special then?" Her whole face lit up. "Yeah her name is Jac, well Jacqueline, she's amazing. We met online and just clicked instantly I didn't even realise until that moment what I was or what I was looking for. But I've found her." Wow, how cheesy, but it explained a lot. Elaine turned to Karen. "I'm sorry to barge in like this, I was worried that my mum had told Emily's mum and that she would get to her first,

given that she likes a bit of gossip. I couldn't let that happen."
"No problem, I was just convinced when you barrelled through my door that you'd found out about me and Simon and were here to spill the beans. Which is why I blurted it out the way I did, instead of waiting for him to arrive." "You and Simon, hey?" I said turning to Karen, she looked a little nervous again. "How in God's name did that coupling ever happen?" I sipped my wine, studying Karen's reactions. Her whole face lit up too. Great! Everybody was in love and contented except for me again. I slugged my wine back morosely. "Do you remember that night out where you got so drunk and were dancing on the table in that club ?" "How can I forget, I got manhandled out of the club by the doorman. It was the single most embarrassing thing that has ever happened to me...until today that is! Oh and on my birthday!" "Well, your brother was in the club too, but you hadn't remembered that and I wasn't going to bring it up, then you did." She looked quizzingly at me. "I had a vague hazy memory of him, in a suit, looking out of place, but then he brought it up at Easter." "He'd come straight from work, he looked hot!" I pulled a face at her. "Sorry, was that too much? Too soon?" I nodded, still grimacing. "We got talking and got on really well. Obviously he was with Cassia at the time but we just clicked, you know?" No I wanted to say, I don't know. Having never really clicked with anyone like that. Well apart from Mike but that was now a moot point. "Well, after you got thrown out, he helped put you in a taxi and he messaged me later that night to see if we got home ok and we just carried on talking ever since." She sighed and pulled a face. "It wasn't planned and nothing happened until after he split from Cassia, we've only been on two official dates."
"But he's such a smug twat!" I said. "Not with me, I'm pretty sure all that is all an act for your benefit!"
"Oh my God!" I exclaimed. "You're a bloody cougar!" Karen blushed red. "Appears I am, yes!" The doorbell rang. That'll be

the smug twat himself. Simon appeared sheepishly into the room. "Am I in your bad books?" he asked looking rather contrite for a change. He had a large bunch of flowers in his hand. "Well if it isn't Romeo himself." I grin at him. "Are they for me?" He looked embarrassed. "Nooo, they are for Karen actually," he handed them to her and kissed her on the cheek. You'd have to be blind to have missed the look that passed between them. I felt like the giant gooseberry in the room. "Well, what an evening of revelations!" I declared loudly. We all looked at each other and burst out laughing, Simon's was still of the nervous variety though. "I had to come down hard on mum," Simon admitted. "She became obsessed with finding out who my new woman was." I grimaced at this, while Karen glowed at being called his woman, pass me the sick bucket please. This would take some getting used to. "I was just worried if mum told you instead of us then it might all get a little messy."
"And we wouldn't want that!" I agreed. I just put two and two together. "K not Kay? Karen was just K singular in your phone?" "Yeah, it's how Cassia found out I was seeing somebody else. She just didn't know who." "Also," said Karen "I'm pretty sure she is your peeping tom and your lurker in the bush!"
"She was trying to find out what Simon was up to, we think she might have guessed it was me via snooping on Facebook, and was prowling about knowing that we were friends and neighbours!"
"Yeah that kind of makes sense," I agreed. Glad it was Cassia and not Graham or a random weirdo.
The camera!! Of course, it must have been Cassias who left it at my parents during one of her little pop ins. It wasn't my house that was the object of interest it was Karen's. Phew..

"Shall we eat?" Asked Karen changing the subject. "I'm sure it'll go round four of us." It turned out to be a really good evening after all, if I ignored all the soppy looks flowing between my brother and my best friend. The wine also flowed rather nicely and instead of any awkwardness in the light of all the gut spilling tonight it felt like everything was back to normal. Well as long as the two love birds kept their hands to themselves in my presence, I wasn't sure I was ready to see public displays of affection between these two yet. "I'm still pretty pissed off with you though Elaine!" "What now? I thought you were cool with it, I thought you understood?" She wailed. "No not the lesbian thing, couldn't give a shit about that! The fact you set me up with a fucking midget!" "Oh that, yeah sorry but William is a nice guy." she said huffily, not sounding sorry at all. "I thought you'd get on, opposites attract and all that!"

"I guess it's not his fault he still wears kids clothes, maybe that's why he does all those extreme sports to make up for the fact he has a little willy!" "Wow, I thought you said you didn't get on, but you managed to touch his willy in the space of your twenty minute date?" Touché, things were definitely back to normal. I slapped her with my napkin, while she shrieked with laughter ."Anyway, let's make a toast," Simon said raising his glass. "To no more secrets, good times and everything getting back to bloody normal!" I shot him a look, nothing about this was normal. I don't think I'd ever socialised with Simon anywhere unless it was at our parents house. This might possibly be a first. It felt ok, right now.

Just as we all raised our glasses and clinked. "Cheers!" The back foot flung open and there stood Nicole with my phone held out in front of her, tears running down her face. "Nicole, what on earth is wrong?" I shouted, running to her. Although my gait was slightly staggered. "It's James!! He's been kidnapped!" We all just looked at her, waiting for the punchline. "Look!" She shoved my phone at me.

I HAVE YOUR SON. I'LL EXCHANGE HIM FOR MY KITTENS! CALL ME.

"Cassia has kidnapped James?" I felt confused. Simon, Karen and Elaine all looked shocked at the message. "Cassia couldn't kidnap a fucking cucumber let alone a sixteen year old boy!" declared Simon. "I have to admit though, she is a complete and utter fruit loop!" he added unhelpfully. Karen nodded in agreement. You should see the messages she's sent me when she only suspected I was seeing Simon! "Not helpful guys!" I said crossly, panic gripping me that this complete and utter fruit loop had my son. "Are you sure Nicole?" "There's a photo as well." sobbed Nicole. "Oh God, is he ok? Is he tied to a chair and beaten up?" I felt sick to my stomach. What a sick bitch. There was no way she was getting away with this or having those innocent little kittens back. "Well no," admitted Nicole " he's eating a doughnut, looking perfectly happy but that's not the point is it?" "Well no," I agreed looking at my 'kidnapped' son sitting stuffing his face on what appears to be my parents sofa. All of a sudden I felt like I was having an out of body experience. I felt like I was trapped in a dodgy, slapstick sitcom where nothing made any sense at all, but the audience found it rip roaringly funny. The copious amount of wine I'd consumed tonight wasn't helping with my clear thinking. "Simon phone mum or dad and see if Cassia has taken James there. You never know they might all be sitting together watching Casualty together." "Yep, I'm on it...wait though, no they aren't at home tonight they've gone out with Sandra and Rodger to celebrate their engagement! I spoke to dad earlier." "Yes, that is true." Elaine confirmed. "So Cassia has broken in to our parents house then?" I wondered out loud. "Should I phone Jac?" asked Elaine. "Get her to come over?" I stared at Elaine dumbfounded. "Look, while I'm happy that you're now a lesbian and you've met the love of your life, do you really think now is the right time to invite her round to meet your friends, with all this going on? Seriously we have a situation here!" I said somewhat hysterically. "My son is being held hostage!" She took a deep breath before answering. "She's in the police-force, did I not mention that!" Nope. No you didn't. "Then yes please, that would be a good idea." I said feeling a bit mean at my outburst. Still, at the end of the day my son was being held against his will, at his grandparents house eating baked goods. My outburst was allowed. Was I over reacting? No there was definitely a element of concern, but maybe kidnap was too strong a word for what she'd done. "Right, Nicole go and put the cats in the cat carrier..." "We are not actually giving the Lexus and Lily back to her are we?" she asked aghast. "No. Though if it meant getting your brother back in one piece it would be the price to pay. I'm simply thinking we should take them with us. I'm sure Cassia isn't clever enough, but this whole ridiculous 'kidnap' story might be a ruse to get us out the way and then break into our house and take the kittens back!" "We may have a slight problem here!" said Karen suddenly. We all turned to look at her. "We are all pissed as farts. None of us can drive!" Shit, she was right. I'll have to call a cab. "You could ask Mike mum," Nicole pipes up. "He not long ago knocked on our door again...I told him you were still sleeping. He now thinks you have a chronic sleep disorder, I may have laid it on a bit thick." "No, I'll call a cab!" In the end I tried five different taxi numbers, but all had an hour waiting time. Damn it! "Just ask Mike." Karen whispered. "He'll do it, and clearing the air might be a good thing. We'll stay here and keep watch on the house."

"Once Jac arrives, she'll drive me over, if only to scare the bejesus out of her." Elaine gave me a hug. "He'll be fine, he's hardly at any risk really." No, I think the only thing James was at risk at at this present moment in time was type two diabetes. However there was still a deluded ex girlfriend on the loose making ridiculous threats. Time to swallow my pride and ask for help.

I knocked on Mikes door. Trying to forget that the last time I stood in this very place just hours before I nearly died of shame. I couldn't even look at the letterbox. Instant cringe worthy memories. The kittens miaowed in the carrier by my feet. He answered almost straight away and looked ridiculously pleased to see me. I cut him off before he could say a word. "Sorry Mike, I hope I'm not interrupting anything," I said pointedly. " I'm here to ask a favour actually. I've had a drink but I need a lift, James has got himself into a situation and needs rescuing." "You're awake. Finally." he joked, his eyes sparkling with mischief, damn it, he knew Nicole had been lying for me. And clearly I hadn't been asleep as I'd been drinking enough wine to sink a ship. Thank God for the polo mint. "Yes, I'm awake," I replied stating the obvious. "So where do you need to go?" he asked reaching for his keys. I climbed into his truck. To his credit he didn't even seem to find it strange that I was bringing the kittens with me. I placed them between us. The close proximity to a man I fancied who'd slept with another woman just hours ago was excruciating. Thank God I had James's predicament to take my mind off how nice he smelt and how good he looked in that tight T-shirt. At least he was now wearing a shirt. Concentrate Emily, your son could be in danger. "So where does he need rescuing from?" Asked Mike, pulling away. I waved to the crowd outside my house. They all waved back. It was rather surreal. "My parents house." "Your son needs rescuing from

his grandparents?" Mike had reason to look confused. I agree it sounded ridiculous. "No he's been kidnapped by my brothers crazy ex girlfriend, she wants her kittens back in exchange for my son! For some reason she's taken him to my parents house, they are out for the evening and are unaware their house is being used to hold him hostage. We assume she's broken in. It might all be a ruse to get me out of the way and steal the kittens from my house while I'm gone, hence why I'm bringing them with me." I said it very calmly even though I was nervous as hell. I also felt a little out of breath. Mike looked at me opened mouthed. "There's certainly never a dull moment when you're around is there?" He chuckled. "Look about earlier..." "Can we not do this Mike, it was excruciating enough at the time without having to rehash it over again." I wasn't so much red in the face, but puce and started to have heart palpitations. Mike was silent, for precisely two seconds.
"It wasn't what you thought. What did you think by the way?" "What part of not rehashing it did you not understand?" I felt myself growing redder again. My voice getting higher, I'm pretty sure only dogs could hear me now. "It was my ex wife," he carried on regardless. Would it be childish to put my fingers in my ears and start humming? Ex wife! That makes the story so much more palatable. Not.
"Her water tank burst causing a ridiculous amount of damage to her house, obviously she needed somewhere to go there and then." Well obviously, and the ex husband was her first port of call? Michael certainly wouldn't be mine. "I offered to help," he continued "by giving her, her new husband and my daughter a bed for the night. They've gone now, the insurance company have arranged temporary accommodation." Ok so this wasn't what I was expecting to hear. I wasn't sure how to proceed after hearing this rather welcome news. "Well obviously, that's exactly what I thought had happened." I lied, trying to save face. "Is that why you turned into sleeping

beauty then every time I knocked?" he laughed. Luckily we then pulled into my parents road, discussion over for now. He cut the engine. "What's the plan?" he asked. We looked at the my parents house, which was in darkness apart from the flickering light from the television. "We go in! I'm assuming she broke in around the back, the front looks secure enough. Bring the cats would you please. Just in case she's lurking around waiting to ambush!" We both theatrically looked around us. Nope nothing out of the ordinary. But knowing the daftness of Cassia she could well be wearing one of her wooden dresses and be disguised as a tree! There was still no signs of a break in around the back either, I tried the door and to my surprise it opened. Mike and I looked at each other. "Do you think I need a weapon?" I hissed at him.

"No, you've got me instead I won't let the crazy bitch anywhere near you!" He gave me that intense look, I'll not lie, it gave me butterflies in my tummy. I mentally slapped myself, concentrate Emily, your son is being held hostage by a crazy lady. We crept in, I could hear the television on low. A pack of five doughnuts lay open on the kitchen work top, only two left! If we made this out alive I'd be having words with that boy and putting him back on my healthy eating diet. We crept to the doorway that was ajar. Mike squeezed my hand in support. The kittens mewed pathetically. I pushed the door open and nearly had a heart attack. There was my James, lying unconscious on his back on my parents sofa. Blood covered the front of his T-shirt and he appeared to be frothing at the mouth. What had she done to him? "Oh my God!" I screamed running to him. "Call 999!" Mike got out his phone. I shook James hard. Screaming at him to wake up. He opened his eyes. "Oh thank Christ for that!" I exclaimed before realising three things pretty quickly.

One: It wasn't blood covering his chest it was strawberry bloody jam, from the doughnuts.

Two: He wasn't foaming at the mouth at all, it smelt suspiciously like a banana milkshake moustache.

And Three: He wasn't unconscious, he was merely asleep."

"What's going on mum?" He said sleepily. "Hold the 999 call!" I yelled to Mike, but Mike had already put his phone back in his pocket. He was smirking, probably at the absurdity of it all. "Where's Cassia?" I ask, pulling him up to a sitting position. "Did she hurt you?" He looked confused."Why would she hurt me?" "Because she's bat shit crazy. She sent me a text saying she'd exchange you for the kittens!" "Oh!" He replied. "Is that all you can say? Oh! What did she tell you? How did she get you here?" "She picked me up from football, she said there was a family emergency and that she had to drop me off here and wait for you to call. She bought me a MacDonald's," he said happily. My son, anyone's for a Big Mac! "You didn't think to question this and maybe text me or Nicole what that emergency might be? Cassia and Simon aren't even together anymore!" "Aren't they?" he said, confused. I wanted to shake him! Was he really so dense? Of course he was, he was a teenage boy who only cared about, PlayStation, boobs and MacDonald's, apparently. "Did she break in to Grandma's house?" I asked. "No she had a key," he replied. "But she gave it to me, it's in my pocket."
I surmised she'd probably stolen one during one of her random tearful visits to my mum. "James, whatever happens Grandma must never know about this. Ok? Comprende?" Did I just say Comprende in front of a man? One that I'm attracted to? I'm an idiot. If Mike hadn't ran screaming into night by now

I'd be very surprised. I'd also question his sanity if he was still there standing behind me.
I turned slowly around, yep, he was still there looking amused. I began the tidy up operation. By the time I'd finished it was like we'd never been there. We all climbed back into Mike's truck after that, the atmosphere felt a bit flat. Clearly I was massively relieved that we hadn't had to do the whole hostage negotiation thing with a crazy lady. However, now I just felt a bit of a mug. Why hadn't I just phoned James and double checked that he'd been snatched and all of this could have been avoided. The kittens were going mental in their carrier by this point. I'd be glad to get them home and set them free. Obviously with my son sat beside us Mike and I could not continue our previous conversation, this might work to Mikes advantage, if I'd just witnessed the craziness that Mike had just been subjected too I might have second thoughts about me too. I decided to check in with home. Simon answered straightaway. "Emily thank God! How is James? Have you found him?" He sounded frantic. "We didn't want to call in case the phone went off at the wrong moment " "Calm down, he's safe." I heard Simon shout out to the others that he was safe, a cheer went up. It sounded like a party back there. "Look don't worry, we have Cassia! She's sitting in the back of a police car. You were right, as soon as you drove off she appeared and tried to break into your house. She smashed a panel in the back door,
luckily Jac turned up at that point and arrested her. It was all a bit crazy for a while!" "You're safe," I told James after I hung up the phone "she's been arrested for breaking into our house. Thank goodness I brought the cats with me. Crazy bitch!" James nodded, his expression didn't change. I think he just thought I was being an overprotective mother again. There was a welcoming committee when we arrived back, the police car dominating the space in front of my house. It's blue lights

casting an eerie glow. Simon, Karen and Elaine standing outside, still all sipping wine I might add. Like they were attending a street party. Nicole was at the front room window, she come running out when she saw us. It looked like she about to give her brother a huge hug but instead she grabbed the cat carrier from him instead and marched off into the house. Giving Cassia the finger as she stalked past. Cassia let out a blast of expletives. Rocking about like the crazy person she was. She needed sedating or putting down if you asked me. Simon just shook his head at the sight of her thrashing about. I could read his mind and it was along the lines of 'what the fuck was I thinking?' It turned out that Cassia was my peeping tom, that's how she discovered the kittens were in residence. Damn, I felt a bit bad for accusing Graham now, but Graham definitely had his own issues going on so I wouldn't lose too much sleep over him. Apart from Nicole everyone else treated James as though he was a hero who'd escaped from a prisoner of war camp.

"You ok buddy?" Simon ruffled his hair. Patting him on the back. "Good to have you back." Elaine said tearfully. Squeezing his hand. "You must have been so scared." Karen said squeezing his arm. Yes, it must have been terrifying being driven through the drive through at McDonald's. I rolled my eyes.

James looked rather confused, as well he might, I pushed him on through the crowd of well wishers into the house. I looked round for Mike wondering what he was making of this circus, but he'd disappeared. I sighed, I wasn't at all surprised. I bet he was packing his bags right now. I'd wake up in the morning to find a for sale sign outside his house. Things got a bit blurry after that. Maybe it was all the wine from earlier, but I started to feel a bit sick and shaky. I wanted to confront Cassia but was warned by Jac that it wasn't a good idea. Jac who by the way was a bit of a babe. Quite tall, slim, long dark hair and olive skin. She had a Latino look about her. Sexy. "You're punching above your weight there," I joked to Elaine. She beamed in response. "I know." "Cassia has accused you of stealing her kittens" Jac said, pulling me aside. Simon has confirmed that he gave them to you as a gift, he paid for them and all the equipment that came with them. He has a bank statement to prove it. She's been arrested for breaking and entering your home." "What about kidnap and the blackmail?!" I wondered out loud. "Technically, despite the silly text she sent all she really did was take your son out for tea, I can't imagine a charge of kidnapping will stick I'm afraid." Jac smirked looking amused. "Fair enough." She had a point there. "By the way, it's nice to finally meet you, despite the weirdness of the situation." she said. "I've heard so much about you." "Likewise," I replied."well the nice to meet you but, I didn't know you existed until tonight." "It's difficult coming out."she replied, giving Elaine an encouraging look.

It was time to call it a night. I hugged and thanked my friends for all their help. Jac drove off with the prisoner handcuffed in the back, but not before a lingering goodbye with Elaine who then jumped into a waiting taxi. Simon and Karen disappeared pretty quickly too. I didn't want to wonder too much why they are in such a hurry to be alone. After double locking the front door, I went into the front room, the kittens were getting rid of some of their pent up energy from their confinement and were going crazy. One of them had taken a shit on the sofa she was that pleased to be home. Fab. I wandered into the kitchen and had the shock of my life. A silhouette of a man by the back door. I screamed, making him swear. Hang on... I turned on the outside light, thank god it was only Mike but he was armed with a hammer. He looked menacing for a second there. "I've fixed your door panel," he explained. "Temporary for now, but I'll get a mate round to do it properly tomorrow." I nodded silently, here come the tears. They rolled silently down my face. Mike walked over, thankfully placing the hammer on the worktop first and he enveloped me in a big bear hug. We stood there for a while. Him just holding me. It had been so long since I'd had physical contact with a man that the intensity of it took me by surprise. I took in his warmth and his smell. It was lovely. He kissed me on the forehead. "Get some sleep. We will talk tomorrow." I nodded, unable to say much else without blubbing. "You've been through quite an ordeal," he murmured. I certainly had.

CHAPTER THIRTEEN

"Emily, darling please tell me you are well again. I need you. It's absolute carnage here without you!" Logan's wheedling voice penetrated my eardrum painfully. Why did I answer the phone? I really needed another day to recuperate. My head was all over the place. I coughed. "I'm still not feeling too great to be honest," I coughed again. "Can't you suck a cough sweet then dear?" His voice suddenly sounded a little cooler, I think he was on to me, time to pull out the big guns. "Logan, last night somebody broke into my house and kidnapped my son (may God forgive me for my exaggeration) I've had no sleep (another lie, I slept like a baby) and I'm waiting for a man to fix my smashed door!" I cough again, trying to sound indignant rather than guilty. "Dear girl, that all sounds faintly ridiculous but definitely something that might happen to you." He was back to being caring Logan again. Phew! "I take it your son was found, unharmed?" he asked, sounding concerned. "Yes, eventually." Yes I really should have mentioned that! "He's resting, I don't really want to leave him alone." Obviously he'd be going to school as normal but Logan didn't need to know that. "Of course, of course, I'll have to get Maud to hang up her tabard and be front of house instead then." He sighed dramatically "Michaela has disappeared. Poof, one minute she was there the next she was gone! The final straw. Money is also missing I'm afraid." I really hoped he wasn't accusing me. "Security cameras confirmed it," he added sadly. "But on the plus side I now have an excellent excuse to get rid of Michaela for good!" I wondered if he'd now hire himself some protection if he was going sack her. I would, she was bloody mental. She was terrifying when riled. Being sacked would definitely ruffle her dry, yellow locks. After hanging up, promising him I'd be back tomorrow a sudden thought hit me. Hadn't Michaela said she was having lunch with The Hunk from crime-stoppers? What if he'd done something to her. Unlikely given she was built like a brick shit house, but you never knew. What if he'd made her steal the money? I looked at her text again, realising that I hadn't actually looked at the photo she'd sent me. I clicked on it, yep there was Michaela looking very pleased with herself and there was...bloody hell, not the criminal but my bloody ex husband who looked slightly bewildered and a tad scared. I text him furiously.

WHERES MICHAELA?

He text back.

WHOS MICHAELA?

I sent him the photo of him and Michaela.

THAT WOMAN IS BLOODY CRAZY! SHOVING HER PHONE IN MY FACE WHILE I'M TRYING TO EAT. INVITING HERSELF TO MY ROOM OR IN THIS CASE MY LUNCH TABLE!

BUT WHERE DID SHE GO???

A CURLY HAIRED DUDE CAME RUNNING IN SHOUTING AND HOLLERING. SHE WENT TO DEAL WITH HIM AND DIDN'T COME BACK. THANKFULLY FOR ME.
WHY?

I ignored him I had the information I needed. Curly haired dude? That must have been Graham. Shouting and hollering, yep definitely sounded like him. Oh well, I'm sure she was fine wherever she was. Not my problem. She could look after herself. I just hoped Logan could if she took it badly.
I poked my head in James's bedroom and watched him sleep for a minute, he looked so peaceful. Although there was never any real danger last night it still could have been so different. My sweet little boy. Then he farted loudly and stuck his hand down his pants for a good old scratch so I beat a hasty retreat. I'd give him another ten minutes before I started yelling at him to get up. I thought back to what Michaela had told me previously, she'd definitely told me she'd hooked up with with someone, I wrongly assumed she meant the dodgy looking guy but she must have been talking about Michael!
I also felt rather bad about tarring that guest with a criminal brush, he was probably just a normal guy on a business trip. It wasn't his fault his eyes were too close together making him seem untrustworthy.
I was too quick to judge, I vowed to try better in future. I text Michael again.

YOU'RE A LIAR! SHE TOLD ME SHE SLEPT WITH YOU!! IN THE SHOWER!!

ONLY THE ONCE! WHAT'S IT GOT TO DO WITH YOU ANYWAY?

DICKHEAD!

The cats were mewing for breakfast, I fed them and went to make myself a cup of tea when the doorbell rang. I could see the outline of two familiar figures waiting to be let in. Oh bloody hell what did they want? It was way too early for a parental invasion. "Hey mum and dad," I plastered on a fake smile. "This is a nice surprise, although totally unexpected," Not to mention rather unwelcome. I breezed on, "Come in, come in." Normally I'd get at least a weeks notice before a visit. Enough time to hire someone to come round and deep clean my house. Both looked rather serious. Unsmiling. Unsurprisingly my dad looked rather grumpy, he'd probably been frog marched here against his will. Dad only really visited three places other than home. The rugby club, the golf course and the pub. This would be out of his comfort zone. Mum looked around like she had an unpleasant smell under her nose. This unfortunately was actually the case as I hadn't emptied the cat litter tray this morning and the smell of cat poo was wafting not so enticingly around the room. Mums eagle eye also spotted the peas on the floor and the collection of wine bottles and empty cans of gin and tonic on the side.
I just knew I'd start getting AA leaflets through the post, again, anonymously of course. I had told her I'd stopped drinking midweek. The scene before her showed conflicting evidence. "Tea?" I suggested. I think dad was about to say yes please when mum put out her arm out to stop him. "We're not here for pleasantries," she barked. She was also probably worried he'd catch something from my dirty kitchen. I couldn't blame her. "Is there something you want to tell us?" I wondered if this was about Simon again. Fuck it, I know it wasn't my place to tell her who he was seeing, but I was getting pretty pissed off about it all right now. It was hardly a secret anymore. "Ok so I know who Simons mystery woman is. Sorry I didn't immediately down tools and contact you but I had other things

going on last night," I said, watching mum as she gave dad an 'I told you so look'. "Emily that is such yesterday's news, Simon and Karen announced they were in a relationship on Facebook this morning! I liked it. I've moved on you should too!" she said patronisingly. I resisted the urge to scream. So, could this be about Elaine then? I knew they had been out with Sandra and Roger the night before. Surely they had discussed it. "Elaine's a lesbian, did you know that?" I threw out there. "Of course we know! But should you be spreading it around? I hope you are not being prejudiced Emily, there was a time we thought you was batting for the other side too!" I couldn't bloody win. Dad sighed uncomfortably. I wondered if it could possibly make matters worse if I started tipping the dregs of the empties on my worktop into my mouth. Anything to dull the pain of this visit. "Do you want to admit to anything love?" Dad prompted kindly. I shrugged my shoulders. "Can you give me a hint?" I asked. I did wonder then if it was about last night and James's 'kidnapping' and Cassia's arrest but why wouldn't they just come out with it instead of all this good cop bad cop routine rubbish. "We have some concerns." mum said.

"Anything in particular!" "About James actually." Oh I wasn't expecting that. Had they seen him smoking? Little sod, surely he knew the rules of underage smoking. To hide in parks and fields, behind bushes and don't get seen by Grandma. "Is it true you attacked him the other day?" mum said.

Dad rolled his eyes. "Of course I didn't attack him. What are you talking about?" I said in confusion. Was I dreaming. Yes I must be dreaming. "Did you attack his with a carton of milk?" Mum carried on.

"I did not attack him. I threw an empty milk carton at him." I didn't think she needed to know I'd thrown it twice. "Does that not constitute as attacking?" Mum argued. "An empty milk carton thrown from a distance? No. Not at all. Who told you

anyway?" I knew James wouldn't have, he'd have forgotten about it two seconds after it had happened. "I was on the phone to Nicole at the time and heard it all!"
Yeah, I vaguely remembered Nicole with her phone. That was a bit embarrassing, it wasn't my finest moment. I had been screaming furiously. "They drank all the milk. Six pints in twelve hours. Neer mind that most of those twelve hours they were asleep. I was pissed off. I wanted a cup of tea." "Darling it's milk, losing your temper over something so trivial could be a sign." "A sign that my children are selfish? I agree." "A sign that you're not coping? That you might have a problem?" Her eyes wandered to the empties in the corner. "I do not have a problem with alcohol," I said wearily. "Are you sure? It would explain why your house looks the way it does, and why you have such a short temper lately."
We all just stared at each other. I think my mum and dad have very short memories. They had constantly yelled at me and Simon over the most mundane reasons when we were kids. I obviously learnt from the masters of overreaction! Christ almighty. I'm pretty sure I was once grounded for accidentally knocking over a vase. Albeit a very expensive vase when I was chucking a hacky sack around the room, despite being asked not to, see, overreaction! They both stood there as if they were about to stage an intervention. "Would it surprise you to know we had security cameras fitted in our house?" mum said looking for my reaction. Oh shit. I kept my face impassive. They'd obviously seen James lolling about on their new sofa without a care in the world, massacring a bag of doughnuts spreading their stickiness everywhere. I did not know that!" I admitted honestly. Mum looked like she'd won a small victory here, dad just looked pained. "Do you know why we had security cameras installed?" "No, obviously not as I wasn't aware of their presence." "Nor do we actually," admitted mum. "Your father thought it would be a good idea."

She gave him a look. I gathered there was a beef over the cameras. "But it has come in very handy. Do you know what we saw last night?" "James in your house eating your doughnuts?" I pretended to guess, like I had suddenly become a clairvoyant.

"But why was James In our house eating our doughnuts in the first place? Is he using it as a safe house to get away from here? We saw you shaking him savagely. How did he even get in?" I suddenly felt furious. I let her have it with both barrels. "Ok, I wasn't going to tell you this, I didn't want to worry you both, but last night Cassia, sent me a text saying I could have James back in exchange for her kittens!" Mum and dad looked at each other in puzzlement. "You mean she took him against his will?" dad asked sounding confused, then bloody furious. "Yes!" I confirm. I neglected to mention the bribe of a Big Mac, that information was strictly on a need to know basis. They definitely didn't need to know. "She picked my son up from football training telling him there'd been a family emergency, she took him to your house, using a key to get in. Then told told him to wait for a phone call! James is sixteen, he is clueless and was perfectly happy and oblivious to what was happening."

"She had a key?" Mum said looking bewildered. "Yes this one," I handed her back her key. Mum examined it and nodded, yep it was definitely her key. "It's the spare from the drawer." I ignored her.

"She did it to get me out the way here, so she could break in and steal back the cats! She smashed my door and was subsequently arrested by Elaine's policewoman girlfriend." Mum and dad just looked at me with open mouths. "I assume that when Cassia popped in on her many random visits she was left alone and had access to the spare key?" Mum nodded, white as a ghost. Dad looking furious with her. "I told you befriending that girl was a mistake." He barked.

"Especially after Simon had dumped her, do you never listen?" "I'm also guessing that she was aware the cameras had been installed?" Mum nodded again. "I'm guessing there was no sign of Cassia on your CCTV? She knew where to avoid." I was too tired to be angry anymore, I could kind of understand why they might think there were problems at home and we had been caught on camera in their house in suspicious circumstances. Things had definitely been weird around here lately. But to actually think James would need a safe house. It was hurtful and ridiculous. "Didn't you hear our conversation though?" I asked dad. "It's only pictures it doesn't record sound. We just watched you come in, it looked like you were yelling and shaking James." Dad looked like he wished he'd paid the extra fifty quid for sound so he didn't have to be standing here having this extremely awkward conversation."I thought he was dead, but it was jam on his top not blood. I was yelling at Mike to call 999, until I realised my mistake." "Who's Mike?" Mum asked ears pricking up. "Builder Mike." "Not now Sheila!" barked dad.

Cue the next ten minutes of tears, apologies and begging of forgiveness, well not so much crying or begging but mum obviously felt bad that much was obvious. So she should. I may be a lot of things but an abuser of my child was not one of them. A possible alcoholic, I'll give her that one but not the other. "Emily, just because you are an adult now doesn't mean I don't worry about you. I probably worry more. You're a great mum, but you've had an awful lot on your plate lately. None of us are perfect. Please when it all gets too much just ask for help. I'm sorry for jumping to conclusions."

Saying sorry wasn't easy for my mum. She looked a bit red around the throat. I nodded tearfully, glad the recriminations were over. Mum then directed her anger elsewhere. Dragging dad to the police station to report Cassia for stealing a key to their house. She had a rage on. "I was nice to that girl!! Even when I didn't have to be! Stealing! The absolute nerve of her. I even offered her the chocolate hobnobs instead of the plain ones!" I could hear her chewing off dad's ear as she dragged my poor father down the driveway.

Nicole got up soon after that and left for work. None the wiser that Grandma had been round accusing her poor mother of abuse. I'd forgotten to wake James up so I left him asleep. After his 'ordeal' he probably needed it. Plus it helped my cover story with Logan, not that he'd check of course but it made me feel better. I then spent the next couple of hours cleaning my, quite frankly filthy house.
Mum was right I had let things go of late. I swept, polished, washed and hovered. I decluttered cupboards, tidied drawers. Threw out a lot of old crap to make way for my boxes of memories. It felt good. A good cleansing purge was good for the soul. I finally threw out the sugar puffs, although it pained me to do so. What a waste. I even, changed my bedsheets, not because I was planning on inviting anyone in but you know it was good to be prepared for any eventuality. Mike's mate Shawn popped round and replaced the glass in my door, refusing to accept money assuring me that Mike had 'sorted' it.

THANKS MIKE FOR GETTING MY DOOR FIXED. HOW MUCH DO I OWE YOU? X

YOU OWE ME DINNER AND A DRINK. MY TREAT OBVIOUSLY LOL XX

YOU'RE ON! BUT ON ONE CONDITION! IM PAYING. NO ARGUMENTS XX

TONIGHT?? XX

GOES WITHOUT SAYING XX

A date was made. Yay.

I made a shepherds pie for the kids for dinner. I then spent the next few hours beautifying myself for my first real date in years, well one that actually excited me anyway. One that wasn't with a hobbit. I stayed away from the blunt razor blades this time for obvious reasons..

WHERE ARE WE GOING? XX

A SURPRISE!! XX

I NEED TO KNOW WHAT TO WEAR! XX

YOU'LL LOOK PERFECT WHATEVER YOU'RE WEARING. XX

Not helpful Mike. Not helpful. So I went smart/casual. A long, back maxi dress. It hugged every curve but in a good way, not in a bag of stones kind of way. I added a colourful scarf to make me look less Morticia Addams like. My hair slightly curled for a change, but on purpose not because of humidity. I donned a cute pair of sandals. Toenails and fingernails painted a matching pretty coral colour. I sprayed myself liberally with Channel. I looked and smelt pretty bloody fantastic, even if i did say so myself. Nicole also mentioned how great I looked too, although I wished she hadn't sounded so surprised. She insisted on taking a photo of me. James walked past and said I looked no different from normal. Which in a weird way I took as a compliment. "You're just mum." He shrugged. "No, tonight James I'm going to be Emily again." I then did something I never really did and posted the photograph of myself on Facebook. Why not? A little bit of self gratification never hurt anyone. I just hoped I got some likes though. How humiliating to not receive any.

Both children had strict instructions to wash and tidy up after themselves. After working my fingers to the bone today I wanted the house to stay clean and tidy for twenty four hours at least. I also warned them to keep the doors locked. I know the Cassia risk was now low, but according to Jac who contacted me earlier she was out on bail. I didn't think she was stupid enough to make her situation worse by contacting us again but this was Cassia we were talking about. She was the ultimate fruit loop. I contemplated asking my mum to babysit, but this was met with boos and 'are you freaking kidding me'. There was also the Graham factor to take in to account. Was he still lurking about or had he finally 'done one'! We could all but hope. Mike knocked on the door at eight o'clock sharp, a bunch of sunflowers in his hand. I took a deep breath and opened the door. He smiled and kissed me on the cheek, he smelt divine, I bit my lip to stop myself grinning like a Cheshire bloody cat who got the cream. Dressed in a pair of black jeans and a blue cotton shirt he looked really smart, instead of his usual rough, rugged builder look, which he also pulled off really well. His face dropped when he saw me. "Is that what you're wearing?" He said aghast. "I'm not driving, I'd thought we'd bike to the restaurant, so I can have a drink. Don't worry 'Ive got a spare one in my garage." He pulled a face at me. "Oh, I guess I could change into some jeans..." my face was a blaze of embarrassment. I turned to go back in but he reached out and grabbed my hand. "'ml only joking," he laughed. "You look absolutely beautiful, perfect!" He smiled again before pulling me close to him to kiss me on the cheek. "I'd rather piggyback you there, rather than make you change out of that dress." "Oh, thank you," my face still ablaze but for a totally

different reason now. "I've got a taxi waiting, come on." He held my hand and opened the door for me to climb in.
We chatted easily on the way.

"There's something I've been meaning to ask?" I said when there was a slight pause in conversation. "How come you spent so much time with Karen? I mean I know you spoke to her about me but..." I trailed off because I wasn't really sure where I was going with it or why I was bringing it up now of all times. Mike, took my hand and kissed it. "I like Karen, she's great and she loves you a lot. I wasn't sure where I stood with you, what with you just coming out of a relationship with that Graham," I made a 'pah ha' noise at this. He carried on regardless, grinning. "I liked talking to her, about you mostly but she also needed someone to talk to and unfortunately she couldn't talk to the person she normally talked to," he pointed at me "because you were part of the dilemma. She obviously didn't want to upset you but she really liked your brother." Well, yes that made a lot of sense actually. I squeezed Mike's hand. "Also," I started and he groaned. "Why didn't you have a first impression of me?" I asked petulantly. "You had one of Karen." "I couldn't be honest about my memory of you because you might have thought I was a right weirdo." "Go on, I'm intrigued." "I thought you were the most perfect woman I'd ever seen, for me anyway. I saw you one morning, just chatting and laughing with Nicole and I just thought she's so out of my league." He looked a bit embarrassed, I leant in and kissed him hard on the mouth. "Now if I'd known that was going to be your reaction I'd have told you sooner!" All of a sudden something caught my attention on the radio. Had I just heard right? "Excuse me," I leant forward and spoke to the taxi driver. "Could you turn the radio up?" "Am I boring you already?" Mike laughed. I shhed him and he actually shhed, looking surprised. "Police are appealing for Michaela Brown from Essex to contact the police as soon as possible after neighbours discovered her three young children home alone. It is believed that she went on holiday with a local man, location unknown. The children are now being cared for by family members. Anyone with any information regarding Michaela's whereabouts should contact this number..." I stared at Mike in amazement. That explained Michaela's sudden disappearance. I can't believe she'd leave her children though. That was rather out of character. Is that what she'd stolen Logan's money for? To go on holiday? "Police believe she is traveling with a man named Graham Hardy, who won two point three million pounds on the national lottery just days before they both disappeared..." No way! I looked at Mike in surprise. "That's not Graham as in your ex mental Graham?" He asked incredulously. I nodded, wide eyed and a hysterical giggle escaped my lips. I wondered if it was my line of numbers that won him the money? How funny and ironic if my bra size had helped him win a few quid. I could see it all so clearly now. Graham finding out that he'd won the lottery, coming to find me at the hotel. I remembered what Michael had said about a curly haired dude arriving shouting and hollering. I guessed that Graham had come to brag rather than try to win me back and Michaela had seen a chance and taken it. All hypothetical of course. I couldn't wait to read about it in the papers over the coming months. Logan wouldn't have to hire protection either. Not if she was on the run or eventually in prison. Losing her job would be the least of her problems. "Well, there you go then," I laughed. "All loose ends tied up nicely." I moved closer to Mike and kissed him full on the mouth again. He kissed me back but then pulled away. "Not quite," he answered. I looked at him quizzicality. "Now tell me more about dating midgets and why your parents think you're a sex starved spinster?" His eyes twinkled mischievously. He laughed. A sound I knew I would never tire of. I sunk down in the seat and covered my face. but deep down I knew that this was it. I was where I was supposed to be, with the person who was going to put an end to my sad spinster, sex starved days. Oh and I got eighty nine likes for my photo, a personal best.

CHAPTER FOURTEEN

Three months later

So for years, unbeknown to me, I had rather meanly been labelled a 'sex starved spinster', by my mother of all people. Who needs enemies, hey? Especially when she also thought me capable of unspeakable things concerning James. She had apologised profusely since that day. I'd obviously forgiven her because it had been a very strange time for all of us. Also, you know, I had thrown that milk carton at James, twice. In her defense, if there was one, for being brutally honest about your daughters sex life, since my marriage ended, I'd spent eight years practising celibacy. With the odd dalliance here and there and a disastrous date or two along the way. An unstable man was thrown in for good measure too, completing the car crash that was the back catalogue of my love life.
But now this was no longer the case, I was a spinster no more. Cue party poppers and champagne, well I prefer prosecco actually, I find champagne rather rank if truth be told. Hark at me, the wine connoisseur. I was in a real relationship, with Mike. The last three months had been blissful. I felt for the first time in a long time, content, happy. Nicole and James liked him. Not just tolerated, I mean genuinely liked him. This was without any money even having to exchange hands. They understood that he made me happy, and if I was happy I was less likely to cause them grief and interfere in their personal business. Although James had been warned that if I ever caught him with cigarettes again, I would smash up his beloved PlayStation. Mike's nine year old

daughter Kimberley liked me too. She was a sweet girl, who had seemed a little wary of my intentions at first. She'd never had to share her daddy with anyone else before so I was extremely careful not to ruffle her feathers. I didn't encroach on their time together, giving them space to do their usual daddy daughter things. While I did my usual things, mostly drink wine and Facebook about how happy I now was. There was a dodgy period in the beginning where Kimmy as she prefered to be called kept referring to to me as 'perfect Emily'. It was always said sweetly but I took it to be sarcasm, I guess sarcasm was the default setting in my house. Apparently not though, it appeared that she genuinely liked me and we got on like a house on fire as long as I respected the boundaries and didn't try to make her eat vegetables. Life isn't a fairytale as we all know, and on our three month anniversary, how sickening that we were celebrating every month together like teenagers, we had our first argument. Over a cat poo. In his new shoes. I'd never seen the pissed off side of lovely, funny Mike before. I wasn't sure if he was messing around or not at first. He wasn't, as it turned out. He really was mad. "One of your bloody cats has shit in my shoe!" He shouted up at me from the bottom of the stairs. Holding out his expensive shoe in disgust. Yep, there was definitely a cat turd lurking in there. I wrinkled my nose. "Well, it might not of been one of my cats," I said back. "Maybe one of the neighbours cats came in and pooed in your shoe!" I tried to be diplomatic, but it sounded lame even to my ear. He looked even more furious at my making excuses for my cats instead of just apologising for it. "You're joking surely!" He said incredulously. "They've never left a poo in anyone else's shoe before. Would you like me to sort it out for you? I've got some antibacterial wipes somewhere." I ask reaching for the soiled shoe. "Well, aren't I the lucky one," he said sarcastically, he then grunted something unintelligible at me and stomped off back to his own house, dumping the offensive poo into the green bin on his way. I didn't think it was the right time to call out that the cat shit wasn't on the list of acceptable items that belonged in a green bin. I had the list stuck on my noticeboard. I had to choose my battles. I turned to my cats who were both sitting on the stairs, smug expressions on their little furry faces. "Now look what you've done!"

That argument was then followed a week later by our second one. It was Saturday morning, we'd been out the night before, with Simon and Karen, dinner at an all you can eat Chinese buffet. Which I did. Mike and Simon had become great mates in the last few months. Simon had never hit it off with Michael, so double dating had been out of the question. Not that Michael and I ever really dated or would have wanted to double date with my little brother if we had.
The only downside to the evening was Karen, who wasn't drinking as she was on antibiotics treating a chest infection. I drank for the two of us though and after the meal we went back to mine for a night cap, JD shots for the men, a pot of green tea for the ladies. It was a great night, full of chatter, laughs and promises to do it again soon. The next morning I woke up and I felt rather humpy. Cross even. Something more than a hangover. Something had annoyed me. What could it be? Mike stirred next to me and wound his arm around my waist pulling me closer to him, well he tried to, he was met with resistance, my resistance. "Morning beautiful," he said kissing my shoulder. I grunted at him. He pulled himself up to look at me. "Are you alright?" "Fine." Meaning clearly I'm not fine by my arsey tone. "What's up?" He said a little less warmly. "Do you know how many times you mentioned your ex wife last night?" I spat at him. The memory of Mike chatting to my brother came springing back.

Even though it was irrational, I still felt rather threatened by Mikes pretty ex wife, despite the fact they had been divorced for longer than they'd ever been married and she was now married to someone else. He looked blankly at me. "I mentioned her twice, in response to your brothers questions." He looked puzzled, as well he might. But I was committed to the argument, backing down would have made me look infantile. "Oh so you're aware you're doing it then, keeping count." "Do you know how many times you talk about Michael?" He counteracted crossly. "Err, only when I'm slagging him off saying what a useless twat he is! You were singing your ex's praises!" "Maybe the lady doth protest too much about her rubbish ex. Plus your brother asked me if I knew an interior designer, I do. Her!"
What? Now he was spouting Shakespeare at me. What craziness had I started here. This was beginning to snowball. Mike got out of bed and started to get dressed. "Where are you going?" I asked sulkily. Maybe he was going to make me a tea and bring it up. "Home!" No tea then. "Call me when you've grown up." He called out as he left the bedroom. "Well that won't be any time soon," I retort, then feeling foolish. Then off he went. I waited for the front door to slam. SLAM..

As I lay there I wondered if that argument had been all my fault? As if they knew, the cats padded into my room and sat staring at me from the end of the bed. I picked up my phone, to text and say sorry, then put it down again. I'd give him time to text me first. I jumped in the shower, hoping by the time I got out he'd have left a message. Nope. No message. Then I heard the distinctive roar of his truck. I flew to the window just in time to see him drive past furiously. Where was he going? I bet he was going to see his ex wife. I'd driven him to back into her arms. I then spent a rather miserable morning pacing about the house, my phone clamped in my hand waiting for him to ring me, feeling like a fool. What if he'd decided to leave me, had I pushed him too far? I cleaned the kitchen floor for want of something to do. My mobile rang bringing me back from the awful pictures in my head of Mike and his ex wife together. Oddly enough they weren't having sex in these pictures they were drinking coffee and he was moaning about me to her. That felt worse bizarrely. "Mike?" I sounded pathetic. "No, it's mum. Is everything ok?" "Yes it's fine, I was just expecting a call from Mike that's all." "Your father and I have an announcement to make, can you all make it to our house tonight for six o'clock please?" More over dramatics. I sighed. "It's a bit short notice mum." Wondering who the 'all' might be?

"I'm well aware of that, I'll provide the refreshments." An announcement? Bloody refreshments? Whatever next? A tombola stall in the utility room? I wonder what on earth could be so important that it couldn't be said over the phone. "You and dad aren't getting divorced are you?" I ask aghast, the thought just hitting me. There was silence on the line. "Yes Emily, after forty five years of being together, now that we are in our mid sixties we've decided to go our separate ways and hunt for The One!! Don't be ridiculous! See you at six!" She rang off before I could say another word. My children obviously got their sarcastic streak from my mother. I hoped that the announcement wasn't to tell us all that one of them was dying. Would you feel the need to provide a light buffet if delivering that devastating blow to your nearest and dearest. I could picture the scene now. "I've got an incurable disease kids, I'm a goner, but here have a cocktail sausage. Cheese puff anyone?" Nope it couldn't be that, I was sure.

My evening then got a whole lot worse when Nicole sauntered into the room wanting a 'favour'. "Grandmas just Facetimed me and said about us going round tonight. I was wondering..." she smiled sweetly at me. "Can I drive there tonight?" She wheedled. Now not only did I have to give up a precious Saturday evening to visit my parents, even though I'd seen them just yesterday. I realised if I let Nicole drive her car tonight, with me offering her my wisdom from the passenger seat then I'd have to stay sober. A mother's life was full of sacrifices. I was sure I could manage one evening without wine, at least until I got home anyway. If I got home, that is. Having been out driving with Nicole once before and hit a concrete bollard within thirty seconds the chances were slightly slimmer than if I were driving myself. I allowed myself a little daydream of me being unconscious in hospital, Mike sitting by my bedside sobbing his heart out. "If only I hadn't spent the whole evening out talking about my ex wife, she'd still be conscious." Nicole had just bought herself a little red fiesta, just a crappy little runabout to help her learn to drive. I really hoped Mike hadn't left me to go back to his ex wife and he might offer to sit in the 'death mobile' the nickname I'd given Nicole's car instead. Also there should be a law about old people using modern technology, plus what cheek! "Why was grandma FaceTiming you?" "She said something about practising, I don't know." Whenever I tried to FaceTime Nicole she cancelled the call and would then send a blunt text saying 'what?' "You don't think grandma and grandad are splitting up do you?" she asked looking worried. "Now I think about it, it was all a bit weird, she seemed emotional." "They've been together forty five years and are well into their sixties, why would they now decide to see if the grass is greener on the other side?" I said patronisingly. Nicole had already stopped listening, eyes glued to her phone. I'd just that minute decided to bite the bullet and call Mike and beg forgiveness for my childish behaviour this morning when I heard the unmistakable sound of his truck coming down the road. I hit the floor and combat crawled across to the window, I slowly peeped out over the window sill. Yep it was him. Mike was getting out of his truck, I quickly ducked down again in case he looked over and saw me being weird at the window. James wandered into the front room at this point and did a double take at me lying on the floor. "What are you doing down there?" He asked. "Looking for my contact lens," I replied, willing him to carry on into the kitchen, leaving it at that. "You don't wear contact lenses." Trust James to take such an interest in me now. "I do now," I barked. In desperation I told him there was a packet of chocolate chip cookies hidden in the washing machine and to help himself. That did the trick and he trotted off like a grateful puppy to retrieve his unexpected treat. I counted to ten then slowed eased myself up to look out of the window again and had the fright of my life. A big face, Mike's laughing face was staring back at me. I screamed loudly, making James jump a mile and then drop a bottle of lemonade all over the kitchen floor spraying it everywhere. I wrenched open the door. "You shit Mike, you scared the living daylights out of me! How did you know I was there?" My heart was hammering away beneath my shirt. Mike was standing there doubled up in laughter, I tried not to stare at the huge bouquet of flowers in his hand. I hadn't expected those. I practised my 'you shouldn't have' speech in my head. "I saw your little face peeping at me in my rear view mirror," he was still chuckling to himself. "Sorry, I didn't mean to frighten you but I couldn't resist it." To be fair I was just glad everything was ok between us but I tried to adopt the air of nonchalance as if deciding whether to forgive such behaviour. "They are beautiful," I said nodding my head towards the flowers. "Shall I put them in water?" I'd already decided to take a photo of them to post on Instagram with the caption 'from my gorgeous bf, he's the best', along with some love heart emojis. "Yes please babe, they're for your mum." Thank God I'd already turned my back to him so he couldn't see me blush with embarrassment over my mistake. I mean, why would he buy me flowers, I was the one in the wrong this morning, I should have bought him flowers. "Yeah she phoned me earlier, inviting us round later, I thought it would be a nice touch." "Yes, a lovely thought." Wondering if it would be terrible to still take a photo anyway and upload to social media, nobody would know they weren't actually for me. Nicole upon hearing Mikes voice bundled back into the room begging him to be her driving buddy instead. "I mean mums ok, but she's just a stress head." My phone then beeped indicating a text. Karen.

WE HAVE ALSO BEEN SUMMONED. DO YOU NEED A LIFT? Xx

Mike agreed to Nicole's request and I offered up a silent hallelujah to whoever might be be looking out for me up there. All was well in my world again, plus I could drink wine tonight. So later, whilst climbing into the luxurious leather seats in Karen's car. I had to grin at the sight of big burly Mike folding himself in half as he attempted to get into Nicole's tiny vehicle. We all then watched in fascinated horror as we watched Nicole's fiesta kangaroo bouncing down the road. Should we wait a while?" Karen asked me. I nodded, I wanted to spare Nicole the embarrassment of how terrible she was, if that first twenty seconds was anything to go by. Especially as James was sniggering away next to me, phone at the ready to start recording her misery. As it was we gave them a five minute head start before leaving ourselves, hopefully enough time would had passed and she'd have gotten over her nerves by now and be driving less like a demented kangaroo. I was also worried we'd end up passing a fiesta wrapped around a lamp

post. Mike and Nicole standing at the roadside watching it as it burst into flames. Luckily not though and the little red fiesta was parked on my parents driveway when we arrived, (phew) although there did appear to be a matching dent now in the left side.
I wasn't even going to ask.

We let ourselves in their house, calling out a greeting as we did. Simon and Karen leading the way, holding hands and gazing soppily at each other. God, shouldn't they be over that now. Although saying th,t Mike and I were still in that, holding hands, kissy, I only want to be with you stage too.
I must admit though, since Simon had been together with Karen he'd definitely mellowed. He certainly didn't act like the pretentious twat I'd been so used to for years, she obviously brought out the best in him. Mum was gushing over the flowers Mike had just given her. Dad was pouring the drinks, Cava unless I was very much mistaken. Were we celebrating something? God, had we missed a special anniversary? I look over at Simon to see if he was thinking the same thing but he was too busy playing with Karen's hair. Pass the sick bucket.
We were congregated in their new kitchen/diner that Mike had helped produce. I felt really proud of him. Just a bit of decorating to finish up and then the overall effect would be magnificent. I had nicknamed it the 'west wing' as it was huge, too huge if we were being honest, now that there was only two of them. But it did look absolutely amazing.
We all sat around the big marble island that dominated the middle of the room, on black leather high backed chairs. "How was the drive over?" I asked Mike, before realising I should be asking Nicole. He could tell me the truth later. I turned to her instead. She was beaming. "It was great after I stopped feeling so nervous, Mike's brilliant, so calm. I want him to come out with me every time, no offence mum." None taken, it was like

I'd been pardoned for a crime I was due to serve twelve to eighteen months for. I snuck a look at Mike to see if he looked horrified at the idea, but he smiled and seemed pretty chuffed at Nicole's words. A rather delicious looking spread was laid out in front of us, including a plate of prawn vol-au-vents, my absolute favourite buffet bite of all time. This instantly made me suspicious, what were they up to? Mum hadn't made prawn vol-au-vents since my eighteenth birthday family gathering in 1996. They were trying to butter us up for something it would seem. "Oh look, cheese twists," cried Simon. "I love mums cheese twists, they're my favourite!" he said to Karen, trying to feed her one. Karen avoided my eye, looking embarrassed, taking it from him and popping it in her mouth herself. I sniggered to myself, Karen had always been such a powerhouse it was nice to see she had also mellowed too with my brothers attention. Yep, cheese twists had just confirmed my suspicions. The parents were definitely up to something. We chatted happily avoiding the elephant in the room. The reason why we'd been summoned tonight. "You're probably wondering why you're here?" Mum began. We all instantly stopped our conversations. And waited.... Dad stood up and put his arm around mum. We all held our breaths. James who until now hadn't even looked up from his phone apart from when he was shoving the next sausage roll into his mouth, sausage rolls were his favourite just in case you were wondering, also turned wide eyed to listen to them. We'd ruled out divorce. It seemed unlikely we'd be celebrating an incurable disease.

A lottery win maybe? Yes, that seemed most likely. Maybe they were going to dish out the dosh tonight . "Your mother and I.." dad began. I willed them to just get on with it "..have decided to travel around the world." They stood there waiting for our reaction. There was none. James simply reached for another sausage roll. I looked at my parents then back at everyone else. They also looked rather blank and confused. "You gathered us here today to tell us you are going on holiday?" I emphasised the word holiday as though it were a disease. All this cloak and dagger behaviour, our favourite foods to announce a bloody holiday? Simon spoke first. "Would a phone call not have sufficed?" he asked, a piece of cheese twist stuck to his jumper. Karen noticed and brushed it off. "Well darling, it's not just a holiday. Were you not listening again, that's always been your trouble, it's more than a holiday. We are going on an all around the world cruise." "Ok," I replied. "So you need one of us to look after the house, pop in and gather the post every other day then?" Again she could have popped that on a post-it note. Why were we here? "No, we are hiring a house-sitter, she comes with fabulous references, and is rather reasonable." "Grandma, I would have done it, for free." Declared a disappointed Nicole. My mother pretended she hadn't heard that. Yeah I bet you bloody would I thought, and host wild parties while you were at it. I remember the time Me, Karen and Elaine had gone away to London for the weekend. James was with his dad and I'd trusted Nicole for the first time at home alone. She was allowed one friend to stay with her. Any gatherings of more than four people was banned, still were. I'd phoned and asked her if she was ok the first morning after we'd left. She told me that her friend Annie was there, they'd had pizza and watched a box set of Doctor Who. Like a fool I'd believed her. I'd then arrived home on the Sunday evening to a relatively tidy house, I'd been impressed and proud of her maturity. The next day however, I'd been hovering and for once in my life actually moved the coffee table and found an empty box of drinking games! I was pretty certain that you needed more than one other person to play drinking games. Then I discovered cigarette ash in one of my candle pots. Livid was an understatement. Then instead of pizza boxes in the outside

bin I'd found empty cans of Cider. At seventeen, with a full time job to go to she'd been too old to ground but the next time I had to stay away for the night her punishment was staying at grandmas house, keys taken away from them both. I also laid it on thick how she had broken my trust. She'd never done it again, either that or hid it better from me. Now I was really confused, a house sitter? "So how long is this cruise then?" Asked Simon. "Obviously longer than the usual two weeks then if you're getting a house sitter." Mum and dad looked at each other and grinned nervously. "We'd be gone five months all in all." "FIVE MONTHS!!" I yelled. "That's not a holiday that's practically emigration!" James nearly choked on his sausage roll and Nicole looked close to tears. Simon and Karen had turned pale and were whispering furiously together. "Do you not think we deserve this?" said dad, uncharacteristically getting involved. Sounding rather stern, normally all conversation was left to mum, mostly because he couldn't get a word in edgeways when she was on one of her rants. "We've worked hard all our bloody lives's and when we cashed in a lucrative endowment we thought why the bloody hell not, let's do it now before we're too old or diagnosed with the unmentionable. It's our time, we have always been there for everyone else. We want an adventure." "Well, I think your dad has said it all really," said mum giving him a squeeze an uncharacteristic soppy look on her face. "Excuse us," interrupted Simon taking Karen by the hand and leading her into another room. What was all that about then?
"We can FaceTime Nicole," mum was comforting my inconsolable granddaughter. I couldn't decide if the tears were because she was desperately going to miss them both or if she was mourning the missed opportunity of housesitting my parents house for practically half a year. James looked forlorn too, but I couldn't help but notice all the sausage rolls were gone. I'd give him the benefit of the doubt to the reasons why

he looked so sad. Mike was beaming and enthusing about how cool it all was. Engaging Dad in conversation about what countries they'd be visiting. Giving me a sympathetic glances every now and then as if sensing my shock and sadness but knowing this was an amazing opportunity for my parents. Dad then asked Mike about the bits of decorating that needed doing while they were away. The problem I was facing right now wasn't the fact they were going away for that amount of time even though it was almost unthinkable that I wouldn't be able to see my parents for almost half a year, (HALF A YEAR!) despite social media updates (I really should accept my mums friend request on Facebook before she left) and FaceTiming. It was still a long time to not actually see them in person. Knowing that they were just up the road was a comforting thought. I plastered on a happy face and found that I genuinely was for them, for me rather selfishly not so much. I gave them both a big hug, pushing my still sobbing daughter out the way. "It will be amazing, I'm beyond jealous!" I admitted. Mum went to the drawer and pulled out an inch thick pile of A4 sheets, their itinerary for the next five months. It read less of an itinerary and more of a bragging list. Yep, on the tenth of September when I'd probably be unblocking the staff toilet for the tenth my parents would be arriving in San Tropez. Hang on... "September? Oh my god! You're going in two weeks time?" Cue more hysterical behaviour from Nicole, James then looked up. "What about my birthday?" He asked looking all put out. Of all the selfish things to ask I thought, typical blooming male, actually thinking about it they'd miss my birthday too. "How long has this been planned?" I asked wondering where the bloody hell my useless brother and Karen had disappeared to. "Why didn't you tell us sooner, prepare us for the shock better." "It was a last minute thing," said mum clearly back in the driving seat now of explanations. Dad seemed exhausted after the longest speech he'd ever made. "And we managed to negotiate a fabulous deal with the travel agent. We leave two days after Sandra and Rogers wedding!" Wow that was a lot of information to take in, in just half an hour. I downed my drink and Dad refilled it straight away, seeing to understand that now wasn't the time to start lecturing me on my drinking habits. I wasn't sure I could take many more shocks today. Cue Simon and Karen entering the room again, holding hands and looking rather flushed. Eww what had they been up to? It didn't bear thinking about, I downed another drink, earning a 'look' from my mum this time. "This wasn't exactly how we planned on doing this, but since mum and dad have thrown us their curveball tonight we feel we have no choice," said Simon a huge grin on his face. Karen was glowing next to him.

"We are having a baby!" He announced to a stunned audience. Mum broke the stunned silence first, crying happy tears as she hugged them both. Dad and Mike bringing up the rear to hug and shake hands. Karen was looking at me waiting for my reaction. She went all blurry when my eyes filled with tears, it was either that or I was going blind from alcohol poisoning. I gave her a huge hug. Karen, my best friend, my drinking partner, my agony aunt and my sanity saviour was having a baby. Our friendship was going to change dramatically but not as much as her life. I think our roles would reverse and I'd become her port of call in a storm, having been there and done that. "A baby?" I said. "Not a chest infection?" We laughed. "I'm absolutely terrified," she admitted. "An actual baby at my age." "You'll be an amazing mother," I said meaning it. "The best bit is I'm going to be your baby's auntie. You'll never be able to get rid of me. But it's like the end of an era," I concluded sadly.

"How do you mean?" Karen asked looking confused. "We won't be able to stay up until four in the morning, drinking wine and moaning about our nonexistent love life's anymore," I said. "But you know after I've had the baby." I didn't want to patronise her but I knew from experience that your priorities changed after becoming a mother. I wiped a tear, a happy tear mostly. It had been an emotional night.

"You're going to be amazing, I'm so happy for you." I repeated. She needed to know she could do this and with my support. Always. "Have you decided where you'll live?" I suddenly thought.

"No we haven't really talked about it," she lied badly. There was no way Simon would want to live next door to me in that area, snob that he was. I guessed they would end up buying a big house somewhere together. Definitely an end of an era, but the start of something wonderful. Plus I had Mike now, we had our own journey to go on, one that wouldn't include babies! Although we hadn't actually had that particular conversation, best saved for another day. I gave Simon a hug. He beamed back at me. How things have changed in as little as six months. We then worked out the baby was due two months after mum and dad arrived home. Nicole was looking a little put out. "I hope it's a boy," she said sulkily, not wanting to give up her only granddaughter status. James had started on the cocktail sausages and seemed oblivious to what was going on around him.

No change there then.

CHAPTER FIFTEEN

Sandra's hen party was underway, and I was well on the way to being drunk. Very, very drunk. I wanted to wake up and not remember that I'd just heard a seventy year old woman admit to owning an Ann Summers vibrator and that her and Bert liked it doggy style on a Saturday night. There was also something rather disconcerting about sipping a cocktail out of a penis shaped straw in front of your mother. On second thoughts it was much worse sitting opposite your mother and watching her do the same thing. Karen had cried off, citing morning sickness, damN you pregnancy hormones. It sounded like an excuse but I had always suffered in the evening too. So it was just Elaine and myself doing it for the under sixties. Jac was hoping to pop in too when she'd finished work. I sensed that was an excuse too, she probably hoped the elderly contingent of the party were long gone by the time she rocked up. Tucked up in bed, supping their hot milk by nine thirty. Right now that's what I'd prefer to be doing, instead I was watching an old lady blow up an inflatable man, complete with penis.

Sandra was wearing the obligatory tiara and 'bride to be' sash, very much the blushing bride to be. Although the blush was probably more to do with the huge inflatable penis propped up in the chair next to her, that her neighbour Beryl had so inappropriately decided to bring along, for what reason we hadn't quite worked out yet. There were ten hens all together, wearing name badges and matching pink feather boas. We looked ridiculous. The smell of lavender emanating from the

old hens was overwhelming, wafting through the air. Beryl, who reminded me of Barbara Cartland, but with more pink lipstick slapped on her wizened old lips, seemed to have taken it upon herself to be the unofficial party compere. We had just finished a round of drinks, about to order more when she then declared it was time play some sexy party games. "God no, please! No bloody sex related games!" I said silently.
Everyone turned to look at me. It turned out I'd actually said it out loud and not in my head as first thought. Elaine sniggered next me. "I'm not answering sex questions in front of my mother," I responded primly, when Beryl started calling me a prudish party popper. Heckled by a pensioner, the shame of it. I'd been called prudish once before by the cocky Tommy Jones aged sixteen when I'd refused to go all the way with him. I'd slapped him around the face and stalked off. I wasn't sure that was the correct course of action in this situation, slapping Beryl make be considered rather rude.
Grin and bear it tonight and hope there was nothing said that would damage me for life. I couldn't think of anything worse than talking about sex in front of my mother, except of course my mother talking about sex in front of me! It was bad enough when she told me about the facts of life, leaving a book about sex on my bed when I was eleven. I didn't come out my bedroom for a year after that.
And I'd rather cut my ears off than ever hear the words sexual preferences or positions coming out of her mouth. "We shouldn't have come," I whispered into Elaine's ear. "I know," she agreed visibly turning green as Beryl started dry humping the inflatable penis, while some of the others whooped.
"I think you need to lay of the Bacardi breezers Beryl!" I said out loud, it went unheard over the raucous cheering. The normally placid Carol who was our old school librarian was standing behind her pretending to slap her arse. They didn't get out much that much was obvious. In Beryl's defence, if

there was one for acting like an elderly nymphomaniac on heat in public, at least it wasn't the poor young waiter on the receiving end of her rather questionable gyration technique. She'd been giving that poor lad the glad eye since we'd arrived. If she carried on she'd get herself barred from the basement room at the nice restaurant we were in or at the very least put on the sex offenders register.

His age was still undecided but barely legal was the general consensus. If he was my son, if that were my innocent James trying to earn a few quid to pay for his PlayStation habit and some dirty old lady was flirting, although some might say sexually harassing him, I'd be livid, I'd start throwing around words like exploitation of children and suing. Dinner arrived and things calmed down somewhat. We chatted politely amongst ourselves, Beryl tried to instigate other outrageous behaviour but there were no takers. She sat back in her chair, huffing. Drinking from the wine bottle, like an old soak on the street. The old dears were beginning to flag at the shockingly late hour of ten o'clock.

Thank fuck for that. Desserts arrived, we were about to dig in when my mum stood up.

"I'd like to propose a toast," she began. I groaned inwardly. Why mum? Why?

"To Sandra, we are all so pleased for you and Roger, that you've found each other at this time in your life. Although I did play some part in bringing you both together..." she paused for some recognition at this point. There were some murmurs of acknowledgement, Sandra blew her a kiss. Mum looked disappointed I think she was expecting a round of applause. "You both deserve a lifetime of happiness..." "...and loads of good sex!" Beryl piped up lowering the tone once more, miming a sexual act on wine bottle. That woman had no shame. "...let's raise our glasses to our good friend Sandra." Continued mum ignoring Beryl's outburst. Unfortunately none of us could ignore the fact that Beryl suddenly face planted into her bowl. "Is she dead?" Elaine asked in horror. As we all jumped up in shock. Once we'd pulled Beryl out of her gateaux and had established she wasn't dead just paralytic, we dragged her up the stairs, outside and then Carol went home with her in a taxi, the taxi driver saying he'll fine her if she throws up in his cab. The entire bill was then settled by Rogers credit card.

What an absolute result. I'd always liked that man. Sandra, a little tearful by this time, mostly due to the alcohol she'd consumed rather than distress over Beryls condition, gave Elaine and me a big hug.

"Thank you for being here girls, I know it can't have been much fun for you both being surrounded by us old girls. But it means so much." "I wouldn't have missed it for the world mum," Elaine went all misty eyed too. "I love you mum, I'm so glad you're happy, and Roger's all right too, I suppose. I just wish he'd get rid of those pink trousers he insists on wearing, some men can carry that colour off. Roger can't!" "I'm working on it," Sandra admitted. "I'm not a fan of them either. I much prefer his fawn coloured ones. His bum looks peachy." We both gagged, so did my mother. I gave my mum a big hug too before she climbed into the taxi and she squeezed me back. I really was going to miss her while she was away, even if she drove me completely mad at times. She was quite merry also, but without making a spectacle of herself. I was still able to look her in the eye, because I hadn't heard a single thing about her and my dads sex life. Haleluya for small mercies. "You're a good girl, and I'm so pleased you've found Mike, a nice man, a decent one at last. And you know he's not too bad on the eye either..." "Mum!" "Well it's true and he looks good in a pair of shorts!" Elaine and I then bundled her quickly into the back of the taxi bus with the rest of the elderly gang and waved them off before she could say more perverted things about my boyfriend. The inflatable penis pushed up against the back window twitching obscenely at us as the taxi drove down the road. We both turned to each other and gave a big sigh of relief. Thank God that ordeal was now over. Sandra had enjoyed herself, that was indeed the main thing. We wandered across the road to a wine bar we had frequented before to wait for Jac who'd just text Elaine to say she'd be ten minutes, dropping our name badges and feather boas in the nearest bin along the way. "Beryl was a fucking nightmare, how is your mum even friends with that exhibitionist." I asked confused, sipping my wine. "She's her neighbour and normally very pleasant, maybe her HRT patch was on too tight." Elaine reasoned. "If I ever see that woman again it'll be too soon, that bloody penis! Those images are burned into my poor brain.""She'll be at the wedding," Elaine pointed out pulling a face. "Without any phallic shaped objects about her person hopefully." Jac arrived, all shiny black hair and red lips. I immediately felt like the biggest green gooseberry in the room. They were clearly besotted with each other, witnessing the way they looked at each other made me feel like a voyeur. I felt happy for them of course I did, but I wished I'd hitched a ride with the others and left Elaine and Jac too it, they so needed a bloody room. It was clearly mutual, Jac was a babe but the way she looked at my quirky, gangly red headed friend spoke a thousand words. True love. I wondered briefly if me and Mike made people feel uncomfortable when we were acting all lovey dovey around each other. I couldn't imagine that we did. I'd have to ask people in future or try to gage their reactions when we were together. "Did your mum have a good time?" Jac asked, bringing a bottle of red and three more glasses to the table. We recalled all the good bits and made her laugh with all the horrendous parts, all containing Beryl funnily enough. All of us crying with laughter at my Instagram photo of Beryl face down in a Black Forest gateaux. "Can I tell you something off the record?" Jac said turning to me, clearly needing to get something off her chest.

"The case against Cassia has been dropped, not enough evidence I'm afraid." I'd wondered if that might happen. We hadn't heard anything much about it in recent weeks and as she hadn't caused us any problems since, it wasn't that much of a blow to hear.

"Oh well, I guess there are far more important crimes to concentrate on." You know like rapists, terrorism etc.. "Again, this is off the record too, but it wasn't the first time she'd done it!" "What? She'd kidnapped someone before!" I declared loudly. Luckily the music was loud and no one turned to look at us. Elaine hushed me anyway. "Kidnap is rather a strong word for what she actually did, technically she drove your son to his grandparents house even if the intent was there to threaten." Jac went on to explain that Cassia was a troubled soul, a history of latching on to people and when it started to go wrong which it always did because of her bipolar tendencies, she'd become obsessive about them.

When she was sixteen she'd stolen her ex boyfriends car and smashed it into his front room, while he was sitting there. She'd gotten off of that charge by the skin of her teeth and had received 'help'. Not enough by the sounds of it. Simon really knew how to pick them. I bet he rued the day he picked her up in the frozen aisle section now. Although it seemed she'd probably been watching him for a while and chose him for a reason. His wealth being the main reason. Thank god for Karen, who only ever turned psycho when massively provoked. "And currently, even though you never heard this from me, she was admitted to a secure mental health unit last week and detained for her own safety and that of the publics for the foreseeable future. She had gone for a cup of coffee with a man she'd met on the internet, he'd told her he wasn't interested in having a relationship with her and she had a

meltdown in Costa. Threatened him with a knife, then tried to slit her own throat. She shouldn't bother your family again, by the time she gets out she'll be so medicated up she'll have forgotten who you all are."
Wow that was a lot of information to take in. I decided not to tell my parents all those other details, I didn't want to worry them unnecessarily before their trip.

The day of the Sandra and Rodgers wedding arrived and the weather was perfect. They couldn't have ordered better conditions for their celebration. Brilliant blue sky, the sun was shining brightly and there was slight welcome breeze ruffling our hair. Perfect. Except for heady smell of drugs that was emanating from the group of unwashed teenagers by the bus stop, but no one seemed unduly bothered by this. We were probably under the influence of passive Cannabis smoking, all mellow and monged out. Logan had phoned me this morning too with the news that Michaela had been tracked down at last. Found in the south of France apparently. The police had contacted him to say she was denying taking his money. This made sense actually as she did run away with a lottery winner, but who knew what went through some people's heads at time of stress. She would be facing charges of the abandonment of her children, rightly so. She'd been vilified in the local and tabloid newspapers. She shouldn't except an easy ride. Michaela's 'story' about leaving the children alone was that the father of her youngest was supposed to be looking after them while she was away, which didn't add up, nobody went on holiday for over three months, apart from my parents that is. She'd been found lounging by the pool, no intention of returning. I wondered if my ex husband had cringed when reading it, having had an encounter or two with her. I was surprised he hadn't sold his story to make a few quid.

MY SORDID SEX SHAME WITH HOME ALONE MOTHER!

I could see the headline now. Thankfully not, Nicole and James would never have forgiven him the embarrassment. Plus the photo of Michaela that had been plastered over the news wasn't the most flattering, it wouldn't have done his ego or reputation much good to have been coupled with her. Graham apparently hadn't been found with her, but as he hadn't actually committed a crime they weren't bothered about his whereabouts right now. And Michaela wasn't talking. Like I said to Logan he must have been with her at some point to pay for the expensive villa she'd been staying in. I'm sure we'd read all about it in the papers when she was taken to court for her hideous crime. The small group of us that had gathered to witness the nuptials at the not so indulgent setting of the town hall, wandered into the building and away from the now apparent drug deal going down across the road.

Sandra looked elegant and radiant in a blue coloured trouser suit, a huge smile plastered on her face.

She was being given away by Elaine of course.

Elaine also looked fabulous in a matching blue slim fitting dress. Being a lesbian obviously suited her. She'd never looked so fit before, or so happy. Or maybe it was simply because she didn't have to hide who she was anymore that did it. Roger looking rather dapper in a suit a slightly darker shade of blue, was standing proudly waiting for his bride. Unfortunately he'd decided to grow his moustache back for the occasion, a mistake if you ask me, but nobody was. Maybe Sandra was turned on by that seventies porn star look. My dad as his best man stood next to him, looking as distinguished as ever. Spoiling the effect somewhat by tapping his leg impatiently, wanting his part to be over so he could have a pint. Like father like daughter, my mother might say. I looked around the somewhat dingy little room and remembered the last time I'd been here was my own rather sad little wedding. I'd been six months pregnant, I looked hideous in a cream coloured dress and my hair had been 'done' making me look like my grandma, not when she was younger but in her present state. Michael looked smart for once in a suit, but when I looked back at the photos, not that I ever did, we looked like two twelve year olds playing dress up. We had a handful of guests and it was a pretty dismal little affair to be honest. Onwards and upwards, we couldn't change the past, it was what made us who we were today. I realised that everyone I cared about was gathered in one place today. My heart swelled with love.

Pass the sick bucket, I wasn't normally so soppy but it felt nice to finally feel content. Nicole and James were on one side of me. They'd both dragged their feet about coming today, until they realised it was a week day, meaning a day off school and work. Both looked really smart and I felt extremely proud of them in that moment. I'd managed to bring them up, sometimes dragging them along screaming, on my own. They were a credit to me but mostly to themselves. Michael had missed out on so much by being absent, something he would have to live with. I knew I couldn't have done anything more for them. Well, maybe not have introduced Graham into our lives and maybe drank less but I'm human not a bloody robot. Karen and Simon were behind me. Both only having eyes for each other. Simon's hand covering Karen's non existent baby bump. Despite my initial worries that the two of them being a couple might be weird, it was anything but. It just felt natural. As long as I turned a blind eye to all their personal displays of affection. Which were plentiful. With them sat Jac, looking even more of a babe today. Elaine was very lucky and clearly very much in love. Lingering looks flying between them. Mum was in the front sitting with the rest of the hens, including rather tamer version of Beryl. No penis shaped objects in sight. Mum was looking rather lovely in a plum coloured ensemble, and dabbing her eyes with a tissue already. Probably grateful tears that she'd no longer have to invite the almost married Roger to every special occasion anymore. I reached for the hand of my Mike sitting on the other side of me. It went without saying how utterly gorgeous he looked in a smart suit. I rested my head on his rather broad shoulders and he kissed the side of my head tenderly. It was still early days for us but if these early days were anything to go by then I'd put money on him definitely being my Mr Right. The wedding went without a hitch. All over and done with in a matter of minutes so it seemed. We all spilled out onto the town hall steps, cheering and throwing confetti at the happy couple. Even the great unwashed across the road joined in with the cheers, obviously in even better spirits now their deal had been successful and they were in the money. One kind lad offered the bride a pull of his bung. Cue nervous laughter and a polite no thank you. We made our way happily in the sunshine to The White Horse, where I'd managed to negotiate a good deal with Logan for use of the normally never used back room. I'd decorated it myself, with the help of mum, Elaine and of course Rogers credit card. It looked pretty amazing even if I do blow my own trumpet. All metallic blues, greys and whites. There were only thirty of us altogether, the chef had been prepped and knew exactly what he was cooking as long as he didn't call in sick that is. We'd kept the menu simple, prawn cocktail to start, or the generic tomato soup. A roast chicken dinner, luckily there were no vegetarians amongst us. And chocolate brownie and ice cream to end. Not exactly Michelin star quality but it was executed well and it smelt and tasted delicious. Logan met us in the lobby looking extremely dapper in his dicky bow and suit tails, trays of champagne on the side to greet us. And I'd even managed to get Maud involved, she scrubbed up not too bad and she was giving out pre dinner appetisers, looking less like a frightened rabbit these days now Michaela had gone. She even managed a smile or two. There was hope for her yet. Beryl after too many champagne freebies started the outrageous behaviour again, I vowed to keep an eye on her. When Beryl inadvertently started flirting shamelessly with Logan, not realising he was homosexual, Maud had escorted her respectfully from the premises and put her in a taxi, tucking one of our AA pamphlets into her pocket. Maud had potential yet. But unfortunately still hadn't realised her beloved Logan's sexuality. After dinner the tables were pushed to the side and a disco set up. A good mix of old and modern songs to bop away to too. I loved a good bop, making Mike bop with me. Michaela's replacement, my new colleague Amanda was also there, on hand to help. Pitching in when needed as well as manning reception. Luckily she didn't have a thirty a day habit and came to work, to actually work, a novel idea I know. I'm pretty sure she also wouldn't feel the need to sleep with any of my ex's either. She was happily married to Bob and had two children. I had a feeling that we were going to become good friends over time. Logan come over to me at the end of the evening. "A resounding success, I do believe," he surmised. I nodded in agreement. Watching my family and friends dancing on the dance floor to a cheesy pop song. I clocked James attempting to flirt with Betsy our new young restaurant waitress. And by flirting I mean standing near her looking miserable waiting for her to talk to him instead. Boys, they were so rubbish. It would seem he may have inherited his father's prowess with women. Nature over nurture.

"I've been thinking, since Amanda arrived and she has more motivation in one little finger than Michaela had overall, I don't really need two receptionists." Oh my God! Was Logan making me redundant? Today of all days. I stared at horror at him. "So," he carried on oblivious to my impending heart attack. "I was thinking you could take on the role of my new events manager. This could be your project. This back room has sat empty for years but after tonight, well it's a great venue and you've made it a success tonight. I took the liberty of taking photos of your decoration skills before you arrived. You could use them and take over the website management too, use them for publicity, what do you think?" "I think I love you," and I gave him a huge hug. It was all coming together at last. A new relationship. A new job. A baby niece on the way. My two best friends in the world had found love at last, even if Karen's was with my not so annoying anymore brother. Nicole was learning to drive. James was discovering boobs, it would seem. Mum and dad were off in two days time for an adventure of a lifetime. Graham hadn't been seen for months and Cassia was in a secure unit somewhere. All was good in our world for once. By the time the happy couple departed with the traditional but tacky tin cans tied to the back of Rogers Ford Focus and just married scrawled in shaving foam across the back window, all my nearest and dearest had gathered outside of the hotel to wave them farewell. Logan who had been the unofficial photographer all afternoon and evening had snapped us all in that moment with his camera. Some of us laughing, some wiping tears away, holding hands, hugging and looking all gorgeous, dressed up, drunk, elated even. I knew it would be the perfect photo depicting the perfect day we'd just had.

EPILOGUE

Two carfuls drove to the airport a couple of days later, early in the morning. For once my children didn't moan at being woken up. Simon, Karen, mum and dad in one car. Me, Mike, Nicole and James in the other. The mood somewhat rather sombre. I would be an orphan, an actual orphan, for five long months. It was a long time not to see my mum and dad when I was always used to them being around, however annoying they might be at times. At least I had Mike now for any DIY issues that may occur while they were away. Of course mum was just a FaceTime away. Mum and dad however were bubbling with anticipation at what lie ahead of them. They deserved this, they really did. They were flying out to Corfu to meet their cruise ship. They told us not to worry about coming to the airport to see them off but I think they were secretly pleased we'd all ignored them and insisted on seeing them off properly. We wandered through the airport together, making the most of the time we had left. Nicole sniffing and wiping tears out of her eyes and holding grandad's hand tightly. Part of me wanted to tell her to man up but it just went to prove how important her grandparents were and what a special part they'd played in my children's life's. Both of them being their alternative role models when Michael and I struggled sometimes to do the right thing. James was busy on his phone, I'd bet any money that he was texting Betsy. He'd finally plucked up the courage by the end of the night to ask for her phone number. Cute. Something else to now worry about, let's hope he didn't follow in his dads footsteps and that Betsy was more sensible than me. I knew he'd miss his grandparents too he was just better at hiding it than emotional Nicole. Mum told Simon to look after Karen and her new unborn grandchild, she didn't have to worry on that score I also had Karen's back. She told Mike to look after me and finish their decorating. In that particular order. "And you Emily, you just stay safe and away from any crazy people, you're such a magnet." said mum. We all laughed at that. All the crazy people had disappeared, they wouldn't be bothering us again, any time soon. The time came to say goodbye. Hugs were given, tears were shed, yep Nicole's again but to be fair we were all a bit wet around the eyes as they waved goodbye and walked hand in hand out of sight.

It was probably why nobody noticed the headlines as we walked by on the local newspaper board outside WHSmith.

FORMER MODEL AND MENTALLY ILL WOMAN CASSIA BLAKE ESCAPES FROM SECURE UNIT VOWING REVENGE ON ALL THOSE THAT PUT HER THERE.

      To be continued..

Printed in Great Britain
by Amazon